Dog Walkers

Jack Mallory Mysteries - Book 2

William Coleman

DOG WALKERS

Copyright © 2021 by William Coleman
All rights reserved
First Printing, 2021
ISBN 9798590952670

Dedicated to my lovely wife, Vicki, who has supported me every step of the way through each of my novels by allowing me the time to write, being my first beta reader as well as my main editor. By being my biggest fan and my sharpest critic, she has helped me produce final manuscripts for you to enjoy.

1

Evenly spaced light posts, designed to look like antique gas lamps, lined the walking path of a popular park in the central part of the city. Detective Jack Mallory followed the path, but he wasn't walking for his health. He was there on business. It was two o'clock in the morning and darkness was a thick blanket over the area, broken only by the glow of the lamps. Ahead of him, a young officer stood on the path with a younger nervous looking couple. They waited in silence, watching his approach. Jack noted that the lamp, only a few feet from them, was black as the night. Were it not for the officer's flashlight he would not have seen them until he was almost on them.

"What've we got officer . . .?" Jack let the word linger in the air with the dark.

"Davenport, sir," the officer said. "Officer Richard Davenport. This young couple here was out for a stroll and decided to move off the path for some privacy, into those trees over there. Only when they get in there, they smell something really bad and then they see hair."

"Hair?" Jack turned to the couple.

"Yeah," the boy, no more than seventeen, said. "On the ground, mostly covered with leaves."

"What's your name?" Jack asked.

"Charlie Vincent," the boy said.

"Charlie. I'm Detective Mallory," Jack said. "What did you do after seeing the hair?"

"We got the hell out of there," Charlie said. "As fast as we could. Then we called you guys."

"Good." Jack nodded. "You did the right thing. What about you? What is your name?"

The girl was a year or two younger than her date. "Suzanne Harris."

"Did you see anything more? Maybe something Charlie missed in his rush to get the hell out?"

She shook her head slightly but did not look up. Her body shook uncontrollably.

"You have their contact information?" Jack asked the officer.

"Yes, sir," Richard said.

"Okay," he said to the teenagers. "You two can go, but we may need to ask some more questions, so don't leave town or anything."

They walked away hand in hand, taking quick short steps, moving as fast as they could without running, putting as much distance between themselves and the body as they could. It was not a night they would soon forget. And it would probably be a good long while before they returned to the park.

"Did you take a look, Richard?" Jack looked toward the trees.

"No, sir," the officer said. "I secured the scene and called for a detective."

Jack dug into his pocket and withdrew a pair of vinyl gloves. "Shall we have a look?"

"We, sir?"

"You're going to have to hold the light," Jack said. "Now, put on some gloves and lead the way."

Richard tucked the flashlight under his arm and pulled a pair of vinyl gloves on. Side by side, the two men approached the line of trees about fifteen feet off the walking path. Richard swung the flashlight from left to right, its beam of light illuminating the trunks, until he located the best point of entry near the area the young couple had indicated the body would be found. Jack held a low branch back as Richard led the way in. The detective followed letting the limb snap back into place. From the walking path it appeared no one had ever been there, but for the small bursts of light that escaped the foliage.

Taking slow deliberate steps, the two men searched for what the couple had reported seeing. Under the trees, a thick layer of leaves and twigs covered the ground, and the detective expected the body to be easy to spot. However, it was several minutes before they happened upon what they were looking for, about twenty feet inside the treed area of the park. The overwhelming odor of death brought them to a halt. Richard swept the light a few feet in front of them. The ground had been disturbed, only a thin sheet of leaves covered the clearing and near its center was a tuft of thick black hair. It wasn't a body dump, it was a shallow grave.

Jack directed Richard where to stand and where to aim the light. The detective lowered himself to his knees and used his gloved hands the brush the leaves away from the hair pushing up through the loose dirt. He started to scoop the dirt into a pile next to the scene. Richard stood in his designated place holding the flashlight mostly steady, beads of sweat forming on his forehead. This would be his first body.

Jack moved several handfuls of earth before increasing his pace. After a couple of minutes at the faster speed, he sat back on his heels, turning to the officer. "Step closer. Shine the light right here."

Richard did as he was told and aimed the flashlight just below Jack's hands, illuminating more black hair. Only it wasn't hair. Jack sighed. "Fur."

"Fur?"

"It's a damned dog, Richard." The detective took a sharp breath and released it. "Someone buried their dog here."

"A dog?" Richard leaned closer. The dirty, matted fur was unmistakably a dog. The officer's cheeks flushed. He had called out a homicide detective because someone had disposed of their family pet. "I'm sorry, sir. I . . ."

"Don't worry about it," Jack rubbed his hands together to clean the soil from his gloves. "We better call off the team and get animal control out here to pick up the body."

"Yes, sir," Richard said. "I'll do that as soon as we get to where I can get a signal."

Jack nodded his understanding. He put one hand on the ground and leaned heavily on it as he raised the opposite leg and planted the foot under him. He heaved to rise to his feet but caught sight of something that forced him to stop his ascent.

"Shine that light over here," Jack demanded. Richard stepped up and redirected the beam to where the detective was pointing. Jack dropped back down to one knee, leaned forward, and reached for the object that had grabbed his attention. Brushing at the dirt until it was exposed, Jack sat back again. He looked up at Richard. "Looks like we're going to need the team after all."

The partially exposed body of the animal reminded Jack of a black shag carpet covering the bottom of the hole he had dug. But the object he had just unearthed was the more intriguing detail. Protruding the ground and laying atop the fur was a woman's hand.

2

Jack and Richard retreated to the walking path. The detective told the officer to keep an eye on the area while he walked down the path until he was able to get a cell phone signal. He called dispatch and requested a small team to secure the area and confirmed the coroner and forensics team was on the way.

The silent darkness of the park was about to be disrupted in a major way. Jack strolled back up the path to where Richard stood and joined him in waiting. He took the officer's flashlight and pointed it at the unlit fixture at the top of the light post next to them. There was no obvious damage, but the fact that it was the only non-working light made Jack wonder if it had been tampered with in some way.

He changed his stance and flashed the light to the ground, searching for tire tracks of some kind. It was hard to believe someone would have carried the bodies of a woman and her dog from the parking area. Even at night, there would be a risk of being seen. He turned to the homes on the far side of the park and identified which ones had windows facing them. Had they seen but not reported a car on the walking path at night? He made a list of things to follow up on.

Within a few minutes, the first patrol car arrived. Jack waved them off the path to prevent them from getting too close in case they were able to locate tire tracks close to the scene. Five more minutes and there were a half dozen marked cars, a crime scene van, and the coroner's van. The previously dark area of the park was aglow with emergency lights. The officers on scene set up a perimeter to prevent passersby from entering the scene. At three o'clock in the morning, this was just a formality for the most part. Although, a few residents, awakened by the lights, did wander out in pajamas and robes to search for answers.

The crime scene investigators at the location of the body erected lights that lit up the area like the sun. They went to work excavating, careful to document every step of the way with photos and notes.

The coroner's van parked on the walking path, where it sat for some time before anyone emerged. The driver, a man in his late twenties, walked to the back of the van and started unloading a gurney and other equipment. The passenger, a woman in her thirties, strolled around the van and toward Jack. The detective watched her approach. She held her head high, her shoulders squared.

"Are you Mallory?" She asked.

"And you are?"

"Valerie O'Conner." She held out her hand. "I'm the new medical examiner."

Jack shook her hand. "What happened to . . ."

"Retired."

"When?"

"Two weeks ago," Valerie said. "Thought you would have known that."

"I was off for a bit," Jack explained. "This is actually my first case since coming back."

Jack's last case had caused quite a shakeup in the department. The police chief, his wife, and her brother, a judge, all went down. Another brother, a detective on the force, would have gone down as well, had he not been killed. The backlash from the community and the rest of the department made it difficult for Jack to do his job, so it was decided that he would take a leave of absence before hitting the streets again.

"Well, then," she said. "Welcome back."

"Thanks," he muttered.

"You know what we have in there?" Valerie asked.

"Looks like a woman and her dog," Jack replied. "Buried together. Skin is still intact on her hand, so she hasn't been here long."

"I'll make that determination, detective," Valerie said.

"Not trying to step on your toes." Jack held his hands up. "Just answering your question."

"Sorry." Her shoulders dropped just enough for Jack to notice. "I've had trouble in the past with detectives thinking they knew more than me."

"Because you're a woman?" Jack assumed.

"It came up once or twice." She nodded.

"Did you graduate with a degree in your field?"

"Yes."

"Do you know what you're doing?"

"Yes."

"Then I'll trust you until you give me a reason not to," Jack said. "Welcome aboard, by the way."

"Thank you, detective," she said.

They stood next to each other for the next hour waiting for the CSI team to finish their job. They were going slow to preserve evidence and to avoid damaging tissue on the victim. Jack shifted from one foot to the other, checking his watch at regular intervals.

He wondered how long it would take to dig a grave large enough for a person and a dog. Even a half-hour seemed a long time to avoid being seen. Did he drive her out here then return to the parking area and walk back? Did he catch her on the path and drag her into the trees? How did he subdue the dog? How did he prevent her from screaming or the dog barking? There were a lot of questions to ask, but no one to answer them.

A crime scene investigator emerged from the trees and waved his hand. "Jack? You want to take a look before we hand her over to the M. E.?"

Jack took a few steps forward with Valerie on his heels. He stopped and turned to her. "I believe he called me."

"Thought I'd tag along," Valerie shrugged. "You don't mind, do you?"

Jack looked at her for a moment before turn back toward the trees. "Just stay out of my way."

"Danny!" Valerie called out. "Bring the gurney to the tree line and wait there."

"Yes, ma'am," Danny said. He loaded the equipment onto the gurney and started rolling it across the grass. The uneven terrain caused the gurney to bounce and the equipment to shift. The young man put one hand on the case closest to him and used the other to pull, determined to get to his destination.

Jack reached the trees, nodded at Richard who stood guard there, and pushed his way through the low-hanging limbs. Three sets of lights were set up in a triangle pattern around the grave. Jack slowed, examining the trees as he went. Every snapped twig made him wonder if they had broken it, or had the killer?

Valerie caught up to him and matched his pace. They arrived at the well-lit clearing and halted at its edge. The harsh lighting revealed much more than the flashlight Richard had carried when they had been there earlier. Every tree and blade of grass stood out in stark detail, as did the centerpiece of the CSI's work. Completely uncovered in a shallow hole were the woman and dog. She lay on her back with one arm wrapped around the dog on top of her. Even covered with dirt, her blond hair was in contrast with the dog's black fur. She appeared to be young, maybe college age or a little older. Had anyone reported her missing?

"Find any identification?" Jack asked the investigator closest to him.

"Not yet." The man shook his head. "No purse. Her leggings don't have pockets. Might find something underneath when she's moved."

Jack shot a sideways glance at Valerie. She didn't move. Jack stepped closer to the grave and squatted. He scanned the scene, taking in every detail.

"Did you find anything in the dirt?" His eyes traced the outline of the bodies. Nothing of note presented itself.

"Nothing of note," one of the CSIs said. "We'll be taking a significant amount back to the lab to filter. Hopefully, we'll find something then."

Jack shifted his weight to get an angle on the girl's face. He studied her jawline, the curve of her chin, the distance between her eyes, the shape of her nose. Closing his eyes he tested his memory. When he was satisfied, he rose to his full height. "Let me know if you find anything."

"We always do." The investigator returned to his work.

"She's all yours," Jack said to Valerie as he passed. He was a half dozen steps away when she shouted for Danny to bring the gurney. To Danny's credit, he waited until the detective was out of the way before trying to maneuver his equipment through the trees. Jack stopped about halfway to the walking path and stared at the homes with windows facing the crime scene. His watch told him it was after 5:00 am. Too early to start waking the neighbors for questioning. He checked out with Richard and started down the path to where his car waited.

3

With shift change an hour away, the department was mostly deserted when Jack arrived at the station, the way he preferred it. He sat at his desk, pulled out a folder, and printed Jane Doe across the tab along with the case number. Logging onto his computer, he pulled up the missing persons database and selected blonde aged twenty to thirty in the search parameters. Several dozen results filled his screen. He scrolled through them looking for the face he had seen in the grave, but it was impossible to be sure without more details about the victim. He noted about a dozen where the facial features were similar enough to be a possible match.

The printer whirred to life spooling out a list of the names and contact information for those who had reported them missing. If the victim could not be identified, he would have to make the emotionally draining visits to these families to determine if she was the one they were searching for. Twelve families deserving the opportunity to bury their loved ones. Twelve families hoping it wouldn't be her.

The morning shift started trickling in. A few greeted Jack when they saw him. Most passed by without a word. Though none of them had been fans of Chief Singleton, some had been friends with Detective Bret Peterson, who had been killed as a result of Jack's investigation. They seemed to blame Jack for Peterson killing at least two women. Some of them were angry over the death of Officer Larry Kaninski, who was helping Jack with the investigation and consequently killed by Peterson just weeks before his retirement. Jack was still upset about that one.

"Morning, Jack."

Detective Shaun Travis stood next to Jack's desk. Shaun had also been involved in the investigation that led to Bret Peterson's demise but managed to come out of it without the stigma of Jack. Having only been an officer at the time probably helped him in that regard.

"Shaun," Jack said. "How's the detective training going?"

Shaun was in the final stages of his training which is why he had already received his badge and title. "Actually, that's why I'm here. I need to put in some hours working cases with an experienced detective. Thought I might see if you were working on anything, you know, since you don't have a partner."

"You ever think I don't have a partner by choice?" Jack said.

"I was told it was because no one would work with you." Shaun suppressed a grin.

"Who told you that?"

"Oh, no," Shaun said. "I'm not giving up names. But there was more than one."

"Really?" Jack smiled. "There may be some truth to it then. You sure you want to work with me? It didn't end so well last time."

"You solved it, didn't you?" Shaun said. "Plus you have the highest clearance rate in the department. I want to train with the best."

"Have you cleared it with Chief Hutchins?" Jack asked. "She can't be too excited about you working with me."

After it was discovered that Chief Singleton had altered evidence in a homicide his wife committed and purposely had helped convict an innocent man for the crime; he was fired, arrested, and convicted. Detective Sharon Hutchins was brought in from another precinct as the new chief with a directive from the Chief of Detectives to clean up the department and get it back on track. Being a woman in her position with that as her mission had not made her popular.

Regardless, she had made positive changes within the department. Only those who were benefiting from the old way of doing things were still complaining.

Rumor had it Hutchins kept three lists in her desk. Names of detectives with a future in the department, those who didn't, and those on the fence. On any given day these lists could change. Jack was confident that his name was not on the first one.

Shaun said nothing.

"This was her idea," Jack said. "Wasn't it?"

"She thinks you should have a partner," Shaun admitted.

"You tell her . . ." Jack took a breath. If she wanted him to finish Shaun's training, it probably meant he was 'on the fence'. Better than being on the second list. "Never mind. I can use the help."

"What's the case," Shaun asked. "And where do you want me to start?"

"A woman and her dog were found in a shallow grave last night. We're going to go question the residents across from the park where the victim was found." Jack stood. "See if any of them saw something without realizing it."

"Jack, it's six a.m.," Shaun said.

"Right," Jack said. "I guess we're going to go have a cup of coffee. I'll catch you up on what we know so far."

The coffee shop was abuzz with people coming and going. The tables were full of students studying for exams and researching for papers, blue-collar workers trying to get a head start on the day, job hunters searching and applying for positions they were most likely over-qualified for, mothers enjoying each other's company after dropping the kids off at school and others just there for the liquid caffeine.

Coffee in hand Jack and Shaun found a table as secluded as they could get. The senior detective gave his trainee a quick summary of everything he learned at the crime scene. Twice the college students at the next table turned to them as Jack, even at a whisper, was loud enough for them to hear the gory details. He shifted the conversation to prioritizing the questions that would need to be answered.

"While the medical examiner gets us a time and cause of death," Jack said, "we're going to ask those living by the park about what they may have seen or heard. I want to know how he got the bodies to the middle of the park unnoticed. Or did he attack the woman right there? If so, how did he subdue the dog? It wouldn't have been an easy task to handle the dog and still get the woman before she screamed or ran away. We need to know if the lamp at that location was tampered with making it premeditation. Or was it just burned out offering an opportunity? And what about the grave in those trees? Did he dig it beforehand? Again premeditation. Or was he there with the bodies for as long as it took to dig?"

"Was she targeted?" Shaun said. "Or wrong place, wrong time?"

"Exactly." Jack nodded. "And if she can't be identified, we have to show her picture to a lot of anxious family members who will find closure if she is their daughter, wife, or sister. But will be relieved if she isn't."

"Sounds like a busy day," Shaun said.

"And at some point, we'll have to visit the morgue to hear the medical examiner's findings," Jack said.

One of the students looked at him with revulsion. Jack in turn sneered at her, in an effort to turn her away. The speed at which he proved successful made him grin.

"I hate the morgue," Shaun said.

"Everyone does," Jack said. "But you need to get used to it. So no excuses. You'll be going with me."

"I wasn't trying to get out of it," Shaun said.

Jack set his empty cup on the table and rose to his feet. "We should be going."

Shaun downed the last of his coffee and stood as well. Jack gave the co-ed one more harsh look before the two of them walked out. Shaun shrugged and raised his eyebrows causing the girl to smile.

"Why did you do that?" Shaun asked when they were in the car.

"Do what?"

"Give that girl the evil eye."

"I'm out here trying to make sure she doesn't become the next victim and she's looking at me like I offended her," Jack said. "She's lucky she only got a look."

"It wasn't necessary," Shaun said.

"I know it wasn't necessary," Jack grumbled. "Listen. You're here to learn, not lecture. You don't like the way I treat people like her? Fine. Find you're own way to deal with them. But don't begin to assume you can tell me how to deal with them. Understood?"

"I just . . ."

"Understood?"

Shaun sighed. "Understood."

4

In the light of day, the park and the neighborhood across the street took on an entirely different look. Gone were the low lighting and dark shadows. Instead, the colors were bright and inviting. Jack parked on the street and led Shaun across the park until they were standing on the walking path in front of the yellow tape in the trees, declaring the area beyond, a crime scene.

Walkers, joggers, and cyclists occupied the path. Most of them looked at the two men in their suits with some amusement as they passed. Only a few glanced at the trees.

"That way," Jack pointed to his left, "takes a good fifteen minutes to get to the parking area."

The detective pulled Shaun into the grass as a cyclist raced by them.

"And that way," Jack pointed after the bike, "is at least a half-hour. The shortest distance is from where we parked. But then you're pulling a body out of your trunk across the street from possible witnesses."

"He must have grabbed her on the path," Shaun suggested. "Dragged her into the trees and killed her there."

"That was my first thought," Jack said. "But how do you get past the dog? That was a good-sized dog with her. How do you subdue the woman without losing a hand? Most of these animals are protective of their owners. They aren't just going to sit by and watch their owner get attacked. And if the guy made the move to subdue the animal first, it would have given the woman time to call 911, scream or run."

"Didn't you say there was no signal here?" Shaun pulled out his phone to check. "No bars. Maybe that's the reason he chose this location."

"Good observation," Jack said. "But still. Attack the woman and the dog barks and defends her. Attack the dog and the woman screams and runs. You risk being seen or heard, and reported."

"Except with the lamp out," Shaun pointed. "Someone may have thought they heard something and looked out, saw nothing and decided it was in their head or on their TV."

"Which would explain no one reporting anything," Jack said. "Speaking of the lamp. Was it burned out by chance or did the killer tamper with it?"

The two men approached the post and looked up at the fixture. This drew the attention of a retired couple walking the path at a leisurely pace. They slowed as they neared and came to a complete stop a few feet away, looking up at the lamp.

"Somethin' wrong with it?" the man asked.

"Pardon?" Shaun shifted toward them.

"The light," the man pointed. "Is there somethin' wrong with it?"

"Burned out," Shaun said.

"It is, is it?" The man snickered. "You do know these lights have sensors? Don't come on until it's dark?"

"It was noticed last night," Shaun said. "We're just making sure it hasn't been damaged."

"Has it?" the man asked.

"Has it what?" Shaun said.

"Been damaged," the man said.

"Don't know yet," Shaun said.

"We'll leave you to it then," the man said. As he walked away, he turned to his wife. "You think they'd have a ladder or something."

"Yes, dear," she replied, clearly not caring.

Shaun watched the couple make their way down the path before turning back to Jack. "They're right, you know."

"About what?" Jack was stepping backward, still focusing on the post.

"We would need a ladder to see if someone damaged the bulb or the fixture," Shaun said.

"We would if that's what I was looking at," Jack said. "I asked the CSI team to check it out while they were here."

"Then why are we staring at it?"

"When they tell me the bulb is just burned out," Jack said. "I'll just move on. When they tell me the bulb was broken or loosened or the wires were tampered with, I want to have some answers ready."

"What answers do you have?"

"I know that no one just shimmied up the post to do something to it," Jack said. "I also know that they would need at least an eight-foot ladder. Which is not a small ladder to be dragging out here. Something else to ask if anyone saw."

"What if they used a truck to bring the bodies out?" Shaun said. "He could have easily had a ladder in the truck. Or they could have pulled up to the light and climbed on the roof to reach the light."

"Maybe," Jack said. "If it were me, I would dress like a construction worker and tamper with the light during the day. Everyone would assume I was repairing it and wouldn't even question what I was doing."

"But we're assuming premeditation," Shaun said. "If it was a crime of chance, he probably wouldn't have a ladder handy."

"Follow me." Jack spun on his heels and walked toward the crime scene tape. Shaun followed him into the trees until they came to the open shallow grave where the woman had been found. "First observation?"

Shaun examined the site for a moment. "He had a shovel."

"Smaller than a ladder," Jack nodded. "But still not something you walk around with."

"He would have been digging for a while," Shaun said. "He cut through a lot of roots."

"I don't know if he was confident or stupid," Jack said. "The risk of being seen by someone may have been low at the right time of night, but not zero. How long do you suppose it would take to dig a hole this size?"

"Half an hour," Shaun said. "Maybe more."

"Try an hour," Jack said. "Then he positioned the bodies. He filled it in again. He was probably here for an hour and a half. Longer if he attacked her on the path. Chances are at least one person passed by while he was in here."

"Might be lucky we only have one victim," Shaun said.

Jack stared down into the hole. "Let's get out of here. Time to start knocking on doors."

The two of them made their way across the park back to their car. From there they walked to the house farthest to the left that still had a view of the crime scene, or at least the trees surrounding it. They climbed the steps to the porch of the Craftsman and Jack turned back to be sure. He had a clear view of the lamp post and could just make out the yellow caution tape. He nodded to Shaun who stepped forward and pressed the doorbell.

Several minutes passed and no one came to the door. They were just about to give up when they heard movement inside. Jack knocked on the wood of the door and took a step back. Minutes passed and Jack wondered if the homeowner had a large dog, excusing the thought since there was no barking.

The door opened slowly. A sixty-something woman looked at her two unexpected guests while wiping her hands on her apron. "May I help you?"

"I'm Detective Mallory," Jack said. "This is Detective Travis. We were wondering if you had time for us to ask you some questions. Everyone in the home actually. Is your husband home?"

"Ben passed two years ago May," she said.

"Sorry for your loss, ma'am," Jack said.

"So it's just you?" Shaun said.

"Just me," she answered.

"Okay," Jack said. "We just want to know if you may have seen something out of the ordinary in the park recently."

"Oh, yes," the woman said. "I sure did."

"Could you tell us what you saw?" Jack asked.

"I saw a bunch of police." She leaned out and pointed. "Over there."

Out of her line of vision, Jack rolled his eyes.

"Yes, ma'am," Shaun said. "That was . . ."

"Must have been something awful," she said. "There were so many of them."

Jack stepped forward. "Ma'am, in the past two to three days did you see anyone suspicious in the park? Someone working on the light post near where you saw the police last night? Or perhaps someone lingering in the area of the trees just beyond it? Maybe a man grabbing a woman who screamed for help?"

The woman looked at Jack like she had only just noticed that he was there. "No."

"Are you sure?" Shaun asked. "Take a moment to think about the past few days. Maybe you saw someone who gave you pause, but you dismissed it. It's important that you think about it."

"I understand," she said. "But I don't think I can help you. I didn't see anything."

"You're sure?" Jack said.

"I think so."

"Okay," Jack handed her his card. "Call me if you think of something."

She took the card in both hands and held it close. The men thanked her for her time, and she watched them descend her steps to the street. Only then did she close the door.

5

The next house was an A-frame which had been updated with vinyl siding and modern fixtures that didn't fit in with the original look of the rest of the neighborhood. The two men climbed the steps to the wood-like composite porch. Someone spent a lot of money to take the natural charm out of the home.

Shaun pressed the doorbell. Hearing nothing, he proceeded to knock loudly on the solid wood door. He waited briefly and knocked again. Jack walked along the porch and peered through the window.

"Let's go," Jack said. "The house is empty."

Descending the steps Jack noted that there was no 'for sale/rent' sign in the yard. Assuming the updates were made by an investor, it would stand to reason they would want a return on their investment. Perhaps the new homeowners just hadn't moved in. Perhaps they had just moved out. Perhaps he had killed his wife, buried her in the park, and disappeared in the night.

"Remind me to find out who owns this place," Jack said to Shaun's back.

"Sure thing," Shaun said.

The third home, a two-story Dutch Colonial, was the largest house on the street which made its peeling paint and wood rot that much more noticeable. The yard was not mowed, the shrubs were unkept and the flower gardens overrun by weeds. Jack would have thought the house empty as well but for the light in the upstairs window.

Reaching the front door, Jack forwent the doorbell to go straight to knocking. Minutes passed and Jack knocked again, a little more forcefully, making the glass in the top section of the door shake. Another minute passed before the door finally swung open.

"No soliciting," the elder man said in a graveled voice.

"We're not soliciting," Jack said.

"Then no trespassing," the man said. "Now leave before I call the police."

"We are the police," Shaun said.

"What was that?" the man turned to the younger of his two intruders.

"What he meant to say is that I am Detective Mallory," Jack said. "And he's Detective Travis. We need to ask you some questions. Do you have any family at home?"

"You drove all the way down here to ask me that?" the man said. "No wonder you people can't solve crimes."

Jack let the comment roll off his back. "What is your name, sir?"

"Peter," he said. "Peter Sheridan. My friends call me Pete."

"Are you married, Pete?"

"You ain't my friend."

"Peter," Jack clenched his teeth. "Are you married?"

"Twenty-eight years," Peter said. "No. Wait. It's thirty-eight. Thirty-eight years."

"That's a long time," Jack said.

"You have no idea," the man said in a harsh whisper.

"Is your wife home?" Jack asked.

"Who wants to know?"

"We do, sir," Jack said. "We have questions."

"Alice!" The man yelled over his shoulder.

"What is it, dear?" a gentle, feminine voice came from somewhere in the house.

"Door!" he yelled.

"Coming," the gentle voice said.

They did not need to wait long. A slender woman with silver, grey hair appeared at her husband's side. She examined the two men on her porch. "May I help you?"

"We have some questions for you and your husband," Jack said. "About activity in the park."

"You mean about all the police from last night?" she said.

"It's connected to that," Jack said. "But we want to know about the nights leading up to that."

"The park?" Peter growled. "Bunch of inconsiderates."

"Now, Pete." Alice put a hand on her husband's arm. "Don't get worked up."

"Worked up about what?" Shaun asked.

"You know," Alice said. "Park stuff. Dogs barking. Kids running around at all hours. Lots of shouting."

"Shouting?" Jack said. "You said, at all hours. You ever hear shouting at night? Maybe when there weren't kids out there?"

"Maybe," she said. "I don't really pay attention. It just bothers Pete."

"What about your neighbors?" Jack asked. "Did you ever hear shouting from the house next door?"

"Mr. Fontana?" Alice said. "Oh, no. He's always been a quiet neighbor."

"What about Mrs. Fontana?"

"Oh, she's gone," Alice whispered.

"When did she go?" Jack wondered if she was the woman they had found.

"Let's see." Alice thought for a moment. "She must have passed about ten years ago."

Not their victim.

"When did Mr. Fontana move out?"

"Move out?" Alice tilted her head slightly. "He hasn't moved out. I spoke to him in the yard just this morning while he was tending his garden. I used to do that. Can't do the work anymore. Arthritis, you know."

"Sorry to hear that." They were obviously discussing the wrong neighbor. Jack tried again. "What about the neighbor on the other side of you?"

"No one lives there," Peter chimed in. "House has been empty for years."

"Years?"

"Well it was all run down," Alice said. "Until they fixed it up."

"An eyesore if you ask me," Peter grumbled.

"Did you ever see trucks there?" Jack asked.

"Damn trucks," Peter said.

"Oh, yes," Alice said. "The workers drove trucks."

"Parked them all over the place," Peter continued. "In the driveway. On the yard. In the street. Even on the sidewalk. Reported them for that one."

"How long ago did they finish the work?" Jack asked.

"I don't know," Peter said. "When they were done."

"It was eight months ago," Alice said. "I remember because it was so quiet when they left."

"And no one has been over there since then?"

"The occasional realtor," Peter said. "Maybe others, but I don't know 'cause I'm not nosy."

"I wouldn't even suggest you were," Jack grinned.

"And if you did," Peter pointed at the detective. "You'd be wrong."

"What about in the park? Have you ever noticed someone messing with the lights over there?" Jack gestured toward the park. "Along the trail?"

"I haven't," Alice said. "Pete, have you?"

"Have I what?"

"Seen someone mess with the park lights," she said.

"Damn lights come on too early." Peter wagged his finger at Jack. "Waste of electricity. Not where I want my tax dollars going."

"Sir?" Jack looked the man directly in the eyes. "Have you seen anyone messing with the lights?"

"No." Peter emphasized the word in such a way to suggest he had already answered the question.

"Okay." Jack jotted a note in his pad.

"At least not recently," Peter said.

"Not recently?" Shaun said. "What does that mean?"

"Means it's been a while," Peter said to Shaun. To Jack he added, "Not too bright, that one."

"You were telling us about the lights." Jack steered him back to topic. "What was it you saw?"

"Just that guy working on one of them," Peter said.

"When did you see someone working on the lights, Peter?" Jack said.

"I don't know," Peter said.

"Try to remember, dear," Alice coached.

"I can't," Peter said.

"Can you tell us what you saw?" Jack asked.

"Just a city worker working on the light," Peter said. "What else do you want to know?"

"What did they do?"

"He pulled his truck up to the lamp post," Peter recalled. "Damn guy climbed up on the roof to work on the light."

"He stood on the roof of his truck?" Shaun asked.

"That's what I said," Peter said. "Didn't bring a ladder and he wasn't a very good repairman."

"Why do you say that?" Jack said.

"Light was on when he started," Peter said. "But it wasn't when he finished. Don't know what he was fixing, but he didn't do it right."

"The light was on?" Jack asked. "It was at night?"

"Of course it was at night," Peter said.

"Why do you think it was a city worker?" Shaun asked.

"Who else would work on the lights?" The man rolled his eyes.

"It's really important that you remember when you saw the city worker," Jack said. "Was it a few nights ago? A week maybe?"

"I told you I don't remember," Peter said.

"Do you remember anything?" Jack said.

"No."

"Peter," Alice's voice was soothing. "Try to remember."

"I can't," Peter insisted. "I . . ."

"What is it, dear?"

"I remember when the light went out I couldn't see him anymore," Peter said.

"Couldn't see who?" Shaun asked.

"The worker," Peter gave a sideways look to Jack.

"I know," Jack shrugged. "But he's my partner. What can I do?"

"The department must be desperate these days," Peter said.

"It makes sense though," Jack said. "If the light went out at night, you wouldn't be able to see."

"It wasn't that," Peter said. "It got real dark. You know, because there was no moon."

"The night of the new moon?" Shaun said.

"That's what I just said," Peter rolled his eyes again.

Shaun pulled out his phone and started typing on the small screen.

"Thank you, Mr. and Mrs. Sheridan," Jack said. He handed Alice a card. "Call if you think of anything else."

"We will," Alice assured him.

As they closed the door, Jack could hear Peter grumbling to his wife.

"The last new moon was three weeks ago," Shaun announced.

"Weeks?" Jack said. "This guy's been planning for some time."

"Unless it really was a city worker," Shaun said.

"It wasn't," Jack said. "It was our killer. The question is, with that much time to plan, was the victim an opportunity, or did he target her specifically?"

6

The detectives repeated the same process at each of the remaining houses on the street but were not provided with any new leads. They walked back to the car. Just before reaching their destination, Jack's phone rang. He answered and listened, offering an occasional grunt to let the caller know he was still on the line before ending the short conversation with, "Thank you."

"Where to, now?" Shaun asked.

"Coroner is ready for us," Jack started the car and pulled into traffic.

"That was fast," Shaun said.

"As they should all be," Jack said. "Probably a slow night."

"As they should all be," Shaun said.

They discussed the case on the drive to the morgue, reviewing the little they had learned during questioning. They may or may not be looking for a man in a truck. It was unlikely a city employee would be working at night, accessing the light without a ladder, and essentially breaking rather than repairing the fixture. It was more likely the killer was the one who drove the truck and created a blind spot on the trail. It was also possible someone else had vandalized the light creating an environment for the killer to carry out his crime.

Jack was curious who owned the empty house and why it had no signage in front. Based on what the Sheridans told them, it could not have been a husband killing his wife then moving. But it could have been one of the workers. He could have seen the dark area of the park or even created it himself. It would be easy for a construction worker to carry his victim into the house. Jack's theory of the wife killing husband could still be right. He may have brought the woman from home rather than finding her in the park. They needed to identify the victim and see if she can be traced back to one of the workers who had put in late hours at the house.

Bright lights illuminated the autopsy room. Sanitizing chemicals burned Jack's nose when he entered. One was filled with small refrigerator doors that held the bodies of murder victims and those whose deaths were simply unexplained, waiting for the medical examiner to perform an autopsy. Three stainless steel tables stood in a row under their own harsh lighting, in the center of the room. The smallest of details would be hard to miss in this environment.

On one table lay the woman they had found the night before. On the table next to her was the German Shepherd. The medical examiner stood between the two victims with her back to the men as they entered. She spoke into a microphone as she used a scalpel to open the dog's stomach.

Jack chose a wide path to circle the tables and come up in front of the woman so as not to startle her. Taking the clipboard next to the table with the human victim he scanned through the notes. She glanced up at the motion then continued with the task at hand. A couple of strokes later she lay the stomach in a pan next to the dog's body. Taking a step back, she pulled off her gloves with the snap of latex, reached up to shut off the recording, and turned to the detective.

"Good morning, Detective Mallory." Her smile challenged the dark purpose of the room.

"You said you have something for us," Jack reminded her.

"I do," Valerie O'Conner motioned them to come closer to the table with the woman. "First let me say, I still don't know what killed her. I have some ideas, but nothing concrete."

Jack looked down at the woman on the examination table. Cleaned up, she looked younger than the last time the detective had seen her. Her skin had an ashen tone Jack had come to identify with the dead.

"What ideas?" he asked.

"I'm not in the business of speculating, detective," she said. "When I know for sure, I will let you know."

"Then what do you have?"

"Notice the bruising around the wrists and neck," she pointed as she spoke.

"She was bound," Jack observed.

"She was," Valerie said. "But some of the bruising is also consistent with someone using their hands to restrain her. Some of them are newer on top of older bruises. This woman was abused for a week or more."

"So the theory that he found her in the park, dragged her into the trees, and killed her is ruled out," Jack said. "She was kidnapped."

"That is for you to determine," Valerie nodded.

"Anything that might tell us where she was being held?" Jack asked. "Maybe her stomach contents could tell us where her last meal came from, so we could at least narrow the search area."

"No help there," Valerie said. "There wasn't a lot of food in her stomach. And some of that was dog food."

"Dog food?" Jack said. "He fed her dog food?"

"Either that or she just got hungry enough to steal it from the dog," Valerie said.

"He treated her like a pet," Jack said.

"Actually, he treated the dog better," she said. "Unlike the girl, the dog was well-fed."

"He treated the dog better than the girl," Shaun said. "It could be a power thing? Or he may just hate women."

"What about sexual assault?" Jack asked.

"There are signs of assault," she said. "And before you ask, no, I didn't find any semen. I took some DNA samples; loose hairs, skin flakes. But can't say if they'll lead to anyone."

"How long has she been dead?" Shaun asked.

"I would say about two days," the medical examiner said. "I'll have a more precise time when I finish."

"Have you run her prints?" Jack asked. "It would be easier to determine what happened to her if we knew who she was."

"Yes," she said. "No hits. But I do have something that might help with identification."

"What's that?" Jack said.

"The dog was microchipped," she said. "We scanned it and got an identification number and the name of the veterinarian who implanted it."

"That's great," Shaun said.

"Can we get that printed?" Jack asked.

"On the desk," Valerie crossed the room and lifted a page off the stacks of papers on the small desk. Holding it out to Jack she said, "Hopefully the vet can give you a name for Jane Doe."

7

The information retrieved from the dog's microchip provided the detectives with the address of a veterinarian's office located in the northeast corner of town, several miles from where the victim was found. Jack and Shaun arrived shortly after lunch and the lobby was filled with people and their pets. The two of them stepped to the end of the short line at the front desk and waited in silence.

The receptionist was doing a remarkable job keeping things flowing through the small office. She processed animals in and out, making conversation with their owners, scheduling follow-up visits, and fielding phone calls with skilled efficiency, all with a smile on her face.

"Andrea," she called out. "Take Mrs. Feldman and Peaches to room five. And if you see Darren tell him Bruno needs to be walked."

"Yes, ma'am," Andrea said. "This way Mrs. Feldman."

As they walked away, Jack stepped up to the desk.

"How may I help you?" the receptionist said. She glanced down at the floor, noting the lack of a pet. "Do you have an appointment?"

Jack held up his badge. "We need to speak with Doctor . . ." He glanced at his notes. "Doctor Gardner."

"Dr. Gardner is somewhat busy right now," she said. "Could it wait?"

"No." Jack was abrupt.

"Okay, just a minute." Her smile faltered. She pressed a button on her phone and spoke into the receiver, "Linda to the front."

They could hear an electronic echo of her voice over the speakers in the back of the building. The detectives turned to a hallway leading to the back awaiting Linda's arrival.

The door chimed behind them and a couple entered with a pair of Chocolate Labs. The two dogs followed their owners dutifully and sat on command. Jack glanced down at them.

"Excuse me," the receptionist said. "Could you step to the side so I can help them, please?"

"Oh, sure," Shaun said, moving away from the desk.

Jack took a half step to the side. The couple approached the desk, oblivious of the detective, to be processed and the receptionist's smile returned. Jack felt something on his leg and looked down to see one of the Labs sniffing his shoes. He took another step away.

A young woman bounced into the room and up to the receptionist. "Can I help you, Patricia?"

The receptionist handed a form and pen to the couple then turned to Linda. "Take these two men to Dr. Gardner's office then let him know there are two detectives waiting for him."

"Detectives?" Linda gasped. "Is Dr. Gardner in trouble?"

"Just take them to his office," Patricia snapped. "And find Darren. The dogs need to go out. Starting with Bruno."

"Yes, ma'am," Linda said. "Follow me."

The detectives walked down the hall a couple of steps behind the young woman. As they made their way to the office a Great Dane appeared, dragging a boy behind him.

"Watch where you're going, Darren," Linda said.

Jack was pretty sure Darren had no control over where he was going. The large dog jogged past them as the boy struggled to keep his grip on the creature's leash and maintain his footing. The boy repeated "Excuse me" to each of them as he passed and to anyone else he came across.

Linda stopped in front of a door. "This is his office."

Barking erupted from the lobby. The Great Dane had met the Chocolate Labs and other animals in the room. They could hear Patricia trying to regain control of the room while directing Darren to get Bruno outside.

"I'll let the doctor know you're here," Linda smiled and bounced away.

The two men stepped inside the claustrophobic office. A bookcase on the back wall of the veterinarian's office was filled with books related to his profession. On the walls were charts of dog and cat breeds, as well as framed pictures of animals in various settings. On his desk was a framed portrait of a family; husband, wife, and three children. Next to it was another of the same man surrounded by a dozen or more dogs, all focused on the camera.

"Do you have a dog?" Shaun asked.

"No," Jack said. "Why do you ask?"

"The way that dog was checking you out," Shaun said. "I thought maybe it smelled another dog on you."

"Not me," Jack said. "No time for animals."

"True," Shaun said. "Our hours aren't really conducive to pets."

A short thick man with a gut walked in, easily recognized as the man in the photos on the desk. He was barely inside the door when he stopped. "Can I help you?"

"Detectives Mallory and Travis," Jack said. "We need you to look up a patient for us."

"A patient?"

"Well, a patient's owner, I guess," Jack said.

"I don't understand," the doctor said. "How am I doing this?"

"We need you to use the information from a microchip to identify the owner," Jack clarified.

"Where is the dog?"

"We can't tell you that."

"Okay," the doctor said. "Then how am I supposed to scan it?"

"We already scanned it." Jack held out the paper. "Just look up the number and tell us who it belongs to."

The vet took the paper and rounded the desk sitting heavily in the chair. He took a few minutes to log onto the computer and then to the program. He typed in the identification code and waited. "Oh, yes. Bullet. A black German Shepherd. Beautiful dog. The owner is Susan Fredrickson. I'll write down the address. She'll be glad to be reunited. She loves that dog."

Jack took the address. "Thank you."

"It's unusual to have detectives handling lost pets," the doctor commented. "Must be slow at work."

"We have to be going," Jack said. "Thanks again."

As they made their way out of the building they passed by Bruno and Darren returning from what Jack could only imagine was quite a run for the boy.

"Excuse me," Darren said as the dog pulled him into the lobby prompting another round of chaotic barking.

"And you wonder why I don't have a dog," Jack quipped.

8

Susan Fredrickson's address was in an older middle-class suburb lined with trees on either side creating a canopy of limbs overhead. Jack had grown up in a similar neighborhood and was struck by memories of bike riding and lawn mowing. He was also reminded that he had not called his parents in several months.

He pulled to the curb, parking in front of a nondescript ranch-style home with a light brown brick facade. A walkway of matching brick led to a long narrow front porch enclosed by wrought iron rails with cracked and peeling white paint. A blue sedan parked in the driveway suggested someone might be home.

Jack and Shaun stood at the door and collected themselves. Making notifications was the least pleasant part of the job, and considering the fact that Jack spent considerable amounts of his time examining the remains of murder victims, that was saying a lot. He rang the bell and waited. A man in his late thirties or early forties opened the door, eyed his visitors. There was a sadness in the man's gaze that gave the impression he knew they were coming and why.

"Mr. Fredrickson?" Jack asked.

"How can I help you?" The man leaned into the door frame as if he would fall to the ground otherwise.

"I'm detective Jack Mallory. We are here to talk to you about Susan Fredrickson," Jack said watching the man's face for a reaction. There was none except the quick shift of the eyes to the detective.

"Did you find her?" the man said.

"And you are?" Jack said.

"Blaine Fredrickson," the man said. "Susan's husband. Did you find her?"

"Can we come inside?" Jack gestured to the interior of the house.

Blaine looked from Jack to Shaun then stepped back and held the door for them to enter. The house was eerily quiet. Their footsteps on the hardwood floors echoed as they walked. Passing the kitchen, Jack noted the sink full of dishes and the trash piled high with takeout containers.

The family room was in disarray. Books and papers were stacked on every surface. The leather sofa was made into a makeshift bed with pillow and blanket. The condition of the house looked as sad as its owner.

"Excuse the mess," Blaine said. "Susan was the housekeeper in the family."

"I understand," Jack said. "Do you have kids?"

"Two," Blaine said. "Teenagers."

"Are they here?" Shaun asked.

"I thought it best they get away," Blaine stared absently at the far wall. "They are spending the summer with Susan's parents."

"So it's just you?"

"Yes," Blaine said. "Just me. Did you find Susan or not?"

There was a framed photo of a black German Shepherd on the end table next to the couch. Jack said, "Is that your dog?"

"Are you seriously asking about the dog?" the man said. "Yes. It's our dog. Or it was. Susan took the damn thing for a walk and never came home."

"How long ago was that?" Shaun asked.

"Don't you have all this in your report?" Blaine asked. "She disappeared six months ago. I'm guessing by the way you're avoiding my question that you found her."

"Six months?" Jack said. "They've been missing six months?"

"How do you not know that?" Blaine said. "How can you be on the case and not know that?"

"We found a woman and dog," Jack said. "The dog's microchip led us to you. The dog in the picture there could be the one we found. We are going to need you to come down and . . ."

"Jack," Shaun interrupted.

"We need you to . . ." Jack continued.

"Jack," Shaun was more forceful.

"What is it?" Jack snapped. He turned to his colleague who held a photo in his hand angling it so Jack could see.

The photo was typical of family portraits, all smiles reminiscent of happier times. The kids were early teens and the dog sat between them as part of the family. Blaine had his arms draped over his son's shoulder and around his wife's waist. The daughter was a younger version of her mother. All of them stared into the camera. All of them looked happy. All of them had thick dark hair.

Jack stood and took the photo. "Is this Susan?"

"Of course it's Susan," Blaine said. "Who else would it be?"

"Has she ever colored her hair?" Jack asked.

"No," Blaine said. "What kind of question is that?"

The woman buried with the dog was blond. Susan Fredrickson was a brunette.

"Do I need to identify the woman?" Blaine asked. "Is that it?"

"I'm afraid there's been a mistake," Jack said. "We have your dog. But we have not found Susan."

9

Jack sat at his desk logging into the missing persons database. The dog of a missing woman was buried with another woman. Susan Fredrickson had disappeared six months ago. Where was she? The medical examiner said the woman and dog had only been dead a few days. Where had the dog been for six months? But the question eating at Jack the most was, who was the woman buried with the dog?

He typed in as many details about the victim that he could and waited for the results. It showed him the same list of a dozen possible matches he had seen earlier. At the desk next to him, Shaun was searching for the owner of the empty house across from the park.

"Mallory!"

Chief Hutchins was standing in front of her office with her hands on her hips. Chief Singleton had kept an office on another floor with a secretary guarding his door. Hutchins kept her office just off the homicide department floor. She said she wanted to be near her team. Everyone suspected she wanted to keep an eye on what everyone was doing. When they made eye contact, the chief waved him toward her. He glanced at Shaun before standing and walking to her.

"What's up?" he asked.

"First case since your return," the chief said. "How are you holding up?"

"I'm good," Jack said. "Just glad to be back at work."

"And Travis?" she said. "He's working with you on this one?"

"I assumed that was your idea," Jack said. "But if you feel he's needed elsewhere . . ."

"No," she said. "He can train with you. Any progress?"

"It appears there may be a second victim out there somewhere," Jack said. "We're still trying to identify the first."

"A second?" the chief said. "Are you sure?"

"The dog the victim was buried with belonged to another missing woman," Jack explained. "I am moving forward under the assumption that the missing woman is a victim as well."

"Just remember," the chief said, "two victims make a double homicide. I don't want to hear the word 'serial' anywhere near this. Is that understood?"

"No one's talking about a serial killer," Jack said.

"Good," she said. "Don't need to be stirring up panic. Get back to it."

Jack nodded and returned to his desk and the list of a dozen names.

"The house is a dead end," Shaun said.

"How so?"

"It's owned by the bank," Shaun said. "Repossessed about three months ago. The owners tried to flip it, but ran out of money to make the payments after it was finished."

"So they did the work and lost it to the bank before they could reap the rewards?"

"Looks like it."

"Her eyes were hazel." Jack snapped his fingers remembering the medical examiner's notes. He typed the new detail into his data search. The results were narrowed to three. He printed the information. "Come on. Let's see if we can get a name for our victim."

The first name on the list was Angela Case. The missing persons report was filed six weeks earlier by her parents. Jack and Shaun pulled up to the house and made their way to the door which opened just as they arrived. The couple stood together in the doorway, the woman holding tightly to her husband's arm.

"Mr. and Mrs. Case?" Jack said. "I spoke to you on the phone. I'm Detective Mallory. This is Detective Travis. We need to ask some questions about your daughter."

"We know why you're here," Mr. Case said. "You said you found someone that might be our Angela."

"Can you give us some details," Jack said. "It might help us determine if we're on the right track."

"What do you want to know?"

"Tell us about her disappearance," Jack said.

"Angela's in college," Mr. Case said. "Moved into an apartment at the beginning of the school year. Wanted her independence. She was supposed to come have lunch with us on Sunday but didn't show. We called and she didn't answer. Turned out she had gone to a party Friday night and no one has seen her since. She didn't show for work on Saturday. She wasn't at her friend's dinner Saturday night. She was missing two days before we knew it. And now it's been six and a half weeks."

"The victim we found," Jack said.

"Victim?" Mr. Case said. "So, she's dead?"

"The victim we found is deceased," Jack confirmed. "But it may not be Angela. It's not possible to identify her from the picture you provided."

The mother gasped.

"I'm sorry to upset you," Jack said. "Does your daughter have any distinguishing markings that aren't in the report? Birthmark? Tattoo? Anything?"

"No," Mr. Case said.

"Yes," Mrs. Case corrected.

"What are you talking about, Martha?" the man said.

"She got a tattoo," Martha said. "She didn't tell you about it."

"When did she?" Mr. Case said. "Why didn't she?"

"She knows how you feel about them," the woman said. To Jack, she said, "A small rose on her ankle."

"Thank you," Jack said. "Our victim doesn't have any tattoos. It isn't Angela."

"Am I supposed to be relieved?" Mr. Case said. "I don't know if my daughter is alive or dead. If she's alive, some monster has her somewhere. If she's not . . . I just want her home, detective. I need my baby girl home."

"I understand," Jack said.

"How could you understand?" The man's eyes swelled with tears. "How could you possibly understand?"

The couple stepped back into the house and shut the door. Jack looked at Shaun. "Sometimes I hate my job."

10

The second woman on the list, Lorissa St. Clair, was reported missing less than two weeks ago. The report was filed by the woman's sister, Charlotte Hess. Jack and Shaun arrived at her apartment shortly before dinner time. A man answered the door.

"Mr. Hess?" Jack asked.

"Call me Curtis," the man shook Jack's hand then Shaun's. He let them in without question. "Charlotte is in the kitchen."

The entry hall spilled into the family room, the kitchen/dining room on the right. A short blond woman was at the stove stirring whatever was in the pot. She saw the detectives and quickly stripped off the apron she wore. Curtis rounded the counter and took her place at the stove.

They sat at the kitchen table exchanging introductions.

"Your sister's disappearance," Jack said.

"Lorissa," Charlotte said.

"Pardon?"

"Her name's Lorissa," she said.

"Of course," Jack said. "Lorissa's disappearance was just over a week ago?"

"Yes," Charlotte said. "Ten days."

"Did she live with you?" Shaun asked.

"No," Charlotte said. "She has her own place."

"How do you know she didn't just go somewhere on her own?" Jack said.

"We were on the phone the night she disappeared," Charlotte said. "Making plans to go shopping the next day. It's something we do together."

"She was home?" Jack asked.

"Yes," Charlotte said. "She was fixing Foxy her dinner."

"Foxy?" Shaun said.

"Her Aussie," Charlotte said. "She didn't like store-bought dog foods. She made him a mixture of ground beef with vegetables. Read it was healthier."

"Where is her dog now?" Jack asked, glancing around the apartment. "Do you have it?"

"No," Charlotte said. "Lorissa would normally feed Foxy then take her for a walk. They both vanished."

"She and the dog?"

"That's right," she said.

"You said Foxy was an Aussie?" Jack said.

"An Australian Shepherd." Charlotte nodded. "A red one. When she was young she looked like a little fox. That's where she got her name."

"Any distinguishing markings?" Jack asked.

"On Foxy?"

"No," Jack said. "Lorissa. Does she have any birthmarks or tattoos?"

"Not that she told me about," Charlotte said. "And she tells me everything."

"Had she mentioned any trouble with anyone?" Jack asked. "Maybe a run-in with someone. A neighbor? Someone at work? At the store? A boyfriend or ex?"

"None of those," Charlotte said. "She doesn't have a boyfriend or an ex. Her coworkers love her. I don't know about her neighbors. She never mentioned problems with anyone."

"What about the dog?" Jack said.

"What about it?"

"Any issues there?" Jack said. "Could it have attacked someone or maybe their dog?"

Charlotte chuckled. "Foxy is docile. She is even shier than Lorissa if that's possible. It wouldn't attack a fly."

"So, if someone were to grab Charlotte on the walking trail," Jack said. "Foxy would be unlikely to try to defend her?"

"She might have," Charlotte said. "But she's more likely to lay down for a belly rub."

"What about friendly people?" Jack said.

"I don't follow," Charlotte said.

"Had she mentioned meeting anyone new," Jack said. "Maybe a new man in her life."

"No one," she said. "I told you she's . . ."

"Shy," Jack said. "Okay."

"You think it's her, don't you?" Charlotte said. "This woman you found. You think it's Lorissa."

"It could be," Jack admitted. "We will need you to come in for an identification. Can you come in tomorrow?"

"I . . .," Charlotte started, but couldn't finish.

"We'll be there, detective," Curtis said.

11

The next morning, Jack met the Hesses at the morgue. He had called ahead so that the victim would be ready for a possible identification. When the couple arrived, Jack greeted them and led them inside, bypassing all the checkpoints. Valerie O'Conner was waiting for them, speaking to them about what they would see, to prepare them. They said they were ready. Jack knew no one ever was.

They stepped into the room where the body lay on a table with a sheet over her. Valerie stepped around so that she was facing the couple. Jack stood next to them. There was no gentle way to do it. The medical examiner pulled back the sheet to reveal the victim's face and shoulders. Charlotte inhaled deeply then began to cry. Curtis pulled her into his chest and nodded at Valerie who replaced the sheet.

Jack guided the couple from the room offering his condolences. He had a name. He had a starting point for his investigation. He apologized to the couple, then asked them a series of questions to help him investigate her murder. When he was finished, he assured them he would do his best to find her killer and sent them on their way to deal with their grief.

He pulled out his phone as he watched them drive away. "Shaun. This is Jack. We have a positive ID. I'm going to her place of work. You want to join me?"

An hour later, the two men walked into First Bank and approached the woman at the nearest desk.

"I need to see the branch manager." Jack flashed his badge at the woman.

She pressed a button on her phone and spoke into the receiver softly. When she hung up, she said, "He'll be right out."

A few minutes later a man in a suit approached. "Officers?"

"Detectives," Jack said. "Mallory and Travis. We need to speak to you about one of your employees."

"One of my employees?"

Jack could see the man running through a mental list of his staff, trying to decide which among them could have done something to bring the police. He said, "Follow me."

They walked to the back of the bank and into a large corner office with a view of the parking lot beyond. He sat in his executive chair behind the desk and motioned the detectives to the two seats across from him. The nameplate on the desk read Brendon Watson.

"What is this about?" Brendon asked.

"Lorissa St. Clair," Jack said.

The banker's face softened at the name. "Oh. Lorissa. Do you have news? We've been wondering what happened to her."

"She's deceased," Jack said.

Brendon's face hardened again. "No. How? She was so young."

"Did Lorissa have any issues here at work?" Jack asked. "With you or any of your staff?"

"With me?" the man put his hands to his chest. "Of course not."

"If your staff say otherwise, it won't look good for you," Jack said. "Are you sure?"

"We had no problems," the banker said. "And I don't like your implication."

"We're investigating a homicide," Jack said. "Not concerned about what you like."

"What about your staff?" Shaun said. "Anyone have issues with Ms. St. Clair?"

"She was well-liked here," Brendon said. "We all missed her when she stopped coming to work."

"Was there any indication leading up to her last days here that she was having problems outside of work?" Jack said.

"Not that I know of," Brendon said. "But I didn't work with her very closely. I have a business relationship with the staff, not a social one. She wouldn't have told me."

"We're going to need to interview your staff," Jack said. "Starting with those closest to her."

"Of course," Brendon said. "We have a small conference room you can use."

"Get me a list of your employees and who is here today," Jack said.

Brendon picked up his phone and spoke to someone on the other end. A few minutes later the woman who they had first approached appeared with a piece of paper, handing it to her boss. "Anything else?"

"Yes," Jack answered for him. "We need you to answer some questions. Where's that conference room?"

Susie McKay had been a receptionist at the bank for ten years, two years longer than Brendon had been there. She knew every employee and almost everything about each one. She also liked to talk. By the time they had finished the interview, Jack and Shaun knew about every office romance, every rivalry, and every discrepancy that had occurred over those years. What they didn't know was a single person who had an issue with Lorissa St. Clair.

"What can I say?" the woman said. "Lorissa was sweet and innocent. Everyone looked at her like she was their kid sister. They loved her. They protected her."

"Protected her?" Jack raised an eyebrow. "How?"

"That boyfriend of hers," Susie leaned closer and lowered her voice. "No one liked him. They all tried to talk her into dumping him."

"Boyfriend?" Shaun asked. "She had a boyfriend?"

"Hadn't I mentioned that?"

"No you hadn't," Jack said. "Tell us about him."

"Not much to tell really," Susie said. "He came by from time to time, but not too often. No one here liked him, like I said. They wouldn't come out and tell her that, but they would hint that she should find someone, you know, more like her."

"What didn't you like about him?" Jack asked.

"You know," she said.

"No," Jack said. "I don't. This is the first we're hearing of a man in her life. What about him didn't you like?"

"Well," Susie thought. "He was polite."

"You didn't like him because he was polite?" Shaun said.

"No," Susie said. "You know. He was polite, but you got the sense that it wasn't natural to him. Like it was forced."

"Forced politeness?" Shaun said.

"Yes," Susie nodded. "And he would give Lorissa compliments that weren't really compliments."

"Such as," Jack prompted.

"Like, 'You're a pretty girl'," Susie mimicked a man's voice. "'Why would you wear that?'."

"So, condescending?" Jack said.

"Right," Susie said. "Not always so obvious. But it was there."

"What's this guy's name?" Jack asked.

"Ronnie," Susie said.

"Ronnie what?"

"I just knew him as Ronnie," Susie said.

"Who was Lorissa closest to?" Jack asked.

"Her sister," Susie said. "Without a doubt."

"How about here at work?" Shaun asked.

"That would be Carmen," Susie said.

"Carmen who?"

"Carmen Lopez," the woman said.

12

Carmen Lopez was a Latino woman about the same age as Lorissa. They were hired at the same time and had met during orientation. The two had become fast friends and remained close ever since.

"Thank you for taking the time to talk to us," Jack said as the young woman sat across from them.

"Is it true?" the woman asked.

"Is what true?"

"Lorissa," she said. "Is it true she's dead?"

"I'm afraid so," Jack said.

"And she was murdered?" Carmen said.

"It appears so," Jack said. "That's why we want to talk to you. We're told the two of you were friends. We're hoping you might help us with some answers so we can find her killer."

"Ronnie," Carmen said.

"Ronnie?" Jack said.

"If she was murdered," Carmen leaned forward in her seat. "If she was killed, it was Ronnie. I tried to warn her about him."

"You tried to warn her?" Jack said. "Did you know him?"

"I know his type," Carmen said.

"His type?" Shaun said.

"You know," Carmen said. "Overbearing, control freak. Charming until he gets his claws into you. Then turns into a first-rate asshole overnight."

"It sounds like you're speaking from experience," Jack said.

"I've dated a Jack Prince or two," she said.

"Jack Prince?" Shaun said.

"Instead of kissing the toad and turning him into a prince," Carmen explained. "You kiss the prince and turn him into a jackass."

"And this Ronnie was a Jack Prince?" Jack wasn't fond of the way she used his name.

"Did you know he met her on a Friday and by Saturday he was already dictating her schedule?" she said. "Telling her who she could see and when. Deciding where she was allowed to go."

"Seems sudden," Jack said. "And Lorissa let it happen?"

"He promised her the world," she said. "And I'm pretty sure he didn't have much to give."

"Why do you say that?"

"Lorissa told me his money was tied up somehow," Carmen said. "She had to loan him some cash. Freaking con man."

"What else can you tell us about him?" Jack asked. "His profession? Where he lives? His last name?"

"That's another example of what I'm talking about," she said.

"What's that?" Jack said.

"Lorissa wasn't allowed to tell anyone his last name," she sneered. "Like it was some national secret. I bet she didn't even know what it was."

"Were you aware that her sister didn't know she was seeing anyone?" Jack asked.

"Sounds about right," Carmen said. "He was very controlling. The only reason I knew was because he came in here to check on her sometimes."

"Did he stop coming by when she disappeared?" Shaun said.

"No," Carmen said. "He showed up for two or three days after demanding to see her. He kept accusing us of hiding her from him. Especially me. I saw him sitting in his car watching me when I got off work one day. Asshole followed me home. Or at least he tried. I drove around until I lost him."

"Doesn't sound like the actions of a man who just killed his girlfriend," Shaun said.

"I figure it was the equivalence of calling her phone after," she said. "You know, to show he was looking for her. To throw suspicion off him."

"You said you saw him in his car?" Jack said. "What kind does he drive?"

"An old small one," Carmen said.

"You don't know what kind?"

"It's green," she said. "Sorry. I don't know cars."

13

It took some time, but Jack was able to get a judge to sign off on a warrant for Lorissa's phone records. After the phone company sent them over, it didn't take long for them to narrow down which number in the call log belonged to the mysterious Ronnie. There were more than a dozen calls a day, mostly incoming. The day after her disappearance he had called her almost every quarter-hour. Dozens of times in the days to follow until he finally gave up five days later.

The number was not, as Jack feared, a burner phone. They were able to trace the number back to the name Ronald Dixon. Getting an address after that took no time at all.

The apartment complex was in need of paint. In some areas it had peeled so badly the wood had rotted beneath. The paved parking lot was riddled with cracks, the yellow lines barely visible. Landscaping consisted of an assortment of weeds and shrubs in need of pruning. Carmen had been correct. It was unlikely Ronnie had anything to offer Lorissa.

They located the apartment number listed as Ronald Dixon's residence. Parked in front was an aged green Escort, its faded paint a perfect match for the building that loomed over it. Parking in the next space, the detectives approached the door. Jack wasn't sure there was enough charm in the world for Ronnie to convince Lorissa that he had money that was 'tied up'.

Knocking loudly, they only had to wait a few moments for the door to open. The man was tall and fit, well-groomed, and dressed like a posh professor.

"May I help you, gentlemen?" Ronnie said in a thick English accent, and Jack knew where his charm came from.

"Ronald Dixon?"

"Yes," he said. "And you are?"

"Detective Jack Mallory," Jack said. "This is Detective Shaun Travis."

"Mallory is it?" Ronnie said. "I used to know some Mallorys back home. Are you related to . . ."

"No," Jack interrupted.

"You didn't even let me finish," Ronnie said.

"We're not here to socialize," Jack said.

"Why are you here? Am I in trouble?" Ronnie smiled nervously.

"Do you know a Lorissa St. Clair?" Jack asked.

His smile faded along with his charm. "What did she say?"

"Mr. Dixon." The change in the man's tone made Jack decide a more formal setting was in order. "We need you to come down to the department to answer some questions."

He did not argue. In fact, on the drive back to the station the man hardly said a word. He sat staring out the window like a man who had lost everything. It was an expression he maintained when he was seated in the interrogation room. Jack was convinced they may have found their suspect.

At Jack's insistence, they left him alone in the room for nearly an hour, studying his every move on the monitor in a room across the hall. The man expressed various levels of frustration; yelling at the camera demanding to be heard, pulling at his hair, at one point even crying into his hands. Each gesture and every word convinced Jack all the more that they had their man.

The two detectives entered the room to a barrage of rants about how he should and should not be treated. Shaun stepped to the wall and leaned into it. Jack sat across from the man without acknowledging his concerns. He lay a folder on the table between them and Ronnie fell silent and looked at its bulk.

"Lorissa St. Clair," Jack said.

"Whatever she said I did," Ronnie whined, "I didn't."

Jack remained silent, looking the man in the eyes. Either the man thought the girl was alive, or wanted them to believe he thought she was.

"I'm telling you, I didn't do anything wrong," Ronnie filled the silence. "You know, she might even be a little crazy." He tapped his temple. "Touched. If you know what I mean."

"You don't think crazy is a bit strong?" Jack asked.

"Maybe," Ronnie said. "But, well you know. I mean, sure I said some things I shouldn't have. She said some things she shouldn't have. That's how fighting works."

"Fighting?" Jack leaned forward. "The two of you fought?"

"We argued," Ronnie walked back the image. "She didn't tell you? I assumed that was why we were here."

"Why would you assume that?" Jack asked.

"Well, she was obviously pissed at me, for starters," Ronnie said. "She hasn't spoken to me since. And now here you guys are asking me questions."

"Why don't you walk us through that night?" Jack suggested. "You know, the fight."

"It was just a misunderstanding," Ronnie said. "It was nothing."

"You just said she was pissed at you," Jack said. "Hasn't spoken to you since. Doesn't sound like nothing."

"You ask her," Ronnie said. "You ask her what we argued about. She'll tell you it was nothing."

"I'm asking you," Jack said. "Walk me through that night."

"We fought," Ronnie said.

"I need details," Jack insisted. "What did the two of you do that afternoon?"

"We went to dinner," Ronnie said.

"Where?"

"What?"

"Where did you have dinner?" Jack said.

"I don't understand," Ronnie glanced at Shaun. "How is this relevant?"

"I'd answer the man," Shaun said.

"Where did you have dinner?" Jack repeated.

"The One-Five-One," Ronnie said.

"That new Bistro?" Jack said. "Nice. I heard it was expensive."

"It can be," Ronnie said.

"What did you have?"

"What does it matter?" Ronnie said.

"You were at a nice restaurant," Jack said. "What did you order?"

Ronnie sighed loudly. "I had the Lobster Bisque and a Swordfish steak."

"And dessert?"

"Chocolate Caramel Apple Torte," Ronnie said.

"Torte?" Jack said. "Just a fancy way to say pie, isn't it?"

"Not exactly," Ronnie said.

"What about Lorissa?" Jack asked.

"What about her?"

"What did she order?" Jack asked.

"I don't remember," Ronnie said.

"Sure you do," Jack said. "A man like you remembers every detail."

"A man like me?"

"What did Lorissa order?" Jack snapped.

"Salad," Ronnie said. "She had a salad."

"Sounds . . .," Jack turned to Shaun. "What's the word I'm looking for?"

"Cheap?" Shaun offered.

"I was thinking 'responsible'," Jack said. "But cheap works."

"What does any of this have to do . . ." Ronnie started.

"Who paid?" Jack cut him off.

"Why do you need to know these things?" Ronnie said.

"I've seen where you live, Ronald," Jack said. "Who paid for dinner? And don't lie. There are records. We're going to find out."

"She did," Ronnie said.

"She?" Jack said.

"Lorissa," he said. "Lorissa paid for dinner."

"But she only had a salad?" Jack said.

"Yes," Ronnie admitted.

"Is that what you fought about?" Jack asked.

"No!" Ronnie shouted. "Is that what this is about? I didn't pay for dinner?"

Jack leaned back. "What next?"

"What?" Ronnie asked. "What do you mean?"

"You had dinner," Jack said. "She picked up the check. What next?"

"We went home," Ronnie said.

"Home?" Jack said. "Were you living together?"

"No," Ronnie said. "We went to her place."

"What happened at her place?"

"You obviously know what happened," Ronnie said. "She told you what happened. You're trying to catch me in a lie or something. But for the life of me, I don't understand what I've done to have the police knocking on my door."

Either the man honestly believed Lorissa was alive and in the next room feeding us incriminating information about him, or he was a hell of a liar. But Jack was curious where things were going. "Why don't you tell us your side of the story?"

"Fine," the man huffed. "We went to her place and, you know."

"No, I don't," Jack said. He did. "You need to tell me."

"We had sex," Ronnie said. "Are you happy now? Anyway. Afterward, we were looking for something to watch on TV and her dog jumped on me. The damn thing landed right on my groin, which hurt like a mother. So, I yelled and shoved the dog to the floor. Which is when she got mad at me for hurting her precious Foxy."

"Foxy?"

"The dog," Ronnie said. "And I hadn't hurt it. It had hurt me. That's why I suggested she get rid of the animal."

"The animal?" Jack said. "You suggested she get rid of her pet?"

"I did," he said. "That's when she yelled at me. Told me to get out. Then left to take the dog on a walk."

"What did you do then?" Shaun asked.

"I went home," Ronnie said. "I wasn't going to be talked to that way."

"What kind of dog?" Jack asked.

"If you mean what breed," Ronnie sneered. "It's an Aussie. Australian Shepherd."

"What color?"

"Mostly red," the man said. "With white markings."

"And that night was the last time you saw her?" Jack asked.

"Yes," Ronnie said. "I tried to talk to her, but she refused to answer my calls."

"I see," Jack said. "What about the dog?"

"What about it?"

"Have you seen it since that night?"

"If I haven't seen her," Ronnie said. "How would I have seen the dog?" He looked from one detective to the other. "What aren't you telling me?"

Jack looked at Shaun and nodded. The younger detective pushed himself off the wall and took a step toward their suspect.

"Yesterday evening," Shaun said, "the body of Lorissa St. Clair was found in a wooded area at a local park."

"What?" Ronnie looked confused like he didn't fully grasp the words.

"Lorissa was murdered," Jack said to make it clear to the man.

"Murdered?" Ronnie said. "When? How?"

"When was the last time you saw her?" Jack asked.

"That night," Ronnie said.

"What was the date?"

"The date?" Ronnie thought. "Three Fridays ago. Whatever that date was."

"Three days before her sister reported her missing," Jack said. "Something you didn't do."

"I didn't know she was missing," Ronnie said. "I thought she was avoiding me."

"We're going to need an account of your whereabouts since that night," Jack slid a notepad and pen across the table.

"My whereabouts?" Ronnie stared at him. "You think I did this?"

"You're a suspect," Jack confirmed. "So you need to stay in the area until you hear from us."

"I didn't do this," Ronnie said. "I wouldn't have."

The man's eyes welled up and tears started streaming down his cheeks. Within minutes, he was sobbing so badly his body shook. Jack wasn't sure if it was for the death of the girl or because he was being considered for the crime. Regardless of why, Jack felt the emotions were disingenuous. "After you write out where you've been, add the names of people who can vouch for you being in each location. Also, a separate list of people you think might help in our investigations; friends, enemies, etcetera."

"Friends and enemies?"

"Yes."

"Mine or hers?"

"Both," Jack said. "When you're done, an officer will show you out."

Jack rose to his feet and motioned for Shaun to leave with him. As they opened the door they heard Ronnie muttering.

"What was that?" the detective turned back.

"I was just wondering what happened to the dog," Ronnie said.

"I thought you didn't like the dog?" Shaun said.

"Hated it," Ronnie stared at the notepad. He picked up the pen and started writing. "Was just wondering."

14

Ronald Dixon handed the notepad to Jack when he emerged from the interrogation room. Jack asked a nearby officer to take the man home and to keep an eye on him for a few hours to make sure he didn't get the urge to get rid of evidence or flee the city.

"Mr. Dixon," Jack stopped him on the way out. "Where did she walk her dog?"

"What?"

"Where did Lorissa go when she walked her dog?" Jack asked again.

"There's a walking path behind her apartment complex," Ronnie said. "She walks about a half hour then turns around. Or walked, I guess."

At his desk, Jack studied what Ronnie had written on the notepad. There were hours of time where he indicated that he was home alone, amounting to ample opportunity to kidnap, kill and bury Lorissa St. Clair. Shaun was waiting for him at his desk.

"Have you heard anything back about the warrant for Lorissa's place?" he asked.

Shaun held up some papers. "That's why I'm here. Just came in."

"Great," Jack said. "After we check it out, we're going to follow her walking path. Apparently, she walked for an hour. So it'll be a while. I want to see if we can find where she was taken."

"It's been more than two weeks," Shaun said. "You think there's anything to find?"

"It's probably been mowed a couple of times," Jack said. "So, it's unlikely. But I want to take a look."

They left the department and, armed with the warrant, had the apartment complex manager let them into Lorissa's apartment. They assured the manager they would lock up when they left and practically pushed him out the door.

Lorissa had lived in the one-bedroom for three years. Framed prints and family photos filled the walls. More photos were mixed with decorations on shelving and furniture tops. She was definitely about family. The Hesses were represented prominently, with dozens of pictures of the sisters together. A high proportion of the photos were of a red and white Aussie, as Ronnie had described. A few were of the work friend, Carmen. There were no pictures of the boyfriend.

The two detectives searched every inch of the apartment, trying to find anything at all that would suggest Lorissa might have a killer in her inner circle. It was not a large living space, but it took the better part of two hours to do a thorough search. Every drawer was overturned, every box emptied. Clothing was unfolded, pockets checked. Books were opened and fanned for notes. Seating cushions and the mattress were removed to be sure nothing was hidden underneath. When all was said and done, they had a handful of notes, a diary, a laptop, and a mess.

"Did you find anything about the boyfriend?" Jack asked as he began to thumb through the diary.

"Nothing," Shaun said. "If it weren't for the bank employees I would say he wasn't a boyfriend at all."

"Maybe he wasn't," Jack said. "Maybe for her it was just a fling."

"What about the suggestion that he was controlling her life?"

"Perception," Jack said. "Maybe she was deciding to make changes in her routine and they assumed it was him."

Jack stopped talking as he concentrated on the diary. Shaun read through the notes, which provided little, then opened the laptop. It required a password. None of the notes gave a hint as to what it might be.

"This is interesting," Jack said. "There was another boyfriend."

"Another boyfriend?" Shaun said. "The sister didn't know she had one and there were two?"

"Some guy named Jeremy," Jack quickly turned pages of the diary. "Looks like he lasted about four months."

"Four months can be a commitment to some," Shaun said.

"Maybe he thought it was going somewhere and she didn't," Jack suggested.

"Don't know what Jeremy is like, but I bet he was better than the English creep," Shaun said. "Does it say why they split?"

Jack turned to the last few pages on which Jeremy's name appeared. He scanned the paragraphs and shook his head. "He is the main topic on several pages, then he's gone. No reason. No explanation for no longer mentioning him at all."

"How long before she mentions Ronnie?" Shaun asked.

Jack turned more pages until he found the first occurrence of the name. "Almost a year."

"Doesn't sound like she dumped the one for the other," Shaun said. "Seems like a long time to wait to get revenge over a breakup too."

"You have to look at the triggers," Jack said. "If Jeremy saw the girl who dumped him with another guy, it might have set him off."

"Any mention of a last name?" Shaun asked.

"That would be too easy," Jack said. "You don't want your cases to be too easy do you?"

"I would prefer that they were," Shaun said. "How do we track him down?"

"We talk to the sister," Jack said. "And the friend, Carmen. It's been a while. Maybe they didn't mention him because he was out of the picture. Bag the diary and the laptop and put them in the car. I'll lock up. Then we can check out the walking path."

A few minutes later the two detectives were standing on the walking path that stretched away into the distance in both the east and the west. A couple walked past them, eyeing the men in their suits.

"Ronnie said she walked for a half-hour before turning around," Jack said, turning his head from the left to the right. "I didn't think to ask which way she went."

"So, we could be out here for two hours?" Shaun said. "Wish I'd brought different shoes."

"You'll survive," Jack patted him on the back. "Although you may have to carry me part of the way."

The walkway from the apartments curved into the path so that one would be facing the east, so the detectives decided to continue in that direction. The path itself was about eight feet wide, allowing plenty of room for those choosing to exercise to pass one another. Fifteen minutes into the walk they had already crossed paths with dozens of people walking, jogging, running, and cycling. Some with dogs, most without. It was a busy path during the day. They wondered what time of the day walkers stopped.

They noted several areas where the trees were thick enough for someone to hide when the sunset and there was little or no source of light. Jack stopped them at each of these locations and walked into the trees searching the ground as they went, looking for signs of a struggle. Finding nothing they moved on.

Forty-five minutes into the walk brought them to a small park with trees on either side and a parking area on the far side, closer to the street. Jack stopped and stared at the park for a few minutes.

"This is where I would do it," he said.

"Seems too public." Shaun counted four families and three couples enjoying the park.

"It is at this time of day," Jack said. "But late at night, when those kids are asleep and the parents are exhausted from a long day, there aren't many out here. It might be risky. But you hide in the trees and wait for that window of opportunity when no one is out here but one woman walking the path. You back your car in so all you have to do is pop the trunk and you're gone in a matter of minutes."

"Truck," Shaun said. "He used a truck to disable the lamppost."

"Even easier," Jack said. "Leave the tailgate down until you get her into the back, tied up, and unconscious. Close the gate and drive away."

"Do you think he kills the dog first?" Shaun asked. "It seems the dog would defend her otherwise."

"Subduing them both would certainly be a challenge," Jack said. "But Susan Fredrickson's dog was still alive six months after she disappeared. I think he takes them together."

They moved to the tree line on the west side of the park. It was thick with trees but backed up to homes that would prove difficult to hide if someone were outside or at a window. Crossing the park, they nodded at the families as if it were perfectly normal for two men in suits to spend time in a park. For their part, the parents seemed to corral their kids a little closer until they were far enough away to feel less threatened.

The trees on the east side of the park were less dense, but still provided plenty of cover for someone to hide. In addition, there were no homes behind them, only more trees. The two men walked the edge until they found a gap in the trees with broken undergrowth. It could easily have been animals in the woods, but Jack stepped into the trees to check it out. Shaun followed close behind. A moment later a glint of light caught Jack's eye. He bent down with a gloved hand and lifted the object. He held up an earring with three interlocking circles.

"Did our victim have earings?" Jack asked.

"I don't remember any," Shaun said.

Jack dropped the piece of jewelry into an evidence bag and the two of them searched the area more thoroughly. There were signs of a struggle, that could also be the aftermath of playing children. They found paw prints that may have been from the girl's dog or any number of other dogs passing through the park. They were standing in what could be a crime scene, or just as easily be nothing.

15

Jack knocked on the door of the home of Curtis and Charlotte Hesse and waited. He had seen the couple through a window as he was parking, so he knew they were home. The wait was longer than it should have been, but under the circumstances, Jack didn't let it bother him.

"Oh," Charlotte opened the door. "It's you. Is there news?"

"Could I come in?" The detective stood at an angle to the door, trying to not be intimidating in any way. It was something his ex-wife had taught him. At six feet, with broad shoulders, he sometimes came across as threatening. It was probably the only thing he kept from the marriage. "I have some more questions for you and your husband."

"Of course." She stepped back and allowed Jack to enter.

They returned to the same room they had spoken in earlier, sitting in the same seats. Curtis joined them this time.

"Where is the other detective?" Curtis asked.

"He's working on a lead." Jack decided it would be best to speed things up and sent Shaun to speak with Lorissa's work friend Carmen while he talked to the sister.

"Should you be there?" Charlotte asked. "Working the lead? Whatever you need to talk to us about could wait. We'll be here."

"Detective Travis will do a thorough job," Jack guaranteed. "I felt we could cover more ground quicker this way. And I would rather not wait for the answers to my questions. Every detail could be critical to the case."

"Of course," Curtis put his hand over Charlotte's. "We didn't mean to imply anything. What can we help you with?"

"When we were here before," Jack turned to Charlotte, "you said that Lorissa wasn't seeing anyone."

"That's right," she said.

"Well, apparently she was," Jack said. "She never mentioned a Ronald, or Ronnie?"

"No." The idea that her sister had not shared a relationship with her upset Charlotte. It opened the possibility that there may have been more unshared moments. "How long?"

"Not long," Jack said. "Are you sure she didn't mention the name as something other than a boyfriend?"

"Not that I recall." Charlotte looked at her husband.

"I never heard the name," Curtis assured her.

"Is he the one who did this to her?" Charlotte asked. "Did he kill her?"

"We don't know yet," Jack said. "We're considering him a person of interest. But we're not ready to stop looking elsewhere."

"A person of interest," Charlotte repeated.

"What about the name Jeremy?" Jack said.

"Jeremy?" Curtis' eyebrow raised. "There's a name we haven't heard in a while."

"So you did know the two of them were an item?" Jack said. "I ask because you didn't mention him when I talked to you before."

"We knew they dated," Charlotte said. "But that was a year ago or more and didn't last more than a few months. He didn't even come to mind."

"What can you tell me about him?" Jack asked. "Anything might help."

"We only met him two or three times," Charlotte said.

"There was the dinner," Curtis said.

"Oh, yes," Charlotte nodded. "Hard to believe I forgot that."

"The dinner?" Jack prompted.

"We asked Lorissa to bring him to dinner," Curtis said. "We thought it would be nice to get to know him. You know, since he was part of her life."

"Part of her life?" Charlotte scoffed. "I should say not."

"Care to explain?"

"Well, first he was late," Charlotte said. "My sister was never late, anywhere, ever. But that night they arrived a half-hour after the time we agreed on."

"It was easy to see Lorissa was upset when they got here," Curtis said. "She didn't hide her feelings very well."

"Then he spent the whole evening looking up sports stats on his phone," Charlotte said. "I think he was even watching a game."

"Sports fanatic?" Jack said.

"Wouldn't talk about anything else," Curtis said. "I like a good game, but I don't obsess over it."

"How did Lorissa react to him?"

"She wasn't happy," Charlotte said. "She stepped outside with him and chewed him out. They left shortly after that. A week or so later it was like he had never existed."

"Never mentioned his name again," Curtis agreed.

"Do you know his last name?" Jack asked. "Maybe his profession?"

"She told us what he did," Charlotte said. "Didn't she, hon?"

"Well he didn't tell us anything," Curtis said. "But since you mention it, I think she did tell us."

"He did something in connection to the bank," Charlotte said. "That's how they met. What was it?"

"I remember," Curtis exclaimed. "He drove an armored truck. Or rode in one. He picked up and delivered money at the bank."

"That's right," Charlotte confirmed.

"What about his last name?"

"I'm sorry," Charlotte said. "I don't think she ever told us."

She looked at her husband who shook his head.

"That's okay," Jack said. "There can't be too many Jeremys working for an armored truck company servicing the bank where she worked."

"I bet not," Curtis said.

"One more thing." Jack reached in his pocket and pulled out the evidence bag containing the earring he had found in the park near the walking path where Lorissa was last known to be. "Do either of you recognize this?"

Charlotte took in air so fast Jack thought she was going to faint. Curtis was quick to put a hand on her shoulder to steady her.

"Mrs. Hesse?" Jack said.

"I gave her those earrings for her birthday." Charlotte's eyes swelled with the tears she had been holding back.

Jack sat uncomfortably as Curtis tried to console his wife. You just never know what will set a person off, what will make it real. The detective stood, thanked the couple, and showed himself out.

16

The bank was closed, so Shaun had to look up Carmen's home address. He arrived just as she was seating her two kids at the dinner table. He apologized, but she insisted he come in. The kids, aged three and five, became excited at the sight of their guest and proceeded to try to entertain the detective as only young children could.

"Sorry about them," Carmen raised her voice to be heard. "We don't get a lot of visitors here."

"I didn't realize you had kids," Shaun said.

"Despite the noise," Carmen said, "it's just the two."

Shaun smiled. "Maybe I should come back later."

"You don't have kids," Carmen said. "Do you?"

"No."

"It doesn't get better later," she said. "Give me a minute. Luiza. Tito. Quiet."

The two children became silent. They stared at the stranger in the room intently. Their mother took their hands and led them from the room. A minute later she returned alone.

"They are going to watch a video before dinner," she said. "What brings you here? Are you hungry?"

"I'm good," Shaun said. "I just have some follow up questions."

There was a shrill scream that sounded like the young girl. Shaun's head snapped in that direction.

"Don't make me come down there!" Carmen yelled down the hall and all went silent again. "What questions?"

"We found her diary," Shaun said. "There's a gentleman mentioned in it, named Jeremy."

"Jeremy's no gentleman," Carmen looked as though she had just bitten into a lemon. "He's a macho scumbag."

"You know him then?"

"He's with the armored truck company that comes to the bank," Carmen said. "Asked Lorissa out. Treated her awful."

"Was he abusive?" Shaun asked.

"No," Carmen shook her head. "Nothing like that. He just, you know, ignored her and everything. He didn't want a girlfriend. He wanted someone to come to his apartment and clean up after him."

"You didn't like that?"

"Hell, no," she said.

"What about Lorissa?" he said. "What did she think of him?"

"At first it was all, 'I have a boyfriend'," Carmen waved her hand in the air. "Then it was, 'You know what he did today?'"

"According to her diary they were together a little while," Shaun said.

"She broke up with him more than once," Carmen said. "But he would get all nice and promise to be better. Then right back to the old ways."

"Did he ever get angry with her for dumping him?"

"He'd just try to win her back," Carmen said. "Started giving her gifts to win her back."

"Gifts?"

"Yeah," she said. "He was the one who gave her that dog."

17

"**H**ow long were they together?" Jack asked.

"They lasted about four months," Shaun said. "And he gave her a dog."

"What's wrong with that?" Jack asked, although he had been thinking the same thing.

"Dogs are long term," Shaun said. "You wait at least a year before a gift like that."

"How many relationships have you had that lasted more than a year?"

"None," Shaun said.

"Maybe you should give them a dog," Jack suggested. "Show you're in it for the long haul."

"Didn't help Jeremy, did it?" Shaun said.

"Maybe he thought it would," Jack said. "If he thought he was in it for the long term and she dumped him, he could have been upset."

"I would be," Shaun said.

"Then he finds out he's been replaced by Ronnie," Jack said.

"Do you think that's why Ronnie didn't like the dog?" Shaun said. "Because he knew this other guy had given it to her?"

"Could be," Jack said. "I've seen people get upset for dumber reasons."

"If Jeremy knew what path she took, he could have been waiting for her," Shaun said.

"Since he gave her the dog, he probably knew the path," Jack agreed.

"We need to bring him in," Shaun said.

"Why don't you follow up with the armored truck company?" Jack said. "Get his full name and bring him in if you can find him. I want to talk to the detective on the Susan Fredrickson case. She and Lorissa both disappeared while walking their dogs. I want to see if there are any other similarities."

"Of course," Shaun said. "Two women disappear and one is found buried with the other's dog. The cases must be related."

"That's what I'm going to look into," Jack said. "But we don't stop looking at Ronnie or Jeremy. Or anyone else who becomes a viable suspect. No one comes off the list until we clear them or get enough evidence to name a primary."

The phone on Jack's desk interrupted them, and he picked it up. After the initial introduction, Jack sat listening to the caller without so much as a grunt until he turned to his computer, saying, "Give me a minute."

The detective navigated through the screens until he came to where he wanted to be. "Got it."

He dropped the receiver back into place. "You may want to see this."

Shaun stepped up so he could see over Jack's shoulder. "What do we have?"

"A clip from one of those video doorbells," Jack said. "Across from the park where we found the earring. An officer canvassing the neighborhood got it for us."

Jack clicked the play button. The image was dark save for a single street lamp and the circle of sidewalk and pavement directly below it. These types of doorbells typically record only when motion is detected. Jack studied the screen trying to identify the motion that had initiated this recording while also trying to determine where on the screen the park might be.

Headlights flared to life on the left side of the screen. Both detectives focused on them and watched as the vehicle pulled to the street and turned. It was off the screen in seconds.

"What did you see?" Jack asked.

"Not much," Shaun said.

"I didn't ask what you didn't see," Jack said.

"Headlights," Shaun said. "And a vehicle leaving the screen."

Jack hit play again focusing on the dark area of the screen where he now knew the vehicle was. There was absolutely no visibility until the lights came on. He tapped the image. "There was no interior light. Assuming this is the vehicle Lorissa was abducted in, there was no interior light when the driver got in."

"Unless the driver was waiting inside and a partner did the grab and loaded her in the car," Shaun said.

"A team?" Jack considered.

"I thought about a team before," Shaun said, looking at the image. "But . . ."

"But what?"

"I was basing that on the fact that the woman and her dog were taken," Shaun explained. "I thought it would be easier if there were two abductors. One for the woman and one for the dog. This video suggests the driver remained in the vehicle. Which negates the reasoning of two victims, two assailants."

"Unless," Jack said. "As I said, there was no interior light."

Jack paused the video where the vehicle was just about to leave the range of the camera. At the distance the vehicle was to the camera it was mostly a blurred image. "What can you tell me about the car?"

Shaun leaned closer. "By its size, it could be a pickup truck."

"What else?" Jack encouraged.

"The man who disabled the lamppost drove a pickup," Shaun said.

"About the image," Jack said. "What else do you see?"

"Nothing," Shaun said. "It's too blurry."

"Its shape," Jack said. "It's either an SUV or a pickup with a topper."

"You're right," Shaun said. "Either way, easy to hide dogs and bodies."

18

Detective Maureen Weatherby was a bright young detective hired by Chief Hutchins while Jack was on leave. He knew nothing about her other than what he heard from coworkers. There was, at the time, a lot of anger over promoting detectives from outside the department, especially with less seniority than those she was promoted over.

Since then there had been feedback, both positive and negative, about her abilities as an investigator. Most of the negative feedback came from the older, more experienced members of the department who were most likely threatened by the changes taking place. Jack suspected the criticisms had less to do with her skills than they did with her gender and race.

She was sitting at her desk with her face buried in a case file when Jack sat in the seat next to her. She raised her head and her dark, piercing eyes leveled on his.

"Mallory, isn't it?" she said.

"It is," Jack said. "And you're Weatherby."

"I hear you found my dog." Maureen put the file down.

"We found Susan Fredrickson's dog," Jack confirmed. "That's why I'm here."

"My vic's dog was buried with your vic," Maureen laid out Jack's thoughts. "You're wondering if there is a connection between the two women besides being dog owners."

"I thought we could share details," Jack said.

"Why don't you just bring me your case file?" she said.

"Excuse me?"

"Bring me what you've got," she said.

"And why would I do that?" Jack met her gaze.

"The cases are obviously related," Maureen said. "Mine was filed first. I've been on it for two weeks. You've been on it for what? Two days?"

"I'm not handing my case file over to you," Jack said.

"You think because I'm a black woman I can't handle two related cases?"

"Your case is a missing person," Jack pointed out. "Mine is a homicide. It has nothing to do with you being a woman or black. It has to do with you being in the missing persons unit and my being a homicide detective. If your victim turns up dead, you'll be giving me your case."

"We're not there yet," Maureen said. "What do you want to know?"

"My victim, Lorissa, worked at a bank." Jack looked at Maureen expectantly.

"District manager, beauty supply chain," Maureen said.

"Where was your vic abducted?"

"As far as we can tell, she was jogging the track at North High School with her dog," Maureen said. "One of her neighbors who knew she went there daily saw her that night. But she never returned home. Yours?"

"Walking path behind her apartment complex," Jack said. "Have you come across the names Ronnie or Ronald Dixon or a Jeremy?"

"Does Jeremy have a last name?" Maureen asked.

"Not yet," Jack said. "Has the name come up?"

"No," Maureen said. "Neither has Dixon. Are they suspects?"

"Persons of interest," Jack said.

"I'll alert the media." Maureen did not try to hide her sarcasm. "Do you have any other suspects?"

"Not at this time," Jack said. "What about you?"

"She walked her dog at approximately the same time every night. Her husband seldom went with her." Maureen cited the highlights of her case. "The Shepherd was intended to keep her safe. Their marriage seemed strong, so he doesn't seem a likely suspect. And according to her parents, siblings, and friends, she was happy and had no reason to leave on her own."

"Have you looked at Susan's circle of friends?" Jack asked. "Maybe she and Lorissa knew each other from church or something."

"Why do you do that?" Maureen said.

"Do what?"

"Use their first names," she said. "Like you know them?"

"I try to know every one of my victims," Jack said.

"Doesn't that just make it harder when you're not able to solve the case?"

"I guess I better solve the case then," Jack looked Maureen in the eyes.

"They don't know each other from church," she said.

"How do you know?"

"The Fredricksons moved here about a year ago from the east coast," she explained. "Where they grew up together as best friends before falling in love and getting married. They had been here less than six months when Mrs. Fredrickson disappeared. They were still settling in. They hadn't made any connections outside of work yet."

"So you know your vic pretty well," Jack said. "Almost well enough to call her by name."

"Maybe," Maureen said. "You really think they knew each other?"

Jack stood. He brushed at his pant legs to straighten them out then looked at the female detective. "I hate to think what it means if they didn't."

19

Shaun parked in front of the armored car company headquarters. There were a number of armored vehicles lined up on the side of the building, inside a tall chain-link fence. Otherwise, the business looked deserted. He entered the door that was not marked with an "employees only" sign. A chime announced his arrival, but the thick, angry-looking woman behind the desk had already spotted him.

"What can I do for you?" she said. The tone of her voice completely defied the expression on her face.

Shaun held out his badge. "Looking for one of your employees. First name Jeremy. His route includes . . ."

"What'd he do?" Her tone shifted more toward her expression.

"Just need to ask him some questions," Shaun said. "As I was saying his route . . ."

"I know who you're looking for," she said. "Only one Jeremy here. He's out right now. Should be back soon if you want to wait."

"That would be fine." Shaun stepped away from the desk and leaned against the wall.

"You want an application while you wait?" the woman asked. "Lots of cops work here part-time for extra income."

"No, thank you." The detective pulled out his phone and started scrolling through messages to let her know he wasn't interested in conversation.

After about ten minutes one of their trucks drove around the building toward the fenced parking area. Shaun watched through the windows.

"That's not him," the woman announced. "Should be the next one."

Fifteen more minutes passed and Shaun was still staring at his phone, though he had finished reading long ago. Another truck circled the building to park. He looked at the truck and then at the woman.

"That's him." She picked up her phone and pushed a button. She paused then said, "Hey. Send Jeremy to the office when he gets inside."

Shaun nodded to her and pushed away from the wall. A few minutes later the door behind her opened and a blond man approximately thirty years old walked in.

"What do you need, Ruby?" the man said.

"Not me." She pointed at the detective. "Him."

Jeremy looked at Shaun with confusion. "Who are you?"

"Detective Shaun Travis," he introduced, flashing his badge. "You're Jeremy?"

"Yes," he said.

"Last name?"

"Jones," he said. "Jeremy Jones. Shouldn't you already know that?"

"I have some questions for you," Shaun said. "We can step outside and speak privately, or I can run you downtown."

"Am I in trouble?"

"Should you be?"

"No," Jeremy said. "I just don't understand why you're here."

"Let me ask my questions and I'll explain," Shaun said.

"And if I say no?"

"I'll handcuff you and take you in," Shaun said. "Is that what you want? If you haven't done anything wrong, what are you hiding?"

Jeremy glanced at Ruby. Shaun was pretty sure his company would frown on him having a record.

"Yea," he said. "Okay."

The two of them stepped out the front doors and found a spot near the detective's car. Shaun asked to see Jeremy's license. Jeremy asked to see his badge again.

"What does the name Lorissa St. Clair mean to you?" Shaun asked.

"Lorissa?" Jeremy whistled. "Haven't heard that name in a long time. I know her. We dated briefly about a year ago."

"You gave her a dog?"

"Sure did," Jeremy said. "Cute little Aussie pup."

"Did it bother you when the two of you split and she kept the animal?" Shaun asked.

"Bother me?" Jeremy said. "Of course not. It was a gift. Besides my landlord wouldn't allow pets. What was I going to do with it?"

"What about now?" Shaun asked.

"What?" Jeremy said. "What do you mean by 'now'?"

"Do you still have a landlord that doesn't allow pets?" Shaun said. "Are you in the market? Did you perhaps decide you wanted the one you gave Lorissa?"

"She lost him, didn't she?" Jeremy became animated. "And she's blaming me? It's been a year. Why would I suddenly want it now?"

"Where were you Friday two weeks ago?" Shaun said. "In the evening specifically?"

"I wasn't stealing her dog," Jeremy said. "I can't believe a missing dog would warrant a detective."

"Where were you?" Shaun pressed him.

"I don't know," Jeremy said. "Two weeks ago? Friday night? Wait. I remember. I went to a club that night."

"Can anyone corroborate that?"

"I went with friends," he said. "They'll tell you."

"I need a list of their names," Shaun handed him a small notepad and pen. "With contact information."

"This is an awful lot for a dog," Jeremy took the pad and started writing.

"Were you aware that Lorissa was dating someone new?" Shaun asked.

"What?" Jeremy said. "No. But good for her."

"You gave her a puppy shortly after you started dating," Shaun said. "Then she dumped you. Moved on. You weren't a bit jealous?"

"Jealous?" Jeremy smirked. "I don't get jealous. I don't get that involved."

"A puppy is a long term kind of gift," Shaun said. "You didn't think your relationship was going somewhere?"

"Oh," Jeremy drew the word out like he suddenly understood. "Listen. A girl gave me that puppy. And I wasn't particularly into her and I couldn't have pets like I said. So, I re-gifted it. To Lorissa. There was no thought to it. I had a puppy I couldn't keep and Lorissa said yes when I asked if she wanted it."

"And that's all?"

"That's all." Jeremy handed the notepad back to Shaun. "That's everyone I went with that night."

Shaun looked at the list. There were almost a dozen names. Shaun looked up at the man.

"It was someone's birthday," Jeremy shrugged. "Don't ask me whose. I don't remember."

"Okay, Mr. Jones," Shaun handed Jeremy his card. "If you think of anything about that night, call me."

"Why so much effort for a missing dog?" Jeremy studied the card. "Wait. This says homicide."

"Lorissa was murdered, Mr. Jones," Shaun said. "The killer took her dog."

Jeremy stood slack-jawed as Shaun walked to his car and drove away.

20

"I called some names on the list," Shaun told Jack. "They all say that Jeremy Jones was at the club with them celebrating a friend's birthday. Jeremy got wasted and one of them drove him home. Had to take him back the next morning to get his car."

"Don't suppose he drives a truck?" Jack said.

"An old Mustang.," Shaun said. "He's not our guy."

"What did the friend who drove him home drive?" Jack asked. "Maybe they worked together."

"He's not our guy," Shaun repeated. "He left the club far too late to grab Lorissa."

"Okay." Jack sat forward in his seat. "I didn't get much on the Fredrickson investigation. Weatherby isn't into sharing."

"I heard she was pretty tight-lipped about her cases," Shaun said. "Claims it's part of her process."

"Well, what we did discuss didn't put any light on how the two women might be connected to one another," Jack said. "I keep waiting for us to find Susan with Lorissa's Australian Shepherd. There has to be a connection. We just aren't seeing it."

"What about Lorissa's laptop?" Shaun asked. "Maybe there's something on it."

"The techs in the lab got in," Jack shook his head. "There's nothing on it that would suggest she knew Susan or that she was having trouble with Ronnie or Jeremy. There wasn't much on it at all."

"Which leaves us where?"

"It leaves us at a dead end," Jack made a guttural noise and smacked his desk with the palm of his hand. "Damn it. There's got to be something we're missing."

A uniformed officer entered and scanned the room until he saw Jack. He took as direct a path as he could to the detective's desk.

"What is it?" Jack was gruff.

The officer glanced at Shaun before answering. "A woman was found."

"A woman?" Jack stood. "Is it Susan Fredrickson? Is she okay?"

"I wasn't given a name," the officer said. "They found her in a shallow grave east of town."

Jack fell back into his chair. "A body. So she's dead."

"And they told me to mention," the officer said, "she's buried with a dog."

"Of course she is," Jack said.

"Give me the address," Shaun said. "Let them know we're on our way."

"Yes, sir," the officer said.

"Hey!" Jack called out.

The officer turned.

"Tell Detective Weatherby to meet us there," Jack said. "This might close her case for her."

The officer nodded and changed course for the Missing Persons Unit.

"I was hoping we might find her alive," Jack said. He pulled himself to his feet and the two detectives made their way out of the building.

A half-hour later they were following a narrow dirt road into wooded land a quarter-mile off the rural highway. This was completely different from being next to a walking path in a public park. This was public land, but no one would come there at night. This was a place someone could take their time digging a grave and dragging bodies from a truck to bury.

They had seen the flashing lights long before they left the highway. But a lone vehicle with its lights off wouldn't be noticed.

"He didn't want this one found," Jack said.

"Maybe he's more connected to Susan," Shaun offered.

"How did anyone find the body out here?" Jack pulled off the road next to a row of highway troopers.

They left the car and walked into the crime scene showing their badges as they went. One trooper intercepted them just before they entered the tree line.

"You Mallory?" the tall man said. His jaw was set and looked like chiseled stone.

"I am," Jack said.

"Trooper Bruce Montgomery." He nodded his head in greeting.

"You have a woman buried with a dog, I understand," Jack said.

"We do," Bruce said. "And it's my understanding that makes it your case."

"It does," Jack said. "Can I ask who found the body? It's not exactly the kind of place one just happens upon."

"Three teenage boys on motorbikes," the trooper said. "They were riding in the area and cutting through the trees to add a little danger. One of them hit the grave which was loose soil. Front wheel sank and threw him. When he pulled the bike out, he pulled a leg up with it."

"I'm guessing the woman's," Jack said. "Not the dog's"

"That's correct," Bruce said.

"Where are the teens now?" Jack asked. "I didn't see them back at the cars."

"Sent them home," the trooper said. "It was getting late, and we had all we needed from them."

"We did?" Jack challenged. "I didn't speak to them. You sent my witnesses home without giving me the chance to question them?"

"With all due respect, detective," Bruce stood to his full towering height. "At that time it was my case, not yours. And I wasn't keeping kids out here at night just because they found a body. You think they killed her, you feel free to question them."

"Are we talking nineteen or thirteen?" Jack asked.

"Thirteen and fourteen," Bruce said.

"Okay," Jack said. "I'll talk to them if I need to. But if I could have your notes, I can probably leave them out of it."

"That works for me," the trooper pulled out his notes, tore two pages out, and handed them to Jack. "For what it's worth, I hope you catch the bastard."

"Me too, Trooper," Jack said.

A car pulled up to the area and parked. Detective Maureen Weatherby stepped out and jogged across the tall grass to where the three men were standing.

"Thanks for the heads up," she said to Jack.

"No problem," Jack said. "Thought you might want to be here."

The three detectives walked on to the trees and followed the lights to the grave. Similar to Lorissa's burial site, it was surrounded by trees on all sides. The body was laying on its back with the dog laying on top. They stared at the crime scene, at the bodies.

"That's not Susan Fredrickson," Maureen said.

"And that's not an Australian Shepherd," Jack added.

21

The three detectives stood at the edge of the road watching the medical examiner and her assistant emerging from the woods carrying a gurney. The sun was low in the western sky and the long shadows it cast gave Jack a chill in his spine. Reaching the van, they lowered the wheels and lined it up with the tracks inside. Leaving it up to her assistant to finish loading the van, Valerie O'Conner walked to where the trio was waiting.

"Maureen," she greeted. "Gentlemen. Are you all on this case?"

"Detective Weatherby came to see if it might be one of her missing persons," Jack said. "Detective Travis and I are here because we go where the bodies are."

"Does that make you the lead?"

"I guess it does," Jack said. "What can you tell us?"

"They've been out here a while," Valerie said. "With the weather being cool and dry and because she was buried, the decomposition process will have slowed. My best guess based on what I've seen is roughly four to eight weeks."

"That's quite a range," Shaun said.

"I'll narrow it down once I finish the autopsy." Valerie turned at the sound of doors being slammed. "That's my cue. I guess I'll see some of you in my autopsy room later."

The detectives remained where they were as the medical examiner retreated to the van. Once inside, the vehicle moved away, bouncing over the uneven terrain until it reached the dirt road. It sped off, leaving a cloud of dust in the air that drifted slowly after them.

"Four to eight weeks is after Susan Fredrickson disappeared," Maureen broke the silence.

"And before Lorissa," Jack added, staring at the trees where the body had been. "I really don't like which way this is headed."

Shaun turned to Jack. "You think it's a . . .?"

"Don't even say it," Jack interrupted. The generally accepted criteria for a case to be elevated to a serial killer is to have three or more victims over more than a month's time. If connected, the cases they were looking at definitely spanned the required time frame. But they only had two bodies, although it seemed likely Susan Fredrickson could be a third victim. "I'm not ready to go there."

"Speaking of going," Maureen said. "I better be getting back. Not my case after all. Thanks for the heads up. Glad it wasn't my girl though."

The three of them turned and walked toward their cars.

"We'll let you know if we find another." Jack stood next to the open driver's door.

"I hope I don't hear from you, then." She disappeared into her car, started the engine, and drove away.

"A redhead this time," Shaun said. "Might be easier to track down."

"We'll see," Jack said.

"What now?" Shaun asked.

"That looked like a Yellow Lab, or a mix of some kind," Jack said. "Not a small dog. And Susan's German Shepherd. Women often get these dogs to protect them from predators. How is this guy getting to them without losing a hand?"

"Maybe he uses a tranquilizer," Shaun offered. "Or he may drug them with something."

"That may be how he subdues the women too," Jack said. "But dosing a woman and dosing a dog would be different. We may be looking at someone with a medical background."

"That would narrow our suspect pool a little," Shaun said.

Jack pulled out his phone and dialed. "Maureen, Susan's husband wasn't a doctor, or something like that, was he?"

"No," Maureen answered. "Accountant. Why do you ask?"

"Just a thought," Jack said. "Doesn't matter until we know the cases are connected."

22

Jack sat at his desk looking through the trooper's notes on his interview with the boys who discovered the body the night before. A cup of coffee sat on the desk next to him, steam rising steadily as the liquid-cooled. The notes were better than Jack had expected them to be. The trooper had asked all the right questions and written the responses down clearly. He included all the contact information for the boys, but Jack didn't think he was going to need to talk to them again.

Shaun was at the next desk reviewing the information they had on Lorissa and Susan for any connection they might share in the medical arena. So far that had not turned up anything, but they had not asked about doctors, therapists, and such while interviewing the families. It was something they would need to touch base on if they wanted to find a common thread.

Jack's cell phone rang, and he had to adjust his posture to dig his hand into his pocket to retrieve it. Pressing it to his ear he said, "Mallory."

"Detective?" the woman said. "I almost gave up on you."

"Who is this?" He looked at Shaun and shrugged.

"Valerie O'Conner," she said. "Listen. I checked and this dog has a microchip too. I just sent you the information we retrieved from it."

Jack thanked her and pulled up the email she had sent. He printed it out and spun his chair to face Shaun. "We have another vet issued microchip. This one's office is in the west part of town. Let's hope we can identify the victim this time."

The drive across town took more than thirty minutes. Like the first victim, it was nowhere close to the location the woman's body was found. She could have driven the extra distance after finding a vet she trusted. She may have moved after she got the dog. And of course, there was the obvious option. The killer may have taken the woman near her home and transported her to another location where he killed her, then taken her even farther from home to dispose of the body.

This veterinarian's office was a large operation on some acreage with a barn so they could treat horses and cattle. When Jack parked, there was a truck and trailer backing into a loading area. A man in his twenties was guiding the driver, using hand signals to direct him. A young woman stood off to the side holding two dogs on leashes watching the process.

The detectives entered the lobby which was packed with people and animals. Dogs barked, cats hissed and a bird tweeted. Three women sat behind a long reception desk checking people in and out. A woman walked out of the back with a cat carrier, a frightened Siamese inside. She handed the carrier off to a couple standing at the desk. The husband paid their bill while the wife used baby talk to try to calm the feline.

Another woman came from the back and escorted a woman with a small dog to a room. Jack and Shaun took their place in line and watched the constant flow as they made their way to the front. The young woman who had been walking the two dogs came through with only one dog, a mid-sized mutt. Immediately the dog began to growl, bark, and lunge at the other animals in the room. The woman gave command after command to no avail, finally dragging the dog back toward the hallway.

"Shelly!" The woman behind the reception's desk closest to her yelled. "Have Tanner work with him."

The woman with the mutt sneered.

"Just do it," the woman said. "Dr. Parks needs an assistant anyway."

"Okay, Nancy. I'm going." Shelly said turning abruptly and disappearing to the back.

Jack and Shaun were next and as a woman with two small children dragged a puppy away on a leash, they stepped up to the free receptionist.

"Hello," Nancy said. "Name and which doctor are you here to see?"

"We aren't here for an appointment," Jack said. "I'm Detective Jack Mallory and . . ."

"Oh!" The woman jumped out of her seat. "Just a minute."

Jack was left mid-sentence watching the woman half-jog down the hall.

"That was odd," Shaun said low enough only Jack would hear.

Jack watched the woman move down the hall, her ponytail bouncing from side to side as she went. She tapped a door with her knuckle and stepped inside. A moment later she reemerged and walked back down the hall. She stopped at the edge of the room and waved Jack toward her.

"This way, detective," she said.

Several heads raised to get a look. Jack and Shaun pushed their way to the woman and followed her back down the hall. Nancy took them past all the rooms and through a set of swinging doors. They turned sharply to the right, past a row of double-stacked kennels, each containing a small or medium-sized dog. Barking erupted and continued after they were well past them.

The woman leading them stopped next to an open door. "He'll be right with you."

The detectives stepped inside an office with two desks that were in disarray. When they turned back to the door, the woman was gone.

Shaun sat in one of the chairs while Jack moved to one wall and started reading the names on the degrees that hung there. Doctor David Parks was on two of them. Doctor Samantha Bedford had two as well. As did Doctor Judith Stevens. Doctor Keith Stevens had five. Below them all was one for a Doctor Luke Ramsey.

"Gentlemen," a deep voice broke the silence they hadn't been aware of.

Both men turned to the door where a tall slender man with salt and pepper hair stood.

"I suppose you have news." The man crossed to the larger desk and sat facing Shaun.

"News?" Jack sat in the chair next to Shaun. "News about what?"

"My wife," the man sat forward. "Aren't you here about her? Linda said you were detectives."

"Detective Jack Mallory," Jack leaned forward and offered his hand. The man took it in an iron tight grasp and shook.

"Shaun Travis," Shaun said. The two of them shook hands as well.

"And you are?" Jack prompted.

"Doctor Keith Stevens," the man leaned back. "Which you would have known had you been here to talk to me about my wife. So, why are you here?"

Jack pulled the information he had printed earlier out of his pocket, unfolded the paper, and handed it to the veterinarian. "We need to know who owns this dog."

Keith held the paper and looked at it without really focusing. "You found a dog? Two detectives for a dog? It would be nice if you guys put this much effort into my wife's case."

"We're not on your wife's case," Shaun said.

"I don't think anyone is," Keith said.

"Look up the owner of this dog," Jack said, "and tell me about your wife."

"You don't have to pretend you're interested," Keith pulled his keyboard to the center of the desk and started typing.

"I'm not pretending," Jack said. "I wasn't aware of the case. Now I am and I want to know what you're dealing with."

"What I'm dealing with, as you put it," Keith said, "is that my wife disappeared."

"So she's a missing person?" Shaun said.

"That's right," Keith punched a few more keys and the printer behind him came to life. "Almost a year now."

"We don't do missing persons," Shaun said. "But we can talk to them when we get back."

Keith snatched the page of the printer and held it out to Jack. "You don't do missing persons. You do missing dogs. Maybe you should be more ambitious."

Jack took the paper. "Doctor Stevens, we are from homicide. You don't want us on your wife's case. But I would like to hear the circumstances of her disappearance."

"Homicide? So the owner of the dog is dead?" The veterinarian glanced at the name on the computer screen.

"We don't know who is dead," Jack said. "We are hoping this information will get us closer to an identification. Now, about your wife."

23

"Like I said," Keith explained. "She disappeared almost a year ago. She left work a little early that day. When I got home her car was there, but she wasn't."

"She worked here?" Jack twisted in his chair to the framed degrees. "Judith Stevens?"

"That's her," Keith nodded. "We started this business together."

"And how was business?" Jack said. "At the time. Was it good or bad?"

"I don't know," Keith said. "It has ups and downs. I don't remember which it was at that time. Judy did the paperwork."

Jack scanned the mess on the desk. "The two of you weren't having any troubles, were you?"

"No, detective," Keith said. "Our marriage was good, is good. I just need her home."

"Do you remember why she left early that day?" Jack asked.

"She was expecting a delivery, I think," Keith said. "That's right, it was one of those meals in a box things, where they send you the ingredients and you prepare it yourself. She wanted to be sure it got into the refrigerator as soon as possible. Come to think of it, I never saw it."

"So, your wife left work early for a delivery," Jack said. "And when you got home, she and the delivery were gone?"

"That's right," Keith said.

"How much time had passed?" Jack asked.

"Pardon?"

"Between the time she left work and you arrived home," Jack said. "How much time are we talking about?"

"Three," Keith tilted his head trying to see something not there. "Three and a half hours maybe."

"And how long after that before you called the police?" Shaun asked.

"I tried calling Judy first," Keith said. "Then I called her parents, her brother, her friends. I went from nervous to full panic in about an hour when I realized no one had seen or heard from her. I called the police about a half-hour after that. But they wouldn't do anything."

"Because she hadn't been missing for twenty-four hours," Jack said.

"That's what they said," Keith grimaced. "So, I waited twenty-four hours and one minute and called them again."

"I assume they canvased the neighborhood to see if anyone saw anything," Jack said.

"They did," Keith said. "But we live in an almost rural suburb. The lots are two to three acres. The houses are staggered so you aren't directly across from your neighbor. It's not where you can sit and watch everything going on."

"They came up empty?"

"No one remembered seeing her," Keith confirmed. "They did mention some cars driving by, but nothing panned out."

"Her car was there," Jack said. "So she made it home."

"Yes."

"Maybe she came home to find someone stealing the meal off the porch," Shaun suggested. "They took her so she couldn't call the police."

"You think someone took her?"

"Either that or she left," Jack said. "You said your marriage was good. That leaves kidnapping. But if Detective Travis is right, it would suggest they didn't want to kill a witness. They could be holding her, not knowing what to do next."

"You're saying that's a best-case scenario?"

"Your sure nothing else was missing?" Jack asked.

"Besides the meal in a box?" Keith said. "Just Judy. Oh, and the dog."

"The dog?" Jack sat forward. "Your dog is missing as well?"

"Now you're interested?" Keith said. "I guess I should have started with the dog."

"You should have," Jack said. "What breed is it?"

"Border Collie mix," Keith said. "Someone left it in a crate in front of our clinic. Only had three legs. Judy loved that dog."

"Could she have taken the dog for a walk?"

"I'm sure she did," Keith said. "Why?"

"You said the homes in your neighborhood are on large lots," Jack ignored the question. "Are there any parks? Somewhere a parked car might not look out of place?"

"There's a picnic area at the edge of the neighborhood," Keith said. "This is sounding familiar to you?"

"I don't want to jump to conclusions," Jack said.

"But you're homicide detectives," Keith said. "You're here hoping to identify a victim using a microchip. And when I mentioned our dog went missing when Judy did, your questions became about the dog. You know something. You think Judy's dead don't you?"

"Don't do that to yourself," Jack said. "We don't have any reason to think your wife's disappearance has anything to do with our case."

"She's been gone a year, detective," Keith said. "Even an optimist would have trouble putting a positive spin on that."

"When we get back, I'll follow up with the detective assigned to your wife's case," Jack said.

"Judy," Keith said. "Her name is Judy. She's not just a case to me."

"I understand," Jack said.

"I hope so," Keith said. "Now if you'll excuse me, I have patients waiting."

The tall man rose from his seat and stepped into the hall with the detectives. The young man who had been guiding the trailer in the parking lot was there with the mutt the female employee had brought to the lobby. The dog was sitting next to him without a hint of the aggression it was displaying earlier.

"Tanner," Keith said to the employee, "could you show these gentlemen out?"

"Yes, sir," the man mumbled. He patted the dog on the head and with a command, they started down the hall. "Follow me."

They trailed behind man and dog as he led them toward the entrance. The dog obeyed every command, each step of the way. The detectives were anticipating what would happen when they reached the lobby where Shelly had lost control of the dog before.

They reached the destination and the dog began to growl as expected. A sharp command by Tanner and the mutt sat on his haunches and became silent. Shaun thanked him as they continued to the exit. Outside, Shelly was walking a large poodle with a cone around its head. It was a busy place. Jack wondered what a hardship it must be to be short a veterinarian.

24

The owner of the dog found buried with the second victim was named Angel Garcia. The address linked to the dog's microchip was near the vet they had just left, so Jack drove straight over. The home was a duplex in a low rent community. There were two cars in the driveway, though one was missing the front driver's side tire and the hood was open partway.

The detectives stepped onto the porch and knocked on the door. A barrage of barking from multiple dogs greeted them. They took a step back and remained guarded until a man appeared, yelled to silence the animals, and stepped outside with his visitors.

"What do you want?" The man barked.

"I'm Detective Jack Mallory," Jack introduced. "And you are?"

"Eduardo Ramos," the man said. "Why are you here?"

"We're looking for an Angel Garcia," Jack said.

"Angel?" Eduardo chuckled. "You're about two years too late."

"What happened to her?" Shaun asked.

"Nothing happened to her," Eduardo said. "She moved out. Packed up while I was at work and took off. Real class act."

"Did she have a yellow lab?" Jack asked.

"Took it with her," he said.

"Do you know how we could get ahold of her?" Jack looked past the man into the house. It wouldn't be the first time someone murdered their wife or girlfriend and claimed they moved out.

"I know exactly where she is," the man said. "She's with that no good son-of-a-bitch Marcus Valdez."

"Not a fan, huh?" Shaun said.

"He was my best friend," Eduardo said. "Now he's nobody."

"Do you have an address?" Jack asked.

"I do."

The new address was another ten minutes away. It was a small apartment complex standing in a horseshoe shape. According to Eduardo, Marcus Valdez and Angel Garcia lived in the third apartment on the second floor.

The detectives climbed the stairs to the walkway that spanned the front of all the second-floor apartments. They knocked on the third door. It was opened by a young woman with a brilliant smile. "Hello?"

"Angel Garcia?" Jack said.

"Yes?" the woman said.

They had not expected to find the woman. If this was her, she was obviously not the woman in the grave. Jack said, "I'm Detective Jack Mallory. Do you own a Yellow Lab?"

"I did." Her brow wrinkled. "But not for a while."

"Can you tell me what happened to the dog?"

"Am I in trouble?" she said. "I haven't had the dog in two years."

"About the time you moved out of Eduardo's place," Shaun said.

"Did he send you?" she said. "He said he didn't want him."

"What happened to the dog?" Jack asked again.

"The landlord here doesn't allow pets," Angel said. "I had to find him a new home."

"Do you happen to know who you gave him to?" Shaun asked.

"Sure," Angel smiled. "I gave it to a woman I used to work with. Her name's Brea Wiseman."

"Used to work with?"

"I left there shortly after," she said. "But I think Brea is still there."

25

The office where Angel Garcia and Brea Wiseman worked together was a locally owned insurance company. Jack guided the car into a parking space directly across from the entrance. He and Shaun were greeted at the door by a jelly doughnut in a dress.

"Welcome." The woman smiled broadly. "Are you interested in a new policy today?"

"We need to speak to Brea Wiseman," Jack said.

"Excuse me?" She cocked her head to one side.

"Brea Wiseman," Jack repeated.

"I'm sorry," she said. "I'm kind of new here. Let me get someone else."

She waddled to a nearby office and leaned through the door. A moment later she returned, followed closely by a middle-aged woman in a pantsuit. The receptionist settled into her place behind her desk. The pantsuit stopped just short of the men.

"May I help you, gentlemen?" Her dark eyes betrayed her toothy smile as they scanned the men with cautious interest.

"Are you Brea Wiseman?"

"No," the woman said. "But I would be glad to help you."

Jack held up his badge. "I need Ms. Wiseman."

"Oh." Her face flushed a bright red. "I'm sorry. No. Brea is no longer with us."

"Do you know where she's working now?" Jack asked.

"I'm afraid not," she said. "She just stopped coming to work."

"How long ago was that?" Jack said.

"About three months ago," the woman said.

"And you didn't find that unusual?" Shaun asked.

"Not really," she said. "She had been talking about a career change. We expected a two-week notice. But when she stopped coming to work, we assumed she had moved on. Why? What's this about?"

"We need you to get her home address for us," Jack said.

"I'm not sure I can give you that," she said.

"I wasn't asking," Jack lowered her eyes, focusing on hers.

"I don't know that you are who you say you are." She took a step back. "How do I know she didn't stop coming to work because she's trying to hide from you? I'm not giving you her address."

"I can respect that," Jack said. He pulled out his phone and pulled up a picture. "Can you tell me if this is her?"

He turned the phone to her and she shrank away. "Oh my God! Why would you show me that?"

All eyes in the office turned their way. Jack remained focused on the pantsuit. "We are trying to identify a body. We have reason to believe it may be Brea Wiseman. Do you think this is her?"

"Poor Brea." She tried again to look at the picture but diverted her eyes quickly. "I don't know. It doesn't look like her, but it could be."

"That's why we need her address," Jack said. "With any luck, we'll find her there."

"Of course." She nodded and walked back to her office, returning a few minutes later with a small piece of paper. "This is the address we have on file. I hope it helps. I hope she's okay. God. Is that why she stopped coming to work?"

Jack took the paper from her and mentally estimated the distance from where they were. If she had been taken three months ago and killed four to eight weeks ago, the killer had kept her alive for one to two months. To the woman, he said, "Let's hope not."

The address the woman provided was an apartment building on the north end of town. It had eight levels, four more than any other building in the area. According to the room number, Brea was located on the fifth level. The detectives took the elevator up and knocked on the appropriate apartment.

"Hello?" The door was opened by a mousy little man.

"May we speak to Brea?"

"No Brea here," he said, shutting the door.

Jack kicked his foot out to block it.

"Hey!"

"Is she not here?" Jack demanded. "Or do you not know her?"

"I don't know her," the man said. "Now move your foot or I'll call the police."

"How long have you lived here?" Jack continued.

"Moved in three week's ago." The man pulled out his phone.

Jack moved his foot away and pulled the door closed.

"What now?" Shaun said.

"There was a leasing office on the ground floor," Jack said. "We go there."

"Do you think he'll call the police?" Shaun hooked his thumb back down the hall while they waited for the elevator to arrive.

"I doubt it," Jack said. "That would just bring more people to his door."

Back on the first floor, they made their way to the back corner stopping at a door that was marked with a plaque identifying it as the manager's office. They hesitated, not sure if they should knock or enter. Jack chose the latter and opened the door. They stepped into a small space with a single desk and a sliding glass door on the opposite wall leading to a pool and patio. The blond behind the desk forced a grin and raised her puffy eyes to them. "Are you looking to lease?"

Jack held out his badge. The woman's smile faded. "We're looking for one of your tenants."

"I assure you," she said. "We do thorough background checks. Whoever you're looking for doesn't live here."

"A Ms. Brea Wiseman," Jack said. "Supposed to be in room five-fourteen."

"Oh, her," the woman said. "She's no longer here."

"Let me guess," Jack said. "Three months ago?"

"About that," she said. "Missed two rent payments, so we evicted her. Her belongings are in storage."

"She didn't move out then?"

"Just left," she said. "Didn't take anything with her either."

"And you didn't think to call the police?" Jack asked. "Maybe file a missing persons report?"

"I rent apartments," she said. "I'm not a den mother. I'm not their keeper. If someone's missing, their friends and family would know."

"Evidently not," Jack said. "Did you have an emergency contact on file for Ms. Wiseman?"

She opened a file cabinet and thumbed through folders at the back of the drawer. She pulled one out and looked at the pages inside. "There's a cosigner."

"I'm surprised you didn't call them about the overdue rent," Shaun said.

"The original agreement was for a twelve-month lease," the woman said. "Brea had been here for four years. The renewed agreements did not require, nor did they have cosigners. If they had, I would have called."

"Four years?" Shaun shook his head. "Four years and she stops paying her rent and leaves her things behind and you didn't notify anyone?"

"Give us the contact information for the cosigner," Jack said. "Then we'll get out of your hair."

26

The cosigner for Brea Wiseman's apartment was a Walter Wiseman. The address was not local, so Jack waited until they returned to the department to place a call to the man.

In just a few minutes, Jack learned that Walter was Brea's father. Neither he nor Brea's mother had heard from their daughter in several months, however, that was not unusual. They were not aware that Brea was missing and became very distressed by the news. At Jack's request, they agreed to email the detective a recent photo of Brea.

When Jack disconnected the call, Shaun was hovering over him.

"What?" Jack asked.

"O'Conner wants us in the morgue," the young detective said.

"Did she say why?" Jack rose to his feet and stretched.

"I assume she has some information for us," Shaun said.

"Of course she has information," Jack said. "She's not inviting us to lunch. We have two victims down there. She didn't say which one this was about?"

"No," Shaun said. "I didn't think to ask."

They took the elevator to the basement level and followed the long corridor to the morgue. They passed by the front offices, walking directly into the autopsy room where Valerie stood over the body of their most recent victim. She was concentrating on the task at hand and did not acknowledge the men. When she finished, she lay her instruments on a side table, pulled off and disposed of her gloves, and approached them.

"Thank you for coming down," she said. "I have the results of the St. Clair autopsy."

She gestured for them to follow her and walked back toward the offices. She took them to her office which, in contrast to the autopsy room, was dimly lit. She sat behind her desk and turned on the small lamp on its corner. The detectives took the seats across from her and waited.

"From the scientific data," Valerie tossed a folder at Jack, who caught it in a less than graceful fashion. "The victim was buried within a day of her death. About three days before her body was discovered."

"That means the killer had her for about a week before he killed her," Jack thought aloud.

"That sounds about right," Valerie said. "There are signs of abuse over time. Bruises at varying stages of healing. Cuts on her wrists that suggest she was bound show the same signs of different stages of healing. And she was sexually assaulted several times."

"And how did she die?" Jack said, reading through the report.

"Some kind of poison," Valerie said. "We have bloodwork out for analysis to determine what kind. Strange thing, there, is the dog seems to have died the same way."

"He poisoned them both?" Shaun said. "Seems like an odd choice."

"We also found a residue under her fingernails that is at the lab," Valerie said. "Along with some wood-shavings that we found on her body like she was laying on it. It was in the dog's fur as well."

"Wood shavings?" Jack considered. "Could mean we're looking for a carpenter, or someone who works with wood as a hobby."

"She had a broken arm," Valerie said. "The bone wasn't set."

"So he broke it," Shaun said.

"Or she did," Jack said, "trying to get away. What kind of fracture was it?"

"Comminuted," Valerie said.

"Which means?" Shaun asked.

"It means the bone was broken into several pieces," Valerie explained. "Like it was crushed."

"Something that could be caused by blunt force?" Jack said. "Possibly being stomped on?"

"That's a possibility," the medical examiner said. "But I can't say one way or the other what caused the injury."

"I understand," Jack said. "But this girl suffered a lot of trauma at the hands of her killer. I'm going to assume he purposely broke her arm until someone proves otherwise."

"You can assume whatever you want, detective," Valerie said. "Just catch the bastard who did this."

"I'm going to do my best," Jack said. "Anything on the other body yet?"

"I've only just started on her," Valerie said. "I can tell you what I've found so far."

"That's all I ask."

"She appears to be a woman in her mid to late twenties," Valerie said. "I'm sure you're wondering if being buried with a dog is a coincidence or if there is a connection. There is the same or similar residue under the fingernails. There are also the same wood shavings. And although I've only just begun the autopsy, I can tell you that this girl suffered a significant amount of trauma."

"Any broken bones like Lorissa's arm?" Jack asked.

"Not that far along," she said. "I'll have more tomorrow."

The detectives returned to their desks armed with new information. They needed to re-interview witnesses to ask about acquaintances with medical backgrounds as well as possible carpenters or woodworkers.

Jack opened his email and saw that he had one from Brea's parents with an attachment. They had promised to send a recent photo and had followed through. He double-clicked the attachment and a portrait filled his screen. The young woman smiled broadly, her eyes bright with life. It was a portrait of a happier time, a time that was probably gone. The feature that stood out most was the hair. She wore it in a braid that draped over her shoulder and continued past the bottom of the image. Long and golden, Rapunzel came to mind. Not the red-haired victim buried in the trees.

Two bodies. Two dogs belonging to two other missing women; three if you counted Judith Stevens. Five possible victims. Jack worried that there maybe even more.

27

Throughout the course of the day, Jack and Shaun revisited family, friends, and coworkers of Susan, Lorissa, Brea, and Judith both in person and over the phone. They worked separately to cover as much territory as they could as quickly as possible.

They learned that other than doctor's appointments, the only medical contact between them was a friend of Lorissa's that was a nurse. The petite woman was unlikely to be the killer they were looking for, although they didn't take her off the list as it was always possible she was working with a partner in crime.

Brea had an uncle who had a woodworking shop, but he lived six hours away and had an allergy to dogs. The Fredricksons had some work done on their home, but it had taken place three years ago. The Stevens had a barn at their clinic repaired, but the man they hired was retired and, although he owned a truck, it was hard to imagine him climbing up to disable the lamppost in the park.

Susan Fredrickson was thought of fondly in her inner circle, often referred to as smart and witty. She, unlike the other women, was in her forties. She was a department head at the accounting firm where she worked. Her subordinates sang her praises. Her bosses respected her. Outside of work she had a few close friends and family members she kept in touch with on an almost daily basis. None of them knew of anyone in her life who had a problem with her.

Lorissa St. Clair had a very close family and her friends were distraught by the news of her death. She was a teller at a small bank and her coworkers thought highly of her. The boyfriend and ex-boyfriend might be viable suspects for her murder but, as of yet, there was no connection between either of them and the other women.

Brea Wiseman was a receptionist at an insurance office. Her family was from out of town and did not know she was missing. Not exactly close. Her coworkers assumed she had quit without notice and never checked on her. So far the detectives were unable to track down any friends the woman had. The few comments they received suggested that Brea was shy and alone.

Judith Stevens was a veterinarian, a partner with her husband in their clinic. Her family and friends had positive things to say about her and Keith. The employees at the clinic gave a mix of comments, varying from sweet and a terrific boss to stern and mean. One person mentioned that she showed favoritism and praised those staff members while degrading the others. All agreed that she was a great vet and was missed by clients.

Little was known about their Jane Doe. She was in her twenties and had red hair. Other than that there was no way to know much more without making an identification.

Two married, two single, one unknown. Three twenty-somethings. One thirty-something. One forty-something. Different heights and builds. Different hair colors. The only similarities between the women were their ownership of dogs, with the exception of the Jane Doe which they just didn't know yet.

Jack slammed down the phone after ending his last call. He wanted answers and none were coming. He was waiting for lab and autopsy results on their Jane Doe. He was dreading combing through missing persons files for redheads.

"Mallory," Chief Sharon Hutchins called across the room. "Can I see you in my office, please?"

Jack stood. He wasn't sure what the chief could want with him. At the same time, he had never had a chief ask him to the office so nicely. All the same, he knew it couldn't be good. He reached her door and tapped a knuckle on the framework before walking in.

"What's up?" he said.

"Have a seat, Jack," Sharon said.

He paused for just a second before lowering himself into a chair.

"Everything okay, Jack?" she asked.

"Everything, sir?" Jack sat up a little straighter.

"How's the case coming along?" she said. "Any promising leads, suspects maybe?'"

"Are you checking up on me?" Jack asked.

"I'm checking on the progress of a case under my jurisdiction," her tone shifted. "Do you have a suspect or not?"

"I don't," Jack said. "Well that's not true. I have several suspects. It's just none of them seem good for all the killings."

"All?" she said. "You're working the case with the girl and the dog?"

"Two girls, two dogs," Jack said. "And we've added three missing women to the group. And at least one missing dog."

"Is that why you're trying to break your phone?" she asked.

"You saw that?"

"I did."

"Just hit a point where I'm waiting on others," Jack said. "I'm not that patient."

"Do I need to light some fires under some asses?" the chief asked.

"No," Jack said. "They're working. As I said, I'm just not patient."

"Maybe you and Travis should call it a day," the chief said. "Fresh mind. Fresh perspective."

Jack didn't say anything.

"Yeah," the chief said. "That sounded better in my head. Go home, Jack. Get some rest so I don't have to buy you a new phone."

28

Jack's alarm went off and the detective sat up with a jolt. He normally woke before the alarm and was surprised to hear the offensive noise. The chief had been right apparently. He needed rest. But he was not going to let her know that. He took a quick shower and dressed. Refreshed and his mind sharp, he was ready to attack the case anew.

He stopped at a coffee shop close to the department. He stepped in line and started checking his phone for messages. A tap on his shoulder brought him around.

"Morning," Valerie smiled. "Don't think I've seen you here before."

"I usually go to bed at this hour," Jack said. "Which is why I need coffee. What's your excuse. You're already too perky for this time of day."

"Perky?" she laughed. "I guess I'll accept that characterization. But I'm here because if I don't get my cup of java, the perkiness wears off. And I assure you nobody wants that."

"Really?" He crossed his arms and sized her up. "I wouldn't mind seeing you chew someone out."

"What if it's you?"

"I'll take that chance," he grinned. "Besides, this whole happy routine doesn't really go with the job description."

"I'm supposed to be all doom and gloom?"

"You take bodies apart for a living." Several people looked Jack's way. He waved them off. "Not exactly uplifting work seeing what the worst of society can do to another human being."

"Well now you're depressing me," Valerie said. "Move up."

Jack turned and took a couple of steps.

"I don't look at my work the way you do," Valerie said. "I look at my work the way you look at yours."

"How do I look at mine?"

"We each do our part to catch the killers," she said. "It's rewarding work."

"That's not at all how I look at my job," Jack said.

"It should be." Valerie put a hand on his back and pushed him forward. "How do you look at it?"

"I hunt down the scum of the earth and put them behind bars," Jack said.

"That's what I said," Valerie declared.

"Sir?" The young man behind the counter interrupted. "Can I take your order?"

"Medium Coffee," Jack said.

"We have tall, grande, and venti," the clerk said.

"The one in the middle would be the medium," Jack said.

"Yes, sir." He moved away to get Jack's coffee.

"Tell me how what I said differs from what you said," Valerie continued.

"Because in my version," Jack turned to her, "I know that there is a never-ending supply of scum."

"Two-seventy-five," the clerk rang up the sale.

"For coffee?" Jack said. "No wonder I usually make it at home."

"Just move so I can order," Valerie said. She rattled off her order, something Jack wasn't entirely sure was even a drink, let alone coffee. "Your problem is you need a better attitude."

"My attitude is fine," Jack said.

Her beverage arrived, and she paid more than twice what Jack had without blinking an eye. She even thanked the young man.

Jack watched the whole transaction. "Okay. Maybe my attitude isn't fine. But it's good enough for my needs."

"You should spend the day with me," Valerie said. "I could give you pointers on being happy."

"Can't," Jack said. "Too much scum to catch. But thanks for the offer."

"Well the lab results came back on the St. Clair girl," Valerie said. "So you'll be spending part of the day with me anyway."

"I'll be there," Jack said. "What about the new one? Autopsy done?"

"Not yet," she said. "But soon."

They left the coffee shop and Jack stopped in front of his car. "Where are you?"

"Oh, I walked," Valerie said.

"From the station?"

"From home," she said. "And now to the station."

"Do you want a lift?" Jack asked.

"Oh, no," she said. "I walk because I want to."

"What on earth for?" Jack looked at her with scrutiny.

"I'll see you in my office later." Valerie turned and walked away while Jack slid into his department issue vehicle.

About an hour later Jack called ahead to be sure she would be ready to see them, then he and Shaun rode the elevator to the basement level. In the morgue, they let an assistant know they were there and waited in Valerie's office for her arrival.

She entered the room with her coffee cup in hand. Jack had finished his long ago. She greeted the men and circled the desk to sit behind it. Perching the cup on a stack of folders, she pulled a short stack toward her. Spreading them like a fan, she took hold of one of the tabs and pulled that folder out of the pile.

She scanned the contents with the occasional "hmm" and "oh". When she finished, she looked up at the detectives who waited impatiently.

"The wood shavings," Valerie said, "are red cedar."

"Red cedar?" Shaun said.

"Typically used as mulch or animal bedding," she said. "They're soft and repel insects."

"Makes sense," Jack said. "keeping the dogs. Having bedding for them."

"Which brings us to the residue under her nails," Valerie turned the page. "it is a disinfectant spray primarily used in kennels. It was also on her arms, legs, and in her hair."

"Are you saying she was sprayed with disinfectant?" Jack leaned forward.

"I'm not saying anything," she said. "But it is possible."

"Her bloodwork was inconclusive," Valerie read. "But her stomach contents and that of the dog gave us the cause of death for both. They were fed a mixture of hamburger and Oleander leaves that were heavily seasoned. That would be necessary because Oleander does not have a particularly good flavor."

"He fed the girl and the animal the same poisonous concoction?" Jack thought aloud.

"It appears so," Valerie said. "There was some dog food in their stomachs, more in the dog's than the girl's."

"So he starved the girl to be sure she would eat the poisoned meat when he gave it to them," Jack said. "A rather unpleasant way to die."

"Very," Valerie said. "But he gave them enough that it should have been fast."

"I suppose that's a good thing," Jack said. "Have you got anything else?"

"Not on Lorissa," she said. "We were able to get prints off of the Jane Doe, but there were no hits."

"Do you know when you'll be finished with that autopsy?" Jack asked.

"Should be done later today," she said. "I'll let you know when my report is complete."

Jack stood, "Thank you for your time, doc."

"Doc?" Valerie said. "Why don't we stick to Valerie?"

"Okay, Valerie," the detective moved to the door with Shaun following close behind. "We'll wait to hear from you."

They excused themselves and returned the way they had come. They settled into their desks and Jack pulled up the missing persons' database. Under the filter column, he chose red hair and female. Although the parameters narrowed the search, there were still far too many.

29

Narrowing the search parameters even more, using age, Jack also eliminated any that went missing more than a year or less than two weeks ago. There were only two names remaining on the list. A Glenda Stokes and a Meghan Quinn. He stared at their faces on the screen wondering which one, if either, they had found.

"With the red cedar shavings," Shaun said, "should we drop the carpenters from our search?"

"Carpenters still produce wood shavings," Jack said. "Drop them to the bottom of the list, but don't take them off. And with all the new information, I think we should focus on locations that board animals. Get a list of all the breeders, veterinarians, rescue shelters, dog trainers, kennels, and whatever else you can think of that might have facilities for dogs."

"That's a lot of names," Shaun said.

"And doesn't include the ones that are unregistered," Jack said. "But it's a place to start. Once we have the list, we'll need to eliminate any that don't use red cedar."

Shaun pointed at Jack's screen. "Is one of them our victim?"

"They are the most probable matches," Jack said. "But she may not be either one. I'm hoping the autopsy results will eliminate or confirm one of them."

"I'll get to work on the dog facilities," Shaun turned to his computer. "Maybe I can narrow the list down to two."

"I doubt that," Jack said. "But go ahead and try."

Jack printed the files on the two girls and set them on the corner of his desk.

"My God," Shaun said. "There are hundreds listed here."

"Eliminate the big public facilities," Jack suggested. "You can't hide a girl unnoticed with a lot of foot traffic."

"Taking out the big box pet stores, the government-run shelters, and the larger clinics," Shaun typed as he spoke. "That leaves us with one hundred thirty-eight. You have to be kidding."

"Divide the list into zones," Jack said. "We'll have uniforms check them out."

"I'm still not used to the fact that I'm not the uniform anymore," Shaun said.

"Well get used to it," Jack said. "You'll need a list of questions for them. Type of bedding, type of disinfectant, type of tranquilizers."

"Tranquilizers?" Shaun said. "They didn't find tranquilizers in the bloodwork."

"Saves us the time from having to go back and ask again later," Jack said.

"In case we do find something later," Shaun nodded.

"Right." Jack stood and picked up the papers he had printed. "I'm going to go talk to missing persons. See if there's anything not in these files."

Jack arrived in the missing persons department and saw Detective Weatherby working at her desk. He approached her with a wave of the hand. Seeing Jack heading her way, she sat back and waited.

"You keep coming down here and people are going to start talking, detective," Maureen said. "What brings you this time?"

"Let them talk," Jack smiled. "I'll spread a few rumors myself."

"Just what I need," Maureen said.

Jack held out the pages about the two redheads. "I have a couple of yours that I need more detail on."

"Couple of mine?" she took the papers and scanned them. "These aren't mine."

"I meant collectively yours," Jack said. "Your department."

"What do you want to know?" Maureen asked.

"Did either of them have a dog?" Jack asked. "Particularly one that went missing the same time they did?"

"Oh," Maureen said. "The girl in the woods. You think one of these might be her."

"The thought crossed my mind," Jack said.

"Let me see what I can find," Maureen said. "Give me a minute."

She rose from her seat and crossed to a detective who tried to look busier than he was. She handed him one of the papers. He looked at it, opened a folder on his desk, shook his head, and handed it back to her. Maureen showed the detective the other paper and pointed. The man spoke with his hands, gesturing this way and that. Maureen nodded sharply and walked away.

She returned to her desk and Jack. "Glenda Stokes did not have a dog. And she turned up with her boyfriend in Colorado. Both are being brought home."

"What about Meghan Quinn?"

"Seems that case was assigned to Detective Xavier Grey," Maureen said.

"I saw that," Jack said. "I haven't seen him since my return."

"He quit the force about a month ago," she said. "Just before I was transferred. His cases were reassigned, but Quinn's may have fallen through the cracks."

"No one's been working her case?" Jack said a little louder than he meant to.

"It doesn't look like it," Maureen said.

"Well, detective," Jack took the paper from her hand. "Want to join me in questioning her family?"

30

At Jack's suggestion, Detective Shaun Travis was able to divide the names of the businesses that fit the profile into smaller, more manageable lists and distribute them to uniformed officers to follow up on. He kept one list for himself, not wanting to delegate the visit to the Stevens' place.

He made two stops before arriving at the veterinary clinic. Compared to their first visit, it wasn't nearly as crowded. Shaun pulled into a space toward the back edge of the lot so as not to take parking from paying customers. As he walked toward the entrance a large pickup sped into the lot and around the back of the building. Shaun changed course to the edge of the building. He glanced around just as Keith was slamming the driver's door. The veterinarian jogged to a side door and inside.

Shaun looked at the man's truck, pulled out his phone, and took a picture of it before returning to the front door. He pushed his way in and was greeted by a barking, lunging Rottweiler. The owner pulled hard on its leash to keep the dog under control. On the opposite side of the room, a woman sat with a leash wrapped around her legs and a small poodle mix hiding underneath her seat.

The receptionist, Nancy, forced a smile. "May I help you?"

Shaun held up his badge. "I need to ask someone some questions."

"Just a minute." She lifted the phone to her ear and pressed a button. A moment later she said, "There's a detective here wanting to ask some questions. Okay. I'll tell him."

Nancy hung up the phone and said to Shaun, "He'll be right with you."

Shaun thanked her and moved away from the reception desk setting off the Rottweiler again. He sidestepped to distance himself from the dog and the desk alike. A door opened and the assistant named Shelly walked in. Nancy waved her over and the two spoke in hushed voices. The volume increased sharply as the young assistant protested and Nancy chided her. Shelly stopped abruptly and stormed out of the room.

Shaun was watching the door she exited swing shut when he was approached from the hallway leading to the back. The detective turned to see Keith Stevens walking up to him.

"Detective," the veterinarian held his hand out.

Shaun gripped it and shook. "Doctor. I didn't mean for them to bother you. I'm just here to ask some operational questions related to our investigation. It didn't need to be you."

"What do you need to know?" Keith said.

"What type of bedding do you use for your animals?" Shaun said.

"Red cedar shavings or hay," Keith said. "It just depends on the animal and the need."

"What disinfectants do you use?"

"We use a disinfectant by a company called Hillyard," Keith said. "No. Wait. We changed that. Now we are using a product called Rescue."

"And what tranquilizers?" Shaun asked, writing down the information as he spoke.

"Tranquilizers?"

"Yes."

"That is quite a list," Keith said. "It depends on the animal and what the need for the tranquilizer is. I can have Nancy send you the list."

"That would be helpful," Shaun said.

"Anything else?" Keith asked.

"That's it," Shaun said. "Thank you for your time. And I'm sorry I bothered you."

"What is this about?" Keith said. "Is this about the body you found? Or my wife?"

"I can't really tell you that," Shaun said. "We are investigating the murder of the girl. And we are looking into your wife's disappearance. That is all I can say at this time."

"I guess I should be glad someone is trying to find her," Keith said. "Good luck, detective."

"Thank you, sir," Shaun said.

The veterinarian retreated down the hall. As Shaun turned to leave, the door opened and Shelly walked up to the woman with the frightened poodle-mix, coaxed the dog out from under the chair, and led them to an examining room. Soon after, the front door opened and Tanner, another assistant walked in. The Rottweiler, just a few feet away started in again. Rather than shrinking away, Tanner bent over and talked to the dog, putting a handout and closing the distance slowly. Moments later he was petting the animal and guiding dog and owner to another examining room.

"I'll get that list to you," Nancy said.

"Thank you." Shaun exited the building. Just before sitting in his car, he looked back at Keith Stevens' truck.

31

Meghan Quinn had been reported missing by her parents nearly three months ago. The twenty-six year old's address of record was a duplex in an aging neighborhood that was now a blend of elderly couples who had lived there for years, young couples just starting families, and a variety of social statuses.

Detectives Mallory and Weatherby stopped at the duplex first but found it to be empty of furnishings. From there they drove to the parent's home, located in a more upscale gated community. The woman who answered the door looked like an older version of the photo they had of Meghan.

"Mrs. Quinn?" Jack said.

The woman visibly stiffened. "Mrs. Lloyd. Mrs. Quinn is my daughter."

"So, sorry," Maureen said. "We're Detectives Maureen Weatherby and Jack Mallory. We are here to talk to you about your daughter."

"Did you find her?" the woman pleaded. "Is she alive?"

"Let me say, we don't know who we've found," Maureen said. "We've located a body and are trying to identify her. In that interest, we are going to ask a series of questions to help us eliminate your daughter as a possibility. If we are unable to do that we will need you or your husband to come view the body for a possible identification."

"I knew it," the woman teared up. "I knew she was dead. Why wouldn't she come home if she wasn't?"

"You said your name is Lloyd and hers is Quinn," Jack said. "Was she married?"

"Yes," Mrs. Lloyd said.

"Why was it you who reported her missing rather than her husband?"

"She was living with us," she said. "They separated about a month before she disappeared."

"Was her husband ever a suspect?" Maureen asked.

"We thought so," Mrs. Lloyd said. "But the police wouldn't arrest him."

"Why do you think it was him?" Jack asked.

"After she moved out, he acted like everything was her fault," Mrs. Lloyd said. "They went to counseling, but he wouldn't take any steps to reconcile. And when she disappeared, we called him to see if maybe she had gone back to him. A woman answered his phone. And he never checked to see if she turned up."

"Had your daughter ever told you that she was afraid of her husband?" Jack asked. "That she thought he might hurt her?"

"No," the woman said. "But we didn't know they were having issues until she showed up on our doorstep."

"We stopped by the last address we had for Meghan," Maureen said. "A duplex on Huntington."

"That was their place," Mrs. Lloyd said.

"It was empty," Maureen said. "Do you know where we might find Mr. Quinn?"

"No," she stiffened again. "I can't believe he moved. What did he do with her things?"

"We'll find him," Jack assured her. "And we'll find out where your daughter's things are."

"If she's gone," Mrs. Lloyd began crying again. "If she's gone, her things are all that we'll have of her."

"We'll find them," Maureen said.

"Mrs. Lloyd?" Jack said. "Does your daughter have a pet?"

"A pet?"

"Yes," Jack said. "Maybe a dog?"

"I don't understand," Mrs. Lloyd said. "What does that have to do with Meghan's disappearance?"

"Mrs. Lloyd," Maureen said. "The body that was discovered was found with . . ."

"Animal hair," Jack finished giving Maureen a side glance. "We just need to know if Meghan had a dog."

"No," the woman said.

"Okay then," Jack said.

"But her friend did," Mrs. Lloyd said.

"Her friend?" Maureen said. "What friend?"

"The friend she house sat or dog sat for," the woman said. "About a week before she disappeared. Now, what was her name?"

"Do you know where the house is?" Jack asked.

"Why, yes," Mrs. Lloyd said. "The first day she was there she called and asked me to bring her a pair of sneakers so she could walk the dog."

"Did you talk to this friend after Meghan vanished?" Jack asked.

"I wanted to," she said. "But I didn't have her phone number."

"You didn't drive over?" Maureen asked.

"No," Mrs. Lloyd said. "Why?"

"We need that address, ma'am," Jack said.

32

After visiting three kennels, Detective Travis pulled into a no-kill shelter. It was listed as a small operation, however, there were at least a dozen dog runs on the north of the building alone. He parked in a row of vehicles including two cars and two pickups and walked along that side of the building. All but one of the runs was occupied and the residents went crazy growling, barking, and jumping on the chain link. By the time he reached the front, a woman in her early thirties wearing coveralls and her hair pulled back in a ponytail was waiting for him.

"You need something?" She stood with her hands on her hips. "We only show animals by appointment."

Shaun showed his badge. "Just need to ask some questions."

"Let me get you my lawyer's card," she sneered.

"You're a lawyer?" Shaun said. "Wait. No. You aren't in any trouble."

"I've heard it all before," she said. "First you get me into a false sense of security. Then you get me answering questions. Next thing I know you have me saying things that you can take out of context and you're throwing me behind bars."

"Why would I do that?"

"I don't know," she said. "Maybe you have a quota to meet. Or you have a case you're being pressured to solve and figure I will do as well as anyone."

"I wouldn't do that," Shaun said.

"Oh, you said you won't do it," she mimicked. "Then by all means I should trust you. Because no one who ever did something bad to someone else ever lied to them first."

"What happened to you?" Shaun asked. "To make you so angry?"

"Not me," she said. "My husband."

"What happened to him?"

"Don't pretend to care," the woman said.

"I'm not pretending," Shaun said. "What happened to your husband?"

The woman looked Shaun up and down, sizing him up, trying to decide. "He's a good man, my husband. A kind man. He always wants to do the right thing. So, when the detective came to ask some questions, Jeremiah was more than happy to help. The detective asked. My husband answered. The detective would ask more and my husband answered. The detective rephrased the questions and my husband answered. It went on for hours. Until suddenly my husband was being arrested for things he could never have, would never have done."

"He's in jail?" Shaun asked.

"Prison," the woman said. "The detective testified against him. Lied in court, under oath. My husband was convicted and got ten years. That was a year ago."

"Do you remember the detective's name?" Shaun asked.

"I'll never forget it," she said. "Detective Bret Peterson."

Bret Peterson was the detective who, it was discovered, killed three women and a cop all in the interest of protecting his sister. He died in a shootout with Detective Mallory when Jack had found out the truth. It was also discovered that Bret had framed two different men for two of the murders. It did not surprise Shaun in the least that he had done so to someone else.

"Detective Peterson?" Shaun said.

"Bret Peterson," she repeated. "I'm going to make him pay for what he's done. You can count on that."

"He's dead, ma'am," Shaun said.

"He's dead?" She looked at him with her head tilted, trying to decide if it were true. "If he's dead, how are we going to prove he lied? He knows my husband was innocent."

"I need your name and your husband's," Shaun said.

"Why?"

"I can look it up if I have to," Shaun said. "I may be able to help your husband. But I need names."

The woman sighed heavily. "Patricia Hopkins. My husband's name is Jeremiah."

Shaun wrote the information down. "Okay. I'm going to look into this. I'll let you know if anything comes of it."

"I won't hold my breath," Patricia said.

Shaun started to leave but turned back. "I do have some questions. About your business."

"What about it?"

"What kind of bedding do you use?"

"Seriously?" she laughed. "You walked by all those dog runs and you're asking me what bedding I use?"

Shaun looked back at the line of dogs. In the back of each was a wood-frame dog cot.

"My husband built them," she said.

"You don't ever use cedar shavings, do you?" Shaun asked.

"Can't afford that stuff," she said. "Why do you need to know?"

"A case," he said. "That's all I can say. And that's all I need."

He started to walk away. "I'll be in touch. About your husband."

"I still won't be holding my breath," she called after him. But she allowed just a glimmer of hope.

33

Meghan's friend lived in a small house two blocks from the Quinn's duplex. It had a fenced yard, but as Detectives Mallory and Weatherby approached the front door there was no sign of a dog. Jack stopped on the first step so as not to appear threatening in any way. Maureen rang the bell, anticipating the yapping of a crazed dog. None came.

"Maybe she and the dog are out," Maureen suggested. "It's a nice night for a walk."

"It may be," Jack said. "But someone's coming." He pointed at the door.

Through the frosted glass window of the door, they could see the distorted image of a person moving toward them. The door opened and a dark-haired woman in her late twenties peered out at them. She looked from Maureen to Jack and back again. She didn't say anything, holding an expression of anticipation.

"Pardon the intrusion," Maureen said. "Do you by chance know someone named Meghan Quinn?"

The woman's eyebrow raised. "You know Meghan?"

Maureen held her badge out. "Detective Weatherby. He's Detective Mallory. It's come to our attention that she dog sat for you about a week before her disappearance."

"What?" The woman's eyes enlarged. "Her disappearance?"

"Sorry," Jack said, stepping onto the porch. "We assumed you would have known."

"Wait," she said. "You said she disappeared a week after she dog sat for me?"

"Yes," Maureen confirmed.

"That was . . .," the woman reached inside her memories. "That was over three months ago. I knew I hadn't seen her in a while. But three months?"

"We need to ask you some questions," Maureen said. "If you don't mind."

"Of course," she said. "Anything I can do to help. Although, I don't know how I can."

"First of all," Maureen said. "Meghan's mother told us about you, however, she didn't know your name."

"My name?" the woman said. "Karyn Hayes."

"Karyn," Maureen said. "You confirmed that Meghan dog sat for you."

"She did," Karyn nodded. "I just don't know what that . . ."

"Where's the dog?" Jack interrupted.

"Pardon?"

"She dog sat for you," Jack said. "We've been here fifteen or twenty minutes and haven't seen or heard a dog."

"You think I lied about her dog sitting?"

"No," Maureen said. "We just want to know what happened to the animal."

"Nothing happened to the dog," Karyn said. "Casey is out on a walk with my husband."

"Then can you tell us if Meghan mentioned crossing paths with anyone unusual when she took your dog for walks?" Jack asked.

"Unusual how?"

"Someone following her," Jack said. "Maybe someone overly interested in Casey."

"You think she was taken by someone who was actually after my dog?"

"Not exactly," Jack said. "But we are looking for someone who has a connection to dogs."

"A connection?" Karyn said. "Like what?"

"We can't get into details," Jack said. He handed her his card. "If you think of anything after you've had time to mull it over, give me a call."

She looked at the card. "Homicide? I thought you said she was missing. Do you think she's been murdered?"

"We don't know," Maureen said. "We're just trying to find out if there are any similarities between her disappearance and a case we've been working on."

"And are there?" Karyn asked.

"Some," Maureen said. "But nothing definitive."

The detectives thanked her for her time and excused themselves.

"What do you think?" Maureen asked as they drove back to the station.

"If she was taken by the same killer as the other girls," Jack said. "Then it changes the profile of our suspect. We had been assuming that he had positioned himself to target random victims crossing his path, possibly using his interest in their dogs to spring his trap. If he selected Meghan when he saw her walking a dog, it was this dog. But he didn't take her until a week later, without the dog. This would suggest that he finds targets and tracks them. Possibly he crosses paths with them and, again using the dog, builds a rapport, a trust. Then he sets his trap specifically for them."

"He gets to know them and their dogs," Maureen said. "Which allows him to get close enough to strike."

"Instead of an introvert, socially awkward nerd," Jack said. "We could be looking for a charmer."

"Which means," Maureen said.

"Our suspect pool just doubled," Jack sighed.

34

Detective Mallory sat in a corner booth of a local mom-and-pop diner. The dark paneled walls and tin covered light fixtures suggested the place had not been updated since the day they opened. Next to him on the table-top, its finish worn from years of cleaning, was a thick folder. He sipped from his mug trying hard not to look at the pages within. After dropping Detective Weatherby off at the station, he decided to get some dinner. However, after more than half an hour, he had yet to order anything besides coffee.

Even without looking inside, he couldn't get his mind off the folder's contents. In many ways, Meghan Quinn did not fit the profile of the known victims. She did not own a dog and was not taken while walking one. There were similarities. And being the only missing red-haired woman in the system that matched the recovered body suggested Meghan was their Jane Doe. But until there was indisputable proof, Jack had to keep in mind that the woman in the grave could be someone not yet reported missing.

He glanced toward the folder for the hundredth time wondering if there was a significance to the animals. He thought there had been. He was convinced the killer was finding women walking their dogs and using his perceived love of the animals to approach them. Once he was close he could make his move to subdue woman and pet.

But Meghan did not have a dog. For him to use that method with her, he would have had to make his initial move while she was walking her friend, Karyn's dog, a full week before he kidnapped her. That meant he stalked her for at least seven days, getting to know her and her habits. Yet, when the friend returned and Meghan went home, he did not change his plan, he followed her there. He then had to find a different way to get to her. Did Meghan take walks on her own where he could get close to her? Or did he take her from her home? If either was the case, it meant he changed his modus operandi rather than changing target.

"How are you doing?"

Jack looked up at the waitress standing next to him, coffee pot in hand. He set his mug down and slid it her way so she could pour cup number three.

"You ready to order, babe?" She set the pot down and pulled out her order pad in anticipation.

Jack half expected her to start smacking gum. He looked at the menu laying on the table next to the folder, unopened as well. "Have you got meatloaf?"

"We do," she said.

"Okay," Jack picked up the menu and held it out. "I'll have the meatloaf."

"You got it." She took the menu and the pot and spun on her heels and moved on to another table. Jack watched her as she engaged the guests, but especially the way she interacted with the small boy sitting at the table.

"Chick magnets," Jack said aloud. A man at the next table looked at him as if he may be crazy. Jack gave him a look. "Eat your dinner."

Without waiting to see if the man turned away, Jack did and pulled his phone out, dialing Shaun's number.

"What's up?" the young detective answered.

"We've been looking at this wrong," Jack said. "Have you eaten?"

"What?" Shaun said. "Looking at what wrong? And no. I haven't eaten."

"Do you like meatloaf?"

35

Shaun arrived at the diner about the same time the food was being delivered to the table. Shaun extended a hand to Jack and they shook.

"Thanks for coming," Jack said. "Hope you don't mind. I ordered for you."

"No problem," Shaun settled in. "Now what is this about something looking wrong?"

"We are," Jack said. "We're looking at the case and the suspect wrong. We were thinking that he had trouble approaching women but was good with animals. He interacted with the dogs to get close to the women who owned them."

"And that's wrong?"

"Meghan didn't own a dog," Jack said. "She didn't fit the profile. For him to have taken her, he would have had to change his M.O."

"Right," Shaun said. "We already discussed that."

"But I don't think he changed at all," Jack said.

"You think Meghan isn't the girl we found?"

"I think he watches his victims," Jack said. "Yes, he's trying to figure out their patterns so he can plan their abductions. But before that, I think he watches the way they interact with other people. In particular the way they interact with people who have dogs."

"People who have dogs?"

"He doesn't interact with their dogs to get close to them," Jack said. "They interact with his. That's how he gets close."

"He isn't looking for dog owners," Shaun said. "He's looking for dog lovers. It just happens that most dog lovers own dogs."

"Exactly," Jack said. "Meghan didn't own a dog but she must have been a dog lover."

"He saw the way she was with Karyn's dog," Shaun said. "She may have even talked to some other dog owners while she was out."

"Then he formulates his plan," Jack said. "He walks by with his dog, she starts a conversation and he springs his trap."

"That would make sense," Shaun said. "He wouldn't have to hide in the bushes. He could hide in plain sight."

"He could easily follow someone without raising suspicion," Jack said. "And no one would think anything of seeing the same person day after day if he's walking a dog."

"He's killing dogs with the women," Shaun said. "If he owns a dog, do you think he is a dog lover or an abuser?"

"Definitely an abuser," Jack said. "It's unlikely he loves anything. He has a hatred of women. He sees the dogs as a tool. He uses them, then throws them away. Like the women he takes."

"It would be helpful to know where that anger comes from," Shaun said. "Was he mistreated or neglected by his mother? Was he rejected by women? It makes a difference in who we are looking for."

"We have to look at both possibilities," Jack said. "We can't narrow it down without a lot more information. Anyone with a dog, especially working with dogs, and a truck is a possible suspect."

"That reminds me," Shaun said. "Keith Stevens drives a truck."

"The veterinarian who's wife is missing?" Jack opened the folder next to him for the first time since setting down. "When did she disappear?"

"It's been a while," Shaun said.

"Here it is," Jack said. "A year ago. It's not unusual for the first victim in these kinds of cases to be someone the killer knew."

"He doesn't really fit the profile," Shaun pointed out.

"He works with animals, he drives a truck," Jack said. "He's connected to a possible victim and one of the dogs. To not consider him a suspect would be irresponsible."

"I agree," Shaun nodded.

"What have we learned from the canvass?" Jack asked.

"That there are too many kennels and clinics in this city," Shaun said. "Also that there were three locations that use the red cedar shavings as well as the same brand of sanitizer that was found on the victims on my list. Stevens' clinic is one of them."

"Another mark on Keith," Jack said. "Maybe we should visit some of Judith's family and see if she told them anything or if they have their own opinions on the Stevens' marriage."

"I'll research and get some addresses," Shaun said.

"Anything else?" Jack asked.

"I met a woman whose husband may have been framed by Bret Peterson," Shaun said.

The choice had been made, after it was discovered Peterson had framed some men for crimes he had committed, to only review cases related to Mallory's investigation. They made the decision to avoid having to review every arrest Peterson had ever been involved in. They justified it by convincing themselves that the detective only broke the law to protect his family.

"We'll need to look into that," Jack said. "You sure she wasn't just using what she heard in the news to her husband's advantage?"

"She said she wanted Bret to pay for what he'd done," Shaun said. "She didn't know he was dead. Or she's a really good liar."

Jack's phone rang. He answered and listened.

"Okay, thanks." He hung up and looked at Shaun. "Autopsy is complete."

36

On sunny mornings, for a short time, the sun struck the windows of the county morgue at just the right angle to create an almost halo effect. Jack used to wonder if the architect had designed the building with that in mind. He concluded that architects with that much foresight and creative vision probably spent their time designing buildings other than morgues.

He parked in the first empty space he came to although there were plenty for him to choose from. He sat back, drank his coffee, and scanned the case file for that one detail he may have missed the first hundred times he had looked through it. A good ten minutes passed by the time Shaun arrived and parked in the space next to him.

"Morning," the young detective said.

Jack gave him a single nod then took another drink from his Java Joe's house blend. He was nearing the bottom of the cup and the dark liquid had begun to cool. Stepping out of his car, he tossed the remainder into a nearby trash can. Shaun joined him, and they went inside where Valerie O'Conner was waiting.

"Gentlemen." The medical examiner was her usual pleasant self. "I hope you both got some well-deserved rest last night."

"I did, thank you," Shaun said.

"What've you got for us?" Jack pushed.

"You know, I think you're right," Valerie put on a stern expression. "I think there are too many pleasantries in the world."

She stood squarely in front of him, unmoving.

He stared at her for a moment, then said, "Good morning, Valerie."

"Why good morning, Jack," she said. "I'm doing well, thanks for asking."

With that, she spun on her heels and lead the way to the examining room she had set up for their visit. Two surgical lights focused on the autopsy table in the center of the room were in stark contrast to the low lighting elsewhere. The body that lay there with a sheet draped from the shoulders down was the red-haired victim, as Jack expected. The advanced decomposition left few features that would help identify her.

"She's been dead a little over a month," Valerie said.

"Anything that ties her to the other case?" Jack asked.

"Yes," she said. "She and the dog were both poisoned with the same concoction of oleander leaves and hamburger."

"So they were definitely killed by the same man," Jack said. "Did you find anything that might help us figure out who she was?"

"As a matter of fact," Valerie circled the table, "I may have."

The medical examiner pulled the sheet up to reveal the woman's lower legs. Jack stepped forward and examined the misshapen right limb.

"Was that caused by burial?" Jack asked.

"No," Valerie said. "There are signs of the bone mending. It was never set, Jack. It had started to heal in that position."

"To keep her from running?" Shaun asked.

"That," Jack said. "Or possibly he just liked to cause pain. Remember, Lorissa had a similar injury to her arm."

"That's right, detective," Valerie said. "In fact, there is a high probability that the same weapon was used."

"And what kind of weapon would that be?" Jack said.

"You bring me one and I will analyze it," she said. "But without more detail, I can't be sure."

Jack looked at the wound again. "A shoe?"

"Pardon?"

"Could her captor have stomped on her leg?" Jack said.

"It's possible," she said. "It's also possible he hit her with a two by four. As I said, I can't be sure without more to go on."

"If there were signs of the bone mending," Jack said. "He kept her a while."

"I would say three to four weeks," she nodded.

"That's different from Lorissa," Jack said.

"But a lot of things are the same," she said. "The residue under the fingernails, the red cedar shavings. We don't know what the residue is yet, but I assume it will be the same cleaner we found on Lorissa."

"You're assuming?" Jack raised an eyebrow. "I didn't think M.E.s did that."

"Don't hold me to it," Valerie said. "But I think I'm right."

"You said you found something that might help us identify her?" Shaun said.

"I missed it at first." Valerie turned the broken leg toward the detectives. "It was in the damaged tissue, plus the decomp." She took a magnifying glass from a nearby table. "Look at the skin here."

Jack looked then stepped aside for Shaun.

"A tattoo?" Shaun asked.

Jack thought of Angela Case with the rose tattoo on her ankle. Her parents desperate for answers. But she had been a blond, not a redhead.

"It's a butterfly," Valerie said. "I sent a photo to the lab and they are trying to enhance the image."

"Anything else that might help us out?" Jack asked.

"I saved the best for last," Valerie smiled. "I found DNA."

"You saved that?" Jack said. "That's fantastic."

"It's just transfer DNA," Valerie said. "But it's something."

"You sent it to the lab?"

"Of course," she said. "As soon as I found the sample."

"So we're looking at three to five days?" Jack asked.

"Two or three," Valerie said. "I asked them to rush."

"Thank you," Jack said. "As soon as you get them back."

"You'll get them," she assured him.

37

Gordon and Faith Marshall lived on a fully functional ranch about five miles north of town. In total, they had about a hundred head of cattle, a couple dozen horses, and an array of pigs, goats, and chickens on two-thousand acres. A stream framed in the eastern property line. To the north and south white livestock fencing wrapped around to the front drive.

The home proper was set back from the road three-quarters of a mile. Jack and Shaun drove the long gravel driveway lined on either side with large American Elm trees creating a canopy above them. At the end of the allée were a sprawling ranch-style farmhouse and several outbuildings including a barn, a horse stable, and garage.

Farther back stood a livestock barn, hay shed, and storage sheds. Everywhere the detectives looked some type of animal was wandering about. Two Great Pyrenees appeared out of nowhere and escorted them as they drove to the main house. The two dogs sat expectantly outside the car waiting for them to exit.

"Do you think they're friendly?" Shaun watched the dog outside his door.

"Why don't you step out and let me know?" Jack smiled.

As if on cue, one of the dogs let out a deep guttural bark that could be heard from anywhere on the property. Shaun said, "You go."

A man stepped onto the porch. He wore a western-style hat, its crown almost brushing the roof's fascia just before he lowered to the first step. He crossed his thick arms across his chest, stretching his shirt to its limits. He pursed cracked lips and whistled. Both dogs turned immediately and jogged to the man's side where they sat like guardians. Massive hands, hardened from years of hard work, lowered and patted their heads as the man stood, silently waiting.

Jack opened his door tentatively. The animals did not move. He stepped out and stood next to the car stretching his cramped legs. Shaun followed his lead and joined him.

"You need something?" the man called out, his graveled voice deeper than the dog's bark.

"Are you Gordon Marshall?" Jack asked.

"Depends," the man said. "Who's asking?"

"Detective Mallory." Jack took a step toward the man with his badge extended. "And my partner Detective Shaun Travis."

"Did you find her?" the man asked.

"No, sir," Jack said.

"Then I don't have anything to discuss with you!" The man's bark was abrupt and unexpected. He came down the remaining steps but turned sharply toward the horse barn with the dogs on his heels.

"Forgive him." A woman's voice redirected the detectives' attention back to the porch. She was petite but projected confidence and strength. "He hasn't been the same since Judith's disappearance."

"I understand," Jack said. "You must be Faith Marshall."

"I am," she said.

"May we ask you some questions?" Jack asked.

"You're working our daughter's case then?"

"We're looking into it," Jack said, "in connection to a case we're on."

"And if they're not connected?" she said.

"We'll pass on anything we learn to the detective on her case," Shaun said.

"So nothing," she said.

"We'll do what we can, ma'am," Jack said.

"What do you want to know?"

"What can you tell us about your daughter's relationship with Keith?" Jack asked.

"Keith?" She looked at the detective sternly. "After a year, you're looking at Keith? I thought they already cleared him."

"No one has been cleared," Jack said. "He may not be primary, but he is still on the list. Could you answer the question, please?"

"Judy loved that man," Faith said. "I never understood it. Maybe it was the 'save the animals' mindset. Maybe there was something in him that I just never saw. But she loved him."

"What about him?" Jack said. "Did she ever mention that maybe he didn't feel the same way? Or did she ever suggest they were having more arguments than usual? Maybe he was acting differently toward her?"

"That's just it, detective," she said. "My daughter is the one who is hard to live with. Keith was always there to help ground her. He was always the one taking care of her."

"Sounds like a decent kind of guy," Jack said. "Why don't you like him?"

"I like him fine," she said. "He just isn't really Judy's type."

"And what is her type?"

"Outdoorsy," Faith said. "Adventurous and fun. All the things Keith isn't. He's laid back and boring. Not the kind of guy she used to fall for. Not the type of guy to do something to her."

"Maybe he snapped?" Shaun said. "Extreme stress can cause people to behave in ways they may not otherwise."

"What makes you think he was stressed?"

"He said business was up and down," Jack said. "Seems like a recipe for stress."

"Things were fine," Faith said. "She would have told me if they weren't."

"Maybe," Jack said. "Maybe she didn't want to worry you. I understand she has a brother. Are they close? Maybe she would have told him more than she told you."

"Gordon Junior was my husband's son from his first marriage," Faith said. "They never really had a chance to be close."

"He didn't live here?"

"No," Faith said. "He lived with his loser of a mother."

"Could he have been jealous of her?" Jack asked. "He had to live with his mother, who you claim was a loser. Meanwhile, Judith is living on the ranch with their father."

"Really?" she said. "Now you think it was her brother? No wonder no one has found her. Why don't you find some evidence to follow?"

"That's what we're trying to do, Mrs. Marshall," Jack said. "If you could provide me with Gordon Junior's address and the names and addresses of some of her friends, we'll be on our way."

"Who you should be looking at is that no good ex of hers," Faith said.

"Her ex?" Jack said. "She was married before?"

"You didn't even know that?" the woman chuckled. "God help us. You'll never find her. Don't they have any detectives that can actually detect?"

"Add the ex-husband's name and address if you have it," Jack said. "But I'll take that list now."

"Fine," she said, walking toward the house. "I'll get the list. I just hope you don't waste everyone's time not learning what you need to."

While they waited for Faith, Jack noticed Gordon Marshall standing next to one of the barns watching them. Their eyes met, but neither acknowledged the other. A few minutes later the detectives were leaving the ranch on a direct route to Gordon Junior's place.

38

The apartment complex Gordon Marshall Jr. lived in was in the southwest part of town. Jack wondered if he purposely chose a place that was as far from his father as he could get without moving to another city.

Gordon's first-floor apartment had a Harley-Davidson parked on the sidewalk blocking the path to the door. The detectives walked through the grass to the small concrete porch. They knocked loudly and waited.

"Go away!" A gruff voice called out to them.

Jack only knocked louder.

"I said, go away!" The voice responded louder still.

Shaun rang the doorbell.

A moment later the door was yanked open revealing a tall heavy-set man wearing faded jeans and black t-shirt. His facial features resembled his father, but not so much that it was obvious. "What the hell is wrong with you?"

He stared out at the two men and the badges they held before him. Jack inquired, "Gordon Marshall?"

"What's this about?" the big man asked.

"Your sister," Shaun said.

"Did you find her?"

"No," Jack said. "We're just taking another look. You know, with a fresh set of eyes. Mind if we come in and ask you some questions?"

"Uh," he looked over his shoulder and seemed to pull the door closer to him. "This isn't a very good time."

"Your sister is missing," Jack said. "This isn't a good time to help us try to find her?"

"She's been missing for a year," he said. "You really think you're going to find her now? And no. This isn't a good time."

Again he appeared to be narrowing the opening of the doorway by moving the door slightly.

"Are you hiding something, sir?" Jack said.

"What?" Gordon Junior said. "No."

"Is she in there?" Jack asked.

"Who?" the large man asked. "Is who in here?"

"Is that why you live so far away from your family?" Jack asked. "So you can hide Judith from them?"

"What?" Gordon Junior's voice raised several octaves. "Are you insane? You think I could hide her for a year?"

"Then what are you hiding?" Shaun asked.

"I'm not hiding anything." He stood a little straighter.

"Then open your door," Jack said.

"Do you have a warrant?"

"Do we need one?"

Gordon Junior held his ground for a long moment then with a grunt he shoved the door open. "There. Are you happy now?"

Looking past the large man the detectives could see a woman sitting on a couch in her underwear. She waved at the men making no attempt to cover herself.

"Why don't you step out here and answer a few questions?" Jack said. "For your sister. Then you can get back to that."

"Fine," Gordon Junior said. "But make it quick."

The big man stepped out and pulled the door closed behind him.

"You don't seem so concerned with finding Judith," Jack said.

"I'm concerned," the man said. "But it's been a year. Either she doesn't want to be found or she's nowhere to be found."

"Do you have reason to believe she doesn't want to be found?" Shaun asked.

"No."

"She didn't tell you anything?" Jack asked. "Maybe about Keith?"

"No," Gordon Junior said. "But to be honest, she and I don't talk much."

"How old were you when your parents split up?" Jack asked.

"Did the old man tell you they split?" Gordon asked. "He kicked us out. They were married less than a year."

"Is that how you saw it?" Jack asked. "That he kicked you out?"

"That's how it was," he said. "There's no other way to see it."

"And how old were you when Judith was born?"

"Maybe three or four?"

"You don't know?" Jack asked. "Seems like that would be a significant event in your life; your dad having a baby with another woman."

"He kicked us out," he repeated. "I didn't know I had a sister until I was in high school. So forgive me if I don't know when her birthday is."

"How was it to find out that he had another child that he didn't, as you say, kick out?"

"I was pissed," Gordon Junior said. "At first because I wasn't good enough but she was. Then I was pissed at the old man for not giving me the opportunity to know her while we were growing up."

"And after you found out?"

"She looked me up," he said. "That's how I found out about her. Came home from school to find this girl sitting on our steps. My mother was at work or somewhere. She asked me my name. I told her. Then she just blurts out that she's my sister."

"How did the rest of that encounter go?" Jack asked.

"Tense at first," Gordon Junior said. "But it turned out that living with our father wasn't the dream life I had imagined it would be when I was young. We kind of bonded over that."

"You bonded?" Jack said. "With one visit?"

"We're siblings," he said. "Turned out we had a lot in common. Besides, there was more than just the one visit."

"How many more did you have?"

"I don't know," he said. "We would meet from time to time and talk."

"You said you didn't talk," Jack reminded him.

"After she went to veterinary school, and married Keith, we didn't see each other much," he said.

"But you still saw each other?"

"From time to time," Gordon Junior said.

"And she never mentioned having issues with Keith?"

"Not that I remember."

"What about her ex?" Jack said checking the list Faith Marshall had given him. "Dalton Frye?"

"Oh, yeah," Gordon Junior said. "He was the first guy she married. Almost forgot about good old Dalton. Him she talked about."

"They had problems?" Shaun asked.

"Epic," the big man said. "She would constantly complain about him. Found out later that he hit her a couple of times. But she's not helpless. She gave as good as she got."

"How did that go over with him?"

"He tried to be even more aggressive," he said. "But when dad found out what was happening he gave Dalton an ultimatum. He could divorce Judy and disappear or he could find out how good a shot dad was. I think it was the only time I actually admired my old man."

"So they divorced?"

"Of course they divorced," Gordon Junior said. "Otherwise she wouldn't have been able to marry Keith."

"Did she have any more problems with Dalton after the divorce?"

"I heard he had trouble letting things go," he said. "But like I said, we stopped talking as much after that."

"And she never mentioned issues with Keith?"

"I already told you she didn't," he said. "But I'm guessing she ruled the roost in that relationship."

"How do you mean?" Jack asked.

"She's an alpha," he said. "She dominates the relationship, which was part of the problem she had with Dalton. He thought he was the boss. With Keith, that wasn't an issue. She ran the clinic with the intensity of a drill sergeant. Keith is, well, he's Keith."

"You didn't approve of him?"

"Keith?" he said. "He's okay. Just not what I expected."

"That's similar to what Judith's mother said about him," Jack said.

"Well, what can I say?" he said.

"You don't think Keith is capable of harming your sister?" Shaun asked.

"I don't know," Gordon Junior said. "I guess if you push a man, even a weak man, hard enough they might come at you. I just don't see Keith being that man. And if he did, I don't see him coming out on top."

"What about Dalton?" Jack said. "Do you see him harming her?"

"I don't know, man," Gordon Junior said. "They've been divorced for over a decade. Surely he's moved on by now."

39

Trying to locate Dalton Frye led Shaun down a series of roads all ending in frustration until the detective learned that Judith Stevens' ex-husband had been killed in an automobile accident four years ago. They marked his name off the list.

Talking to friends and family, they heard more of what they had already learned. Judith had an alpha personality that could be hard to deal with. Everyone liked Keith, just not necessarily as a partner for Judith. No one thought he was capable of doing anything to her. But Jack's years of experience had taught him that friends thinking someone was incapable did not mean they were.

Shaun sat at his desk reading the file of Jeremiah Hopkins. The husband of the woman who ran the no-kill shelter had been convicted of three counts of armed robbery and two counts of assault despite never being identified by any of the witnesses. Although Mr. Hopkins owned several weapons, all registered, none of them matched the one used in the crimes. Testimony for the defense described the self-employed electrician as a gentle, good-spirited family man. A churchgoer who was always willing to help others in need. No one believed he had committed the crimes. No one but Detective Bret Peterson.

Shaun read through the deceased detective's case notes but could not find anything that directed Bret to the Hopkins. There was no mention of Jeremiah's name. No description that was similar to the man's. It was as if Bret picked a driveway at random and arrested the man who lived there.

It was Bret's testimony that damaged Jeremiah's case. He swore that the electrician had thrown the weapon into a pond to keep from being caught, but under interrogation admitted to what he had done. The defense claimed neither had happened. But at the time it was the word of a man on trial versus a veteran detective.

The internal mail was dropped on the corner of his desk and Shaun picked it up.

"We got the results of the rest of the canvass." Shaun held up a large envelope and several pages of typewritten paper.

"What canvass?" Jack asked.

"Seriously," Shaun said. "You had us asking all the kennels and breeders about their bedding materials, cleaning chemicals, and tranquilizers."

"Oh, that canvass," Jack grinned. "You should lighten up. What did we learn?"

"There are only a handful of locations that use both shaved cedar for bedding and the same brand of disinfectant found on the victim's hands," Shaun read from the report.

"When you say a handful," Jack said. "How many are we talking about?"

Shaun ran his finger down the page. "Twenty-six, including Stevens'."

"That's a handful?"

"Compared to the original list," Shaun said. "Yes, it is."

"Okay," Jack said. "Get me a copy of the list. Include the findings on what tranquilizers each one uses."

"Are we going to get a warrant for Stevens' place?"

"Using products that are common for their business isn't going to get us a warrant," Jack said. "We'll need Judith's body or something else to tie him to the victims."

"Like finding out he was their vet," Shaun said. "Which we would know if we served a warrant."

"Good luck finding a judge who sees it your way," Jack said.

Jack's cell phone rang. He answered, "Mallory."

"Jack, it's Valerie," the woman said.

"Valerie," Jack said. "What can I do for you?"

"Not what you can do for me," she said. "It's what I can do for you."

"All right then," Jack said. "What can you do for me?"

"As you know," she said. "I sent out DNA samples I found on our unidentified victim."

"Yes."

"Well I got the results back," she said.

"And?"

"There are two sets of DNA markers," she said.

"Two sets?"

"That's right."

"The victim and her killer?" Jack guessed.

"Both female," she said.

"Our killers a woman?" Jack said. "Tell me you got hits on them."

"Only one," Valerie said. "And it's not our victim."

"The killer then?"

"Name is Crystal Vaughn," Valerie said. "And Jack. She's been missing for ten months."

40

Crystal Vaughn's image filled Jack's screen. The twenty-eight-year-old single mother of two had been reported missing by her neighbors after the woman's nine-year-old son showed up on their doorstep in tears. It seemed the boy had not done his homework as his mother had asked and after insisting he sit down and complete it, she left the house to take their dog on a walk. She never returned. The boy was convinced she had left him and his little sister because of his defiance.

After ten months, there was still no sign of the woman or the dog. Jack feared neither would be found alive. The detective hoped he was wrong for the sake of the children, but knew he wasn't. A footnote in the missing persons file indicated the kids were living with their maternal grandparents. There was no mention of the father. Jack wondered if the man was out of the picture, or just didn't care. The detective on the case had recently been changed to none other than Maureen Weatherby.

"What can I do for you?" The detective greeted Jack upon his arrival to her desk.

"What makes you think I want something?" Jack asked.

"You're here aren't you?" she said.

"Can't I just stop by to say hello?"

"Is that why you're here?"

"No."

"Just tell me what you want," Maureen said. "I'm kind of busy."

"Crystal Vaughn," Jack said.

"Crystal Vaughn?" she said. "Oh, wait. I just got that file two days ago. Did you find her?"

"We didn't find her," Jack said. "We found her DNA on the victim we just found."

"The one you dragged me out to see?"

"That's the one."

"Any other connection between your victim and Crystal?" Maureen said.

"We still haven't identified her," Jack said. "But maybe you have something. We can look into Crystal's life and see if she knew anyone who could be our victim."

"Are things so slow in homicide that you have to steal our cases?" Maureen asked.

"You know us," Jack smiled. "We won't be satisfied until we are investigating every case in the department."

"Tell you what," Maureen said. "I need to go talk to the family. Introduce myself. Ask some questions. If you have a rendering of what your victim might have looked like, I can ask if they know her."

"You would do that for me?" Jack said.

"I would do it for the victim," Maureen said.

"Fair enough," Jack said. "I'll send you a computer-generated image."

Jack's phone rang. He looked at the screen and saw Shaun's name. "What's up?"

He listened to the younger detective while maintaining eye contact with Maureen. His face tensed. His body stiffened. Maureen sat quietly until Jack disconnected the call.

"What is it?" she asked.

Jack released the breath he hadn't realized he was holding. "They found another body."

41

Jack and Shaun stood shoulder to shoulder approximately twenty yards from where they had located the first victim just days before. The forensics team had arrived before the detectives and were hard at work at the delicate task of uncovering the victim while not disturbing the scene. A photographer walked the perimeter documenting every step of the way.

Standing next to the detectives was an officer whose muscular chest threatened to escape the fabric of his uniform. He stood with his feet at shoulder width, his massive arms at his side. His composure made Jack think he was probably a marine at one time.

"How was she found?" Jack asked.

"Homeless man looking for a place to bunk for the night," the officer said. "Decided to bury his pack to protect it from being stolen while he slept and dug up a surprise instead. To his credit, he found a phone and called it in."

"Any chance he was burying her instead of accidentally digging her up?" Jack asked.

"There's always a chance," the officer said. "But honestly, the man was so freaked out that I can't imagine he would be a viable suspect. Of course, that is up to you detectives."

"I suppose it is," Jack said.

"You want me to arrange for you to interview him?" the officer asked.

"I'm guessing he doesn't own a truck," Jack said.

"No, sir," the officer said.

"Then he's not our man." Jack stepped forward to get a better angle of the open ground.

Two technicians were kneeling at the edge of the grave using hand tools to gently work the soil away within. The bodies were skeletal, draped with patches of light brown fur and remnants of clothing. They had been here for some time. Jack couldn't help but wonder if they might be looking at the first victim, possibly Dr. Judith Stevens?

Dozens of evidence bags filled a plastic bin as more and more items were collected from the grave and the surrounding area. Many of those items would prove useless, but one may help them solve the case once and for all.

"A third victim," Valerie O'Conner appeared at his side.

"Yes." Jack confirmed the point the medical examiner was making. Three victims was the threshold used to categorize a murderer as a serial killer. "You may want to rush this one."

"Why?" She took a defensive tone. "Because your victim is more important than the others that come into my morgue?"

"That," Jack nodded. "And because you'll need the room. I'm sure there are more to come."

42

Louise Vaughn stood in the doorway, a toddler wrapped around one leg. The child looked up at Detective Weatherby with a mix of fear and curiosity. Maureen smiled and waved at the small girl who shrank and shifted to hide more of herself behind her grandmother.

"What happened to the other detective?" the woman asked, one hand on the door, the other on the child.

"Retired," Maureen said.

"Good," she said. "I don't think he tried very hard to find my girl. When were you assigned to the case?"

"Two days ago," the detective said.

"Two days?" The woman pondered. "Something was more important to you than my daughter for two days?"

"I apologize, Mrs. Vaughn," Maureen said. "Unfortunately, Crystal's wasn't the only case reassigned to me."

"Like I said," the woman looked Maureen in the eyes. "Something was more important to you for two days."

A boy ran by the door at full tilt. The grandmother half-turned. "Preston! No running in the house!"

The boy was long gone by the time she finished.

"Sorry," the woman sighed. "He's been a handful since his momma disappeared."

"No need to apologize," Maureen said. "I know you're busy. But would you mind answering some questions? To help me with the investigation?"

"Do you really think it will help?" Louise asked. "It's been so long, do you think you can find her?"

"I'll be honest," Maureen said. "I don't know that we'll find her. What I can say is that we will do everything we can to find out what happened to her."

"I guess I should thank you for your honesty," Louise said. "What do you want to know?"

"The file says your daughter vanished while taking a walk," Maureen said.

"That's right," Louise said.

"Can you tell me?" Maureen asked. "Was she walking a dog?"

"Spongy," the little girl wrapped around her grandmother's leg said.

"I went through that with the other detective," she said. "She took the kids' dog for a walk."

"Spongy," the girl began to cry.

"What kind of dog was it?" Maureen said.

"Cocker Spaniel," the woman rested a hand on the emotional child's head. "And if you haven't guessed, its name is Spongy."

Maureen glanced down at the girl. "Do you know what veterinarian she used?"

"I don't," Louise said.

Maureen reached inside her jacket and pulled out the digital rendering of their unknown victim. She unfolded it and held it out to Louise. "Do you know anyone, possibly a friend of Crystal's, who looks like this?"

Louise took the paper and stared at the not quite realistic face in the image. "Who is this?"

"She's someone who might be connected to your daughter's case," Maureen said.

"You think this woman might have something to do with Crystal's disappearance?"

"No, ma'am," Maureen said.

"Another victim, then," She continued to stare at the image, her face softening. "Poor girl. Is she dead?"

"Yes, ma'am," Maureen said. "But we don't know that there is a connection between this woman and Crystal. We're just asking questions now to see if there is."

"But there's something," Louise said. "Some reason you thought there might be a connection."

"There is," Maureen confirmed. "But I don't want to speculate on what that connection is."

"You think she's dead, don't you?" Louise said. "That's why you're here."

"I don't know that she's dead," Maureen said. "I'm here because I was assigned her case. The image was given to me by a fellow detective so I could ask these questions. I would like to hold on to the hope that we'll find her alive."

"I hope you do, detective," Louise looked down at her granddaughter. "For her sake, I hope you do."

43

Jack walked into the department and there was a buzz in the room. Several heads turned his way without making eye contact. Shaun followed close behind the senior detective. He slowed and glanced from face to face of his coworkers as they walked to their desks.

"How did they find out so fast?" the younger detective asked.

"Never underestimate the internal network," Jack said. "It will make your head spin. I just hope the chief hasn't heard it yet."

As if on cue, the door to the Chief Sharon Hutchins' office opened. She stepped into view along with one of the upper floor brass. They stood in the opening locked in conversation. Jack could not hear the words being exchanged, but he could read their body language. They were both tense, the chief more-so than her superior. There was a good chance they knew. Their discussion ended abruptly and the brass walked away. The chief turned to Jack, "Mallory! My office!"

They definitely knew.

"Sit down," the chief said as he entered.

"What's up, chief?" Jack sat across from her crossing his legs and arms.

"You comfortable?" Sharon looked at him through narrowed eyes.

"Yes," he said. "Thanks."

"Sit up straight," she ordered. Jack did. "This case of yours. I understand you found a third body."

"We did." Jack shifted in his seat. "And we expect to find more."

"More?" She looked troubled. "How many?"

"I can't tell you," Jack said. "I'm pretty sure there are at least three more, but that guess may be conservative..."

"Is he still active?"

"I have no reason to think he's isn't," Jack said.

"Jack." The chief rested her elbows on her desk. "I have to ask this."

"Ask what, chief?"

"This is your first case since your return," she said. "Are you up for it? Do you think you can catch him?"

"If anything, the time off only allowed me to rest up," Jack said. "I'm sharp. I'm eager. This is what I do. I can catch him."

"Okay." Sharon sat back in her seat. "What do you need?"

44

Jack and Shaun moved all of the case files to Conference Room B which the chief assigned to them as their new war room. The senior detective stood next to the oblong table running through the center of the room sorting the papers and evidence bags. Shaun worked to erase dozens of lines of text from the whiteboard mounted on the wall at the head of the table. The information he was wiping away was important to someone, but Jack had told him to erase it all to make room for their timeline.

"Why the hell was I told to report here?"

Jack turned to the door where Detective Maureen Weatherby stood with her hands on her hips.

"Detective Weatherby." Jack stepped around the table. "Welcome."

"What's going on, Jack?"

"You may have heard the rumors that we have a serial killer out there." Jack waved a hand to the whiteboard where Shaun was working. "I am creating a task force to hunt him down. I asked for you to be on that task force."

"I'm missing persons." Maureen studied the board. "Not homicide."

"You think our victims weren't missing before they were found?" Jack took one of the files from the table and handed it to her. "If I'm right, and my gut says that I am, there are more victims out there. And I think we'll find them in your missing persons cases. You can help us determine which ones to look at. And help us catch a killer in the process."

"You couldn't ask me first?"

"The chief asked what I needed and I told her." Jack held out a second file. "I didn't think you wouldn't want to help."

"It's not that I don't want to help." Maureen glanced through the two files. "I do. It's just . . . I haven't been here that long. I'm sure there are others that are deserving of being on a task force. They may not take it well that you chose me."

"You're worried about the politics?"

"I'm worried about making enemies in the department." She lay the files on the corner of the table. "Yeah."

"Listen." Jack looked her in the eyes. "I don't choose people to work with me because they are deserving. I choose people I think I can work with. And people who I think can help me achieve my goals. You are one of those people."

"But . . ."

"Just drop it," Shaun said. "Welcome to the team."

"Fine," Maureen huffed. She looked at the whiteboard where Shaun began to fill in the details they had on a timeline. "What's the plan?"

"Right now, we are waiting for a search team." Jack circled back to where he was standing when she came in. "We're going back to the park to look for more victims."

"You think he's going back to the same places."

"We found two at that location," Jack said. "There's a chance there will be more."

"What am I looking for in the files?" Maureen asked. "Women who vanished with dogs?"

"Exactly," Jack said. "But keep in mind they may not have mentioned the dog. When a loved one disappears, the dog may seem insignificant."

"And how would I know that?"

"Check where they vanished," Jack said. "What they were doing."

"That's a lot of files to go through," Maureen said.

"Keep it within the last year," Jack said.

"That's still quite a few," Maureen said. "I better get started."

The detective left the room and Jack started sorting through the evidence they had. It wasn't much. Most of what had been gathered at the scenes could be discarded trash as easily as it could be evidence left behind by the killer. He separated the bags by victim and then by what was known to be connected to the case, what he suspected to be connected, and what he felt had nothing at all to do with the victim or her killer. Jack placed the last bag in the appropriate pile when his cell rang. He pressed answer and put the phone to his ear.

"You won't believe this." Valerie spoke before he could.

"What's that?" Jack said.

"Your third victim had some unusual dental work," she said. "I ran it through the system and got a hit. We have a name."

"What is it?" Jack pulled out his notebook.

"Rachel Dunlop," Valerie said. "She was reported missing seven months ago."

"Okay, got it." Jack put his notebook away. "Thanks."

"Glad to help," the medical examiner said. "I'll let you know if I come up with anything more. Not a lot to work with on this one."

Jack punched Rachel's name into the database and the picture of a dark-haired woman appeared. She had light brown skin and piercing green eyes. She was smiling in the photo, but her eyes were puffy, the lids heavy. There was no sparkle.

Jack scrolled down. Rachel had been reported missing by her parents seven months ago when they were unable to reach her for three days. According to the report, they went to her apartment to check on her but found no sign of her. They called the police and when they arrived, the landlord let them in. The apartment was in pristine condition, no sign of struggle. Her purse was on the table along with her car keys. The apartment key was not.

The investigating officer spoke with the neighbors, her closest friends, and a boyfriend. No one had any idea where Rachel might be. The officer suspected the boyfriend, but no evidence was found to support his suspicions. The two themes that were constant through each interview were that everyone loved Rachel and that Rachel loved her dog. She had a Samoyed that was with her at all times unless she was at work.

Jack printed a copy of the file and placed it in a yellow folder. He added her name and information to the timeline while Shaun reviewed her file.

"We'll need to follow up with new interviews," Jack said. "See if the officer missed anything."

"I can do that," Shaun said.

There was a knock at the door. The two detectives turned to see a uniformed officer standing there. He did not step in, choosing rather to address them from outside the room. "They're ready, sir."

"Thanks, Dawson," Jack said. "Will you be joining us?"

"No, sir." The officer hooked a finger over his shoulder. "I'm on the desk today."

"Next time maybe," Jack said.

"Yes, sir," Dawson nodded before walking away.

"Let's go." Jack stood and grabbed his jacket from the back of his chair. Shaun followed him down to the garage. With Jack behind the wheel, they headed for the park.

45

When the detectives arrived, the park was filled with uniformed officers and search teams. Two of the teams were cadaver dogs and their handlers for the heavily wooded, uneven portions of the search area. The third was two technicians and a ground-penetrating radar for the easier terrain. They were all in their final preparations.

Jack walked up to the two technicians with his hand extended. "Romano, how have you been, my friend?"

"Jack." The man clutched the detective's hand and shook. "Same as always. Working hard. Living harder. How about you?"

"Same as you," Jack smiled. "You ready to go?"

"You know I am." The technician snapped a lever to lock the handle in place on his equipment.

"Shaun," Jack turned to his partner. "You join one of the dog teams. I'm going to tag along with these guys."

Following orders, the younger detective approached the closer dog handler and introduced himself.

"Carl Lehman." The man did not offer a hand. Instead, he ruffled the fur between the ears of the German Shepherd at his feet. "And this is Major."

"Glad to meet you." Shaun's gaze fell to the dog. "So how does this work?"

"First body hunt?" Carl gave Shaun the once over, one eyebrow raised.

"With dogs, yes." Shaun looked up at the man.

"Well, stay behind me." Carl patted the German Shepherd's neck. "Major here will do all the work."

A whistle blew and everyone started for the tree line. Carl gave a command and Major took the lead, practically dragging his handler to their goal. Shaun followed close behind. He glanced back toward Jack and saw they were almost to the trees with their equipment. They had obviously begun before the whistle.

"How are the wife and kids, Romano?" Jack walked alongside the tech as his assistant cleared the path of debris.

"Guess you haven't heard." Romano fought to keep the equipment on a straight path. "She left me a few months back."

"Left you?" Jack was taken aback. "Thought you two were rock solid."

"Me too." Romano shrugged, nodding without taking his eyes off the equipment. "Turns out she wasn't as happy as I thought she was. Moved in with her mother. I'm trying to win her back, but I have a lot of issues I didn't know I had, you know?"

"Good luck with that, my friend." Jack patted him on the back.

As the trees filled with more voices the two men fell silent and concentrated on the path and the screen on the equipment. They crisscrossed the terrain as best they could for over an hour often stumbling on tree limbs or stones, twice having to back out of paths that had become too narrow for the machine to pass. The voices turned to grumbles as they grew warmer and more convinced there was nothing to find.

A radio broke silence nearing the second hour. "We . . .we've got something."

Jack snatched up his radio. "Who was that? What did you find?"

"Team one, sir," the voice responded. "We've got a body."

Jack started to turn toward the far end of the trees when Romano's voice stopped him.

"Jack," the technician said. "You should look at this."

The detective walked back and followed his friend's gaze to the screen.

"Looks like a body." The man pointed at the hazy image.

"Yes, it does."

Even though Jack had felt like he was right about what they would find, it was soul-crushing to see the image on the screen. They had found two more victims.

46

The search continued into the waning hours. They covered the entire search grid and found three more shallow graves. Five women in all. Each holding a dog. Each in varying stages of decay.

The searchers packed up and went on their way to their different methods of forgetting what they had seen. Officers made a perimeter that covered the five crime scenes to prevent onlookers from getting too close. Forensics crews combed the gravesites for clues, worked diligently to extract the victims without losing any trace evidence, and documented everything with diligence.

Jack and Shaun retreated to the perimeter and watched for hours before finally checking out and returning to the station. They dragged themselves in, physically and emotionally beaten. To Jack's surprise, the captain was still at her desk. He took a direct path to her open door and knocked once.

"Enter," Her somber tone told him she knew.

"Five." Jack held up five fingers to eliminate confusion.

"I've heard." She locked eyes with him. "We catch this guy, Jack. Whatever you need. You catch this guy."

"Yes, ma'am," he said. "We're going to start . . ."

"Go home, Jack," Sharon cut him off. "Forensics is still out there. We won't have anything for you for hours. You and Travis need to get some rest and be ready to go when it starts coming in."

"Captain, I can . . ."

"Go home, Mallory," she snapped. "That's an order."

"Yes, ma'am." He nodded. He stood looking at her for a moment.

"Is there something else?"

"No." He turned back toward Shaun.

The young detective was in the war room staring at the whiteboard, most likely trying to decide where to tie five more women into the equation. Jack would have to remind him they would need more data.

"Five more?"

Jack turned to see Maureen approaching the war room from his left.

"That's right," he said.

"I've got a dozen files that we might use to identify them." She held up the folders. "I can't believe there were five."

"This man's busy," Jack said as they joined Shaun. "And it's our job to stop him."

"Where do we start?" Shaun asked.

"Captain ordered us to get some rest," Jack said. "We start first thing in the morning. Don't be late."

Jack turned and walked out of the room, leaving the other two detectives slack-jawed.

47

Detective Travis pulled into the parking garage at a quarter of seven and took the first space he found. He grabbed his coffee out of the cup holder and stepped out just in time to see Detective Weatherby parking a few spaces away. He waited for her to join him with her own mug in hand. He noted the bags under her eyes that matched his own.

"Morning," Maureen said as they started for the elevators.

"Morning." He glanced past her and saw Jack's car. "I see he's already here."

Maureen glanced at her watch. "Was he expecting us earlier?"

"He's Jack" Shaun took a drink of his coffee. "I don't think he sleeps."

They rode the elevator together and walked into the war room in single file. Jack glanced up as they entered before returning his attention to the files Maureen had brought in the night before. There were stacks of three folders in front of three of the chairs at the table.

"Take your three files," Jack said. "Memorize every detail. When information comes in, I want to know if they are in these files immediately."

The two detectives took a chair and started scanning through the cases. The three of them read in silence for the next half hour until Jack's phone broke the quiet, bringing all eyes to the cell where it rested on the table. The medical examiner's name was on the screen.

"You can't possibly have anything for me yet," Jack answered.

"Good morning to you too, detective," Valerie O'Conner said. "Nothing on the women. But I figured you were anxious, so I checked all the dogs for chips."

"And?"

"Only two chips," she said. "And one collar with an address. I've sent you the information in an email. You should get it any second."

"Thank you," he said.

"I'll update you when I have more," she hung up.

Jack dragged the laptop closer to him and pulled up his email. As promised the document she sent was at the top of the list. He clicked on it and started jotting down the information. His brow furrowed as he wrote down the address from the collar. He set his pen down and looked at the others, who waited expectantly.

"We can identify three of the dogs," he announced. "One from a vet west of downtown. I want you two to go check it out."

"What about the others?" Shaun asked.

"One was chipped at Stevens' clinic," he said. "The other had a collar for the same address. I think it's Judith Stevens' Border Collie mix."

48

Detective Weatherby volunteered to drive and Shaun followed her to the garage. They arrived at the clinic just as it was opening for business. Taking the last sips of their coffee, they stepped out into the air and tried to shake the weariness from their faces. They stepped inside the nearly empty waiting room and approached the woman behind the desk.

"Good morning." She yawned, quickly raising her hand to stifle it. "So sorry. What's the pet's name?"

They held out their badges trying to suppress the chain-reaction yawning the woman had started.

"We need to get an identification on a dog's owner from his microchip," Shaun said.

"We can do that," the woman said. "Just bring the animal in and . . ."

Maureen held out the piece of paper with the data from the chip. "Can't bring the dog in. Just need the owner's name and address."

"I see." She did not attempt to take the paper. "Let me get the doctor."

She stood to leave the room and Shaun called after her. "Let him know this is time-sensitive, please."

The door behind them opened and an elderly woman escorted a Yorkshire Terrier into the lobby. The small dog walked alongside the woman until she stopped. The dog sat next to her foot and looked up at the detectives with curiosity. Maureen smiled and waved at which the Yorkie tilted its head to one side.

"Good morning, Mrs. Wilson. Amy will get you checked in." The man speaking looked from the woman to the detectives. "You two need some information?"

"On a microchip." Shaun held out his hand. "Detectives Travis and Weatherby."

"Dr. Abrams." The veterinarian took his hand and shook. "And the dog?"

"Dead," Maureen glanced back at the Yorkie.

"I see," the man sighed. "So you have the microchip?"

"We have the information from the scan, which brought us to you," Shaun said. "We just need the owner's name and address."

"An awful lot of trouble to go to." The vet gestured for them to follow him. "To return a dead animal to its owner, that is."

"If we could get the information, we'll be on our way," Maureen said.

"Of course," the man bowed his head slightly and turned into an office. "Have a seat."

"We'll stand," Maureen said, holding out the paper with the information.

The vet took it and started typing. He waited a second then typed some more. He studied the screen before continuing. "Cocker Spaniel."

"Anything more?" Shaun asked.

"The owner is," the vet said. "Oh, my."

"What is it?" Maureen asked.

"It's the Vaughn's dog," he said. "They called him Spongy. Beautiful animal. Sorry to hear it's dead. I'll print this off for you."

"Crystal Vaughn," Shaun said under his breath.

"You know her?" The doctor turned to him.

"No." Shaun shook his head. "But I met her husband."

49

Stepping into the morgue, Jack Mallory was assaulted by the smell of decomposition. Three bodies lay on the examination tables in stark contrast to the environments in which they were found. Jack stood in the doorway a moment watching the medical examiner working to gently clean one of the bodies as she examined it for wounds and identifying marks. When Valerie saw the detective, she called him over.

"You're a little early, detective." She dipped her sponge into the pan of water next to her and brushed it along the subject's arm. "I'm only just getting started."

Jack looked at the woman's body and grimaced. "I will never get used to what people can do to one another."

"I hope this is all." Valerie glanced at the other bodies.

"There's another area we haven't searched," Jack said.

"So there may be more?"

"Could be," Jack said. "You aren't doing all this alone are you?"

"I sent my two assistants home for some rest." She continued to clean and document. "They'll be back soon. Then things will move more quickly."

"I'm not here to pressure you," Jack said. "Although we'll take what you get as soon as you can."

"Why are you here?" She looked up at him.

"I need the collar," he said. "I'm pretty sure I know whose dog it is."

"Another of our victims?"

"Maybe," Jack said. "A missing woman. Maybe one of the women we found tonight."

Valerie stopped her work and peeled the gloves from her hands as she walked across the room to a desk on the wall. She tossed the gloves and started searching through a clear plastic tub full of evidence bags, each containing a single item and clearly marked as to what it was and where and when it was found. She pulled one up and held it out.

"Bring it back when you're done," she said.

Jack took the bag and looked at the collar inside. "Thanks. And good luck with . . ." He gestured to the room with his chin.

"Don't worry about me, Jack," she said. "I'm going to get you everything you need to catch this guy."

He gave her a half grin and left the morgue with the collar clutched in his fist.

The drive to the Stevens' clinic seemed to take longer than it had before. It was still early when he arrived and only one car was in the front parking area. The employees were busy walking dogs and tending to the horses and cattle in the barn. The assistant Jack remembered as Shelly walked slowly alongside a Shetland Sheepdog with a cast on its front leg. He parked and entered the building.

Keith Stevens stood next to the receptionist when Jack entered. His eyes shifted to the detective only briefly before returning to the woman. "Call the supplier and ask them when we can expect those bandages. Then call Tanner and see if he's coming in today. Detective. What brings you in?"

"A couple of things," Jack said. "Can we go to your office?"

"Why not?" The veterinarian started down the hall and Jack fell into step behind him. When they reached the office, Keith sat at his desk with the detective across from him. "What is it?"

Jack reached into his pocket and pulled out a piece of paper. He unfolded it and handed it to the man. "Need to know who owns this dog."

Keith looked at the paper and then up at Jack. "Another one?"

"Yes."

The veterinarian turned to the computer and typed in the information. A few minutes later a page scrolled out of the printer, and he handed it to Jack. "Pamela Dickson. Dog was a Standard Schnauzer. Although she was only here a couple of times with him. No record after that."

"How long ago was the last visit?" Jack asked.

"About three years ago," Keith said examining the screen. "She must have found another vet."

"You don't remember her?"

"Not at all," he said. "Will that be all? I have patients coming in."

"One more thing." Jack dug his hand into the pocket containing the evidence bag.

"What is it?"

"Do you recognize this?" Jack laid the bag on the veterinarian's desk.

Keith picked up the bag and his eyes grew wide. "You found her?"

"You recognize it, then?"

"It's the dog's collar," Keith said.

"We found the dog early this morning," Jack said.

"Not her?"

"We don't know," Jack said.

"What do you mean?" Keith looked away from the bag and its contents.

"I mean, we don't know," Jack said. "We found some bodies. They haven't been identified yet."

"Bodies?" Keith said. "My, God. How many?"

"Can't discuss that," Jack said. "But we may need you to come down for an identification. Can you do that?"

"Of course." The man turned his gaze back to the collar. "Just tell me when."

"I'm going to need that back." Jack pointed at the bag in the man's hand.

Keith nodded and held it out.

Jack stuffed the bag into his pocket and stood. "I'll be in touch."

50

The three detectives sat around the table in the war room looking up at the timeline on the whiteboard.

"Keith Stevens identified his wife's dog's collar." Jack laid the evidence bag on the table next to the file for Judith Stevens.

"And the microchip we checked on was Crystal Vaughn's Cocker Spaniel," Shaun said.

"So two of the dogs belong to two of our missing persons," Maureen said.

"Anything on the victims?" Shaun asked.

"Not yet," Jack said. "O'Conner said she would let us know as soon as she had something. But the other microchip gave us the name of another possible victim."

He typed on his laptop and stared at the screen. Pamela Dickson was staring back at him with a smile on her face. Something about her looked vaguely familiar, but he couldn't say why. The owner of the second chipped dog, as the report on the screen showed, was missing like the other women. She had not been seen for over nine months. He read down the page studying the details until he came to one that made him stop.

"Butterfly tattoo," he said.

"What was that?" Shaun asked.

"Pamela Dickson has a butterfly tattoo on her ankle." Jack turned the computer to the others. "Like our unidentified victim."

Shaun looked at the woman on the screen. "Our victim isn't blond."

Maureen pointed. "Look at the roots. Ms. Dickson isn't blond either."

"She's one of the cases Maureen pulled." Jack looked at the table. "Who has her file?"

"Right here." Shaun pulled the folder from his stack and opened it. "Pamela Dickson. Twenty-four years old. Dental Hygienist. Reported missing by . . ."

"I'm looking at that in the report," Jack said. "Tell me what isn't here."

Shaun scanned the file turning the pages as he went.

"Shaun," Jack said. "Is she our victim or not?"

"Went for a walk with her Schnauzer," Shaun read. "A neighbor saw her leave but not return. She wasn't reported missing until two days later when she didn't report for work."

"There," Jack interrupted. "Did he know she was alone? Did he know she wouldn't be missed for two days?"

"That would have given him a lot of time," Maureen said. "He could move her easily if no one is looking for her. But I still don't get why he takes the dogs."

"We think he uses the dogs as a means of establishing trust," Jack said. "If he's good with dogs, or maybe has one with him, the victims may see him as less of a threat."

"Because their dogs have a good sense of judgment?" Maureen asked.

"That," Jack nodded. "Or maybe he stalks them over time and interacts with them or their animal until the time is right. They let their guard down because they have seen him for several days in a row. He's suddenly not a stranger but a fellow dog lover. Then he strikes."

"But why?" Maureen stared up at the whiteboard. "Does he hate women? Did these women, in particular, upset him? Reject him? Or does he just enjoy the violence? Dominating his victim when she feels safe?"

"Maureen," Jack shifted in his chair. "Why don't you contact the family and see if you can get a positive ID? I'll go talk to Crystal Vaughn's mother."

"I'll talk to Vaughn's mother," Maureen said.

"You sure?"

"It should be me," she said.

"Okay," Jack said. "I'll do the ID, and then talk to Rachel Dunlop's parents."

"What about me, boss?" Shaun said.

"I need you to stay here," Jack said. "If the M.E. calls, I want you to start processing the information. Call me if you hear from her."

51

Detective Jack Mallory drove slowly down the street in the quiet suburban neighborhood. Small clusters of children were busy entertaining themselves in various activities. Parents watched their kids at play as he rolled by, and Jack could feel eyes following him. He responded in kind to a few hand waves as he searched the homes for their street numbers until he found the one he was looking for.

The Dickson's house was dark. No children played in the yard. No adults sat on the porch. It reminded Jack of a cartoon he had seen years before of a rain cloud hovering over a single home in the suburbs. He parked on the street and strolled up the driveway.

"There's nobody there, mister." A small boy stood at the edge of the yard rocking on and off the balls of his feet, with an action hero figure clutched in one hand.

"Tommy!" A woman on the porch called out. "Get back over here."

Jack looked up at the Dickson's house then walked toward the woman on the neighboring porch.

"Is he right?" he asked when he was close enough to not have to shout. "About no one being there?"

"Who's askin'?" The woman looked at him suspiciously. It was easy to see she had dealt with more than one salesperson in the past.

Jack held out his badge. "Detective Jack Mallory."

"You here about Pam?"

"Possibly," Jack said. He looked down at the boy who was straining his neck to get a better look at the detective's badge.

"Possibly?" The woman's eyes narrowed. "What does that mean?"

Without a response, the woman seemed to have a revelation.

"Claire," she said. "Take Tommy inside."

"But, mom . . ."

"Don't argue," the woman snapped. "Inside. Now."

Pouting, the two children made their way past their mother and into the house. Only when the door had closed behind them did she speak again. "You found her, didn't you?"

"I need to speak to the family, ma'am," Jack said. "Do you know where I might find them?"

The woman looked long and hard at the house next door. A tear formed in the corner of her eye but refused to break free. "Pamela is my little sister. The day she disappeared broke my family. Sure we kept up appearances, showed a strong face. For four months we were out there searching for her, calling her name, hanging posters, pleading for her return. But we were broken that very first day."

"And your name?"

"Marcy," the woman said. "Marcy Goodwin."

Jack hooked his thumb toward the other house. "And the Dicksons?"

"Four months," she said. "That's how long we held it all together. Then we were looking for her out by the old railroad tracks and dad suffered a stroke. He survived, but not the same. He lives in assisted living now. Mom won't leave his side."

"So sorry," Jack said. He slowly made his way to the porch. The woman either didn't notice or didn't care.

"Did you find her?" Marcy asked.

"We found someone," Jack said. "Could be her. May not be."

"You want someone to identify her?"

"Your sister," Jack said. "She had a tattoo?"

Marcy closed her eyes, trying to brace herself for the worst. "She did. Or does. I don't know what to say anymore."

Jack dug into his pocket. He pulled out a folded piece of paper. He spread it out and held it out to the woman who looked at the image of the butterfly tattoo. Her strength gave way. Tears flowed. She did not say anything. She simply reached down to her leg and pulled up on her pant leg, revealing an identical tattoo.

52

When Louise Vaughn opened her door and saw Detective Weatherby standing on her steps, she did not say anything. She simply stepped aside and let Maureen in. Crystal's children were sitting on the floor playing with toys. On the television, the news was running the story of the hour, about the women found buried at the park.

"We didn't find her," Maureen assured her. "At least we don't think so."

"But you're here," Louise sat at a card table set up in their dining room. "So you know something, or think you do."

"The dog." Maureen lowered her voice so the kids didn't overhear. "We found Spongy."

The woman's eyes lowered to the floor, then drifted back to the news. "She's been gone so long. I knew this was the likely outcome. But . . ."

"We don't know anything for sure," Maureen put a hand on Louise's shoulder. "I wanted you to hear it from me. We're still hoping to find her alive."

"You don't really believe that?" Louise said. "Not now."

"I believe that, until I find out otherwise," Maureen said. "If I give up that hope, what good am I to you and the other families out there looking for their loved ones?"

Louise patted the seat next to her. "Sit with me, detective."

"I need to be going," Maureen said.

"Please."

Maureen looked at the door, her exit. With a slight nod, she sat, turning her attention first to the television and then to the children.

53

Jack drove to the south part of town and found the address listed by Rachel's parents when they filed the missing persons report. He parked on the street in front of the middle-class home. There were flower beds on either side of the front door which appeared to be well-kept. Someone in the house was a gardener.

Jack sat for a long time staring up at the flowers and shrubs. He hated giving notifications. Two in one day was not sitting well with him.

A black sedan came down the street and pulled into the driveway. A black man stepped out of the car carrying a briefcase in one hand and a grocery bag in the other. He looked at Jack briefly before walking up to the house and entering. A few minutes later the man came back out of the house and walked across the lawn toward Jack's car.

"Do you need something?" The man shouted loud enough for Jack to hear through the windows. "Or are you just scoping out the neighborhood?"

He pulled out a cell phone and took pictures of the detective's car. Jack opened his door and stepped out.

"Get back in the car, sir." The man pointed with one hand and took pictures with the other. "Drive away, or I'll call the police."

Jack slowly reached into his pocket and pulled out his badge. "I am the police."

"Why are you watching our house?" the man demanded. "Do you think I've done something wrong? Is that it?"

"No, sir," Jack said. "I need to speak to you. And your wife."

"Do I need a lawyer?"

"No, sir," Jack said. "It's about your daughter. About Rachel."

The man's features softened. His body shifted from a defensive stance to a man with no strength left in him.

"What about Rachel?"

"Can we go inside?" Jack pointed to the house.

"No." The man shook his head. "No. You don't look like a man come to tell me good news. Just, no."

"Sir," Jack took a step forward. "I need to speak to you and your wife. We should go inside."

A blond woman with Rachel's green eyes stood on the porch. Jack had not seen or heard her come outside.

"Let him in, Clarence," the woman said. She disappeared back into the house without waiting for a response.

Clarence walked toward the house. He stopped after a few feet and looked back at Jack. "Are you coming?"

Jack followed. Clarence held the door as he stepped into the foyer. The man pointed to a doorway and Jack moved through it. Inside the living room, the blond woman sat on a sofa with her hands knotted together in her lap. She did not look at Jack as he made his way to a chair and sat across from her. Clarence sat next to his wife.

"Mrs. Dunlop?" Jack said.

"Call me Ava," the woman said. "Everyone calls me Ava."

"Okay, Ava." Jack shifted his eyes to the husband. "I'm Detective Jack Mallory and I'm sorry to inform you . . ."

"No." Clarence squeezed his eyes closed and rocked his large frame. Ava reached out and clasped his leg and squeezed.

". . . that your daughter's body was discovered yesterday."

"No. No. No." Clarence cried. His face scrunched as tears poured from his eyes.

"We don't know for sure," Jack said. "But we believe she was murdered."

Clarence continued to rock, cry and voice his denial. Ava sat stoically, betrayed by tears streaming down her cheeks.

"Can we see her?" Ava still did not make eye contact with the detective.

Rachel had been buried for weeks if not months. All they found were her skeletal remains. Jack knew that the Dunlops were thinking they would see her face, possibly being able to touch her hand or kiss her forehead. It was the closure they deserved. It was not the closure they would be able to have.

"Not at this time," Jack said.

Ava nodded her understanding. Clarence's body shook as he continued to cry.

"I need to ask some questions," Jack softened his voice. "Some of which you may have answered when Rachel disappeared, but we need to look at differently now that it's a homicide investigation."

"I understand," Ava said.

"Your daughter had a dog that disappeared when she did." Jack pulled out his notepad.

"Yes," Ava said. "Why does that matter? Was she killed for her dog?"

"Do you know if she walked the dog at regular times?" Jack asked. "The same time every day?"

"I don't know," the mother said.

"How about you, Mr. Dunlop?" Jack asked. "Do you know?"

"No." Clarence sat up, inhaling deeply to control his emotions.

"Okay," Jack wrote in his pad. "Do you know where she went when she walked him?"

"Her," Ava said.

"Excuse me?"

"Snowball, Rachel's dog," Ava said, "was female."

"Alright," Jack said. "Do you know where she walked Snowball?"

"No." Ava looked at Jack for the first time. "I'm sorry."

"Don't be," Jack said. He looked at Clarence.

The man shook his head briefly, then stopped. "Wait. I know. She used to take her to the park. It was about a half-mile from her apartment. I think there was a walking path she followed."

"Good," Jack continued to take notes. "Did she ever mention anyone she noticed while at the park? Someone watching her? Or following her?"

"No," Clarence said. "I would've gone with her if she mentioned some creep."

"I have to ask," Jack said.

Clarence nodded.

"What about her boyfriend?" Jack flipped his notes. "There was an Eric Bridges interviewed who claimed to be her boyfriend. Do you know him?"

"We know Eric," Clarence said.

"It doesn't sound like you were a fan," Jack said.

"She was my girl," Clarence said. "No one's good enough. Eric was less good enough than others."

"Why is that?"

"I don't know," Clarence said. "He, uh . . ."

"He was an ass," Ava said. "He was so full of himself and never made Rachel first. We wanted her to dump him. But you know how kids are. The more you say he's the wrong choice, the more convinced she is that he's the right one."

"We were just waiting for her to come to her senses," Clarence said.

"Is it possible that she did?" Jack asked. "Come to her senses, I mean? Do you think if she were to dump him that he could have hurt her?"

"Eric?" Ava said. "I don't know. I think he thinks too highly of himself to put that much value in a relationship."

"But if he thought that much of himself and she rejected him," Jack said. "That's quite a betrayal. Could he have become angry? Could he have hurt Rachel?"

"He better not have," Clarence said. "I'll break him in two."

"Calm down, Clarence." Ava patted his leg. "This is all hypothetical. They don't know that Eric did anything. Do you, detective?"

"No," Jack said. "We're just asking questions. Trying to get a picture of her life."

"You have to find who did this to our girl," Clarence said. "You have to find him and give me a few minutes with him."

"I can't do that," Jack said. "We're going to get him. But we're not going to turn him over to you. We can't do that."

"He knows, detective," Ava said.

"Now," Jack said. "Do you know where I can find Eric Bridges?"

54

Jeremiah Hopkins' trial was a sham from the start. Starting with the court-appointed attorney, to the manufactured evidence, to Detective Bret Peterson lying on the stand. Jeremiah had little chance of getting a fair decision. Throw on top, the fact that the judge overseeing the case was Judge Paul Watson, Bret's brother, and his fate was sealed.

Shaun dove into the crime scene evidence, searching for anything that might help him prove the man's innocence. Eyewitness accounts described a burly, bearded man with a sawed-off shotgun that he used like a hammer during the assaults. Jeremiah was five-foot-ten and weighed one-hundred eighty pounds, hardly a match. The weapon was not found on the Hopkins' property and neither were any of the stolen items.

What Shaun focused on however were two police reports filed after Jeremiah's arrest. The reports described two incidents of armed robbery committed by a large, bearded man with a sawed-off shotgun. The crimes were solved, a man arrested, tried, convicted, and sentenced. Shaun compiled the information and made his way to the chief's office, knocking on the door frame.

"Come." The chief did not look up as Shaun entered.

Shaun stepped up to her desk and waited in silence for her to finish reading the papers in front of her.

"Detective Travis." She finally looked up. "Have a seat."

"Yes, ma'am." He sat.

"What can I do for you?" she asked. "Or do you have news?"

"No news yet, ma'am." Shaun didn't say more.

"Why are you here, detective?" the chief asked. "This isn't a break room."

"Sorry, chief," Shaun squirmed a little in his seat. "I've learned something that, well it could be an embarrassment, for the department, I mean."

"Not what I want to hear, detective." Sharon leaned forward in her seat. "How embarrassing are you talking about?"

"Could call into question several convictions from recent years." Shaun shifted uncomfortably in his seat.

"Years?"

"Possibly."

"Details?"

"I think we convicted an innocent man," Shaun said.

"We arrest," the chief said. "We don't convict. That's the district attorney's job."

"Doesn't make him less innocent," Shaun said.

"You said 'think'," Sharon said. "Do you think? Or are you sure?"

"I found evidence that he shouldn't have been arrested," Shaun said.

"And the arresting officer?"

"Detective Peterson," Shaun said.

"Bret Peterson?"

"Yes, ma'am," Shaun nodded.

"And does this case in any way have something to do with his family?"

Bret Peterson had falsified evidence and manipulated facts to convict innocent men for crimes he had committed. The investigation concluded that the crimes were carried out in an effort to protect his family.

"No, ma'am."

"I had a feeling this day would come." The chief sighed. "Give me what you have. I'm going to have to look into it before we bust this department wide open."

"Yes, ma'am," Shaun's cell phone rang, and he stood. "Excuse me, chief."

Sharon nodded and gestured for him to go.

He walked out of the office struggling to pull his phone free of his pocket. The ringing stopped just before he was successful. He stood staring at the number trying to remember if he knew who it was that called when it began to ring again. He answered quickly. "Detective Travis."

"Where's Mallory?" the woman said.

"He's out," Shaun said.

"He's not picking up his cell," she said.

"He may be interviewing someone," Shaun suggested. "Or doesn't have a signal. What's going on?"

"Another woman went missing last night."

55

The address for Eric, which the Dunlops provided Jack, was a small bungalow. The yard was unevenly mowed. The shrubs were untrimmed. Weeds grew freely in otherwise empty flowerbeds as well as in the cracks of the driveway and sidewalk. There was a single chair on the front porch with empty cans laying underneath, some beer, some soda.

Jack opened the screen door and the hinges screeched loudly. He rapped his fist on the door twice and let the screen slam shut again. It was unlikely anyone in the house had not heard. A young woman in shorts and t-shirt opened the door. She did not speak, choosing rather to stare blankly at Jack.

"Is there an Eric Bridges here?" Jack asked.

She still said nothing.

"Who's at the door?" A man's voice called from another room.

"Who are you?" The woman asked on cue.

"Detective Jack Mallory," Jack said. "Is that Eric Bridges?"

"It's a cop!" She yelled over her shoulder but did not move.

Jack moved his hand to rest on his weapon. "I'm going to ask you one more time. Is Eric Bridges in the house?"

"Seriously? Who is it?" The voice was coming closer. When he stepped into view, Jack saw a man a few years older than the woman, also in shorts and t-shirt. "Who are you?"

"Detective Jack Mallory," he repeated. "Are you Eric Bridges?"

"Yes," Eric furrowed his brow. "Why?"

"I need to talk to you about Rachel Dunlop." Jack watched Eric's face for a reaction, but any tell-tale sign was thwarted by the young woman.

"Who is Rachel Dunlop?" She struck Eric in the arm. "Are you seeing someone else?"

"Wendy," Eric snapped. "Go start dinner."

Wendy closed her mouth, mumbled something, and walked away.

"Neat trick," Jack said.

"What?"

"Does she sit and roll over on command too?"

"I thought you wanted to talk about Rachel." Eric lowered his voice when he said her name.

"You two were dating when she disappeared?" Jack watched again for a reaction, but there was none.

"Yes."

"You moved on rather quickly," Jack pointed to the kitchen. "Does Wendy know your last girlfriend vanished?"

"First of all, it's been six months," Eric defended.

"Seven," Jack corrected.

"Whatever," Eric began rocking from foot to foot. "It's been a while. I can't wait forever for her to decide to come back."

"So you think she left you?" Jack shifted ever so slightly with the other man's movements. "Is that it?"

"I think she left," Eric said.

"Are you sure?" Jack stepped closer and raised to his full height. Sometimes, intimidation had a place. "Or maybe did she get tired of being your puppet? Did she tell you she wasn't going to put up with you controlling her life? Is that what happened? Is that why you killed her?"

"Listen, I didn't . . ." Eric stopped rocking. "Did you say 'killed her'? Rachel's dead?"

"You're going to have to better than that," Jack said, "if you want to convince a jury you didn't know."

"Seriously," Eric said. "Rachel's dead?"

"She is," Jack said.

"When?" Eric asked. "Where? I thought she was just gone. I mean took off somewhere gone, not dead gone. God, do her parents know? Of course, they know. You would have talked to them before me. Did they give you my name? Do they think I had something to do with it?"

"Did you?"

"No," Eric said. "God, I was crazy about Rachel. I was heartbroken when she left."

"For a month or two?" Jack pointed toward the kitchen again. "When did you move on to Wendy?"

"I'll have you know, I didn't start seeing Wendy until a couple of weeks ago." Eric started rocking.

"If I ask her, that's what she will tell me?"

"Yes."

"And what about the night Rachel disappeared?"

"What about it?"

"Where were you that night?" Jack asked.

"I was at work," Eric said. "I had to stay late."

"And where do you work?"

"Back then, I worked at a print shop," he said. "And before you ask; Yes. I have witnesses. I couldn't not be there or nothing would have gotten done. The printers don't run themselves."

"Do you know where she walked her dog?"

"Snowflake?"

"Snowball," Jack corrected.

"Whatever," Eric said. "Sure, I went with her a couple of times."

"Do you know if Rachel ever had issues with anyone?" Jack said. "Maybe an ex-boyfriend? Or maybe one of your ex-girlfriends?"

"No," he said. "Rachel got along with everyone."

"What about Wendy?"

"Wendy? What about her?"

"Maybe Rachel knew Wendy was eying you and confronted her," Jack said. "And Wendy took care of her."

"Rachel didn't know Wendy," Eric said. "I only met her a couple of weeks ago."

"Just because you didn't know her doesn't mean they didn't know each other," Jack said. "Maybe Rachel was keeping her away?"

"I think you're putting way too much into Wendy's ability to plan and implement said plan," Eric said.

"You don't think very highly of her, do you?" Jack said. "Seems you would think more of Rachel's replacement."

"What? Wendy?" Eric said. "She's not Rachel's replacement. She's nothing."

"I'm what?" Wendy came around the corner like a feral cat and pounced on Eric. "How dare you."

Jack grinned and backed out of the house. He had heard enough.

56

When Jack left Eric Bridges, he checked his phone and saw that he had missed multiple calls. There were two messages from Shaun. The first was the younger detective informing his partner of the missing woman. The second gave him the address and let him know he and Maureen were on their way. Jack checked the time. It had been twenty minutes since the last call. Jack raced to the scene and pulled in behind Shaun's car where he and Maureen were waiting for him.

"What've we got?" Jack climbed out of his car and joined them.

"Dawn Callahan," Maureen said. "Thirty-two years old. Married with one child. Went for a walk with the family dog last night around eight. When she hadn't returned by ten her husband called the police."

"Last night?" Jack said. "I thought we had alerts set up for women missing with dogs. Why didn't we hear about it before now?"

"The husband didn't mention the dog on the nine-one-one call," Shaun said. "He was distraught about his wife."

"But she hadn't been missing long enough for a standard missing persons," Jack said, flatly.

"Which is why they told him they couldn't do anything for him," Shaun said.

"He called again this morning," Maureen said. "That's when he mentioned the dog. Dispatch contacted us, but she's already been gone twelve to fourteen hours."

"What's the husband's story?" Jack scanned the middle-class neighborhood. From where he was standing, he couldn't see any sign of a walking path.

"He said they usually walk as a family," Shaun said. "Last night their son wasn't feeling well so she took the dog. He stayed home to care for the kid."

"You buying it?" Jack asked. "It doesn't match our guy's M.O. He stalks his victims. If this woman usually walked with her husband, she wouldn't have been a good target. Maybe the husband did something to her and then reported her missing."

"Thought of that," Maureen said. "But the neighbor saw her leave with the dog just like the husband said. And before you ask, the neighbor didn't do it. He's wheelchair-bound."

"It still doesn't feel right." Jack walked to the center of the street to get a better look at the area, the lines of sight, the number of streetlights. "If this is our boy, he suddenly decided to grab a random woman without all the prep work. The other cases we have suggest he is too cautious for that."

"What if he saw us last night." Shaun thought aloud.

"What was that?" Jack said.

"What if he was there, or watching the news," Shaun said. "Then he knew we were in his space."

"His safe space," Maureen added. "And we were taking what he thinks belongs to him, his collection."

"So he's starting a new collection?" Jack said. "Or maybe punishing us."

"Punishing us?" Maureen said. "Pretty sure the victim is the one being punished."

"We took his collection like you said," Jack said. "We also took his safe place. It must have upset him and he decided to make us pay. Taking this victim while we're recovering the others. It could be his way of saying he's still in charge."

"It seems to me that he would have already picked his next victim," Maureen said. "And if Dawn Callahan usually walked with her husband, she wasn't it. So why didn't he take the woman he was already planning to take?"

"Maybe he couldn't," Shaun said. "Maybe she was out of town or had company. There could be any number of reasons she wasn't where she was supposed to be."

"So he took the first woman he came across?" Maureen said. "Without a plan."

"If he didn't plan," Jack said. "If he acted on impulse."

"He may have made a mistake." Maureen finished his thought.

57

Dawn Callahan was walking her dog, a Boston Terrier, when she vanished. And that was where the similarities ended with their other cases. All indications were that the man they were after took time stalking his victims, learning their schedules and routines. Dawn usually walked with her husband and the killer would have never taken time pursuing a target that wasn't expected to be alone.

The victims they had identified were all taken from walking paths in dark, remote areas. Dawn walked her dog on the streets of her neighborhood. There was no walking path within five miles of her home. Everything about the case suggested it had nothing to do with their case. It was the one detail that kept bringing Jack back to it. The dog.

"No one saw her after the neighbor said she left the house." Jack sat across from the others in the war room, leaving officers to canvass the neighborhood for witnesses and clues. "Are we sure she didn't just walk out of their lives?"

"Everyone we've spoken to paints a picture of a happy family," Maureen said. "No financial problems. None of the usual stress markers. And it was highly unusual for them not to walk as a family."

"So our victim leaves the house alone, which is unusual for her," Jack said. "and happens onto our suspect who grabs her without any thought toward planning, something that, up until now, would be unthinkable. And no one saw a thing."

"What if the suspect didn't approach her at all," Maureen said. "She's a nurse. Maybe she thought he was in distress and approached him."

"She walks up, asks if he's okay and he reacts," Jack said. "There could be something to that. But why was he there?"

"Maybe he lives there," Shaun said.

"Lives where?" Jack said.

"Maybe no one saw him because he wasn't out of place," Shaun said. "What if he lives in the neighborhood?"

"All of the other victims were taken from across the city," Jack said. "He's been careful to make it impossible for us to track him. It would be reckless for him to kidnap someone from his own neighborhood."

"Maybe he didn't have a choice," Maureen said. "Maybe Dawn saw something she wasn't supposed to. He had to take her to keep her quiet."

"Then what did she see?" Jack said.

No one responded.

"Neither of you has any ideas?" Jack said.

"The obvious would be that she saw him with a body," Shaun said.

"In the middle of a residential neighborhood?" Jack challenged. "That doesn't seem likely."

"Maybe she knows him," Maureen suggested. "She may have gone to his door. Or maybe she saw him in the garage or back yard and walked up to him. Just being neighborly."

"And she saw another victim," Jack said. "Or maybe just evidence of what he's been doing."

Jack's phone rang and he answered, listening intently to what the caller was saying. When he hung up, he looked at the other two detectives. "One of the neighbors has one of those video doorbells. Seems there's a video time-stamped eight thirty-two of a large pickup truck with a covered bed."

"Could be him," Shaun said.

"Or any number of other people," Jack said. "I need you to go down there and go door to door. See if anyone owns a truck that matches the description we have."

"We just canvassed the neighborhood," Shaun said.

"And you're going to canvass it again," Jack snapped. "Is that a problem?"

"No, sir," Shaun said. "No problem at all."

58

The phone in the war room was louder than most. The ring was a welcome intruder of the intense silence that had suddenly dominated the room. Shaun looked at the phone then turned sharply to leave. When the younger detective was out of the room, Jack lifted the receiver and put it to his ear.

"Mallory," he said.

"This is Valerie." The medical examiner identified herself.

"What've you got?" Jack asked.

"I've got five dead women in my morgue," Valerie said. "I've got four with partially mended bones that were never set. Three are malnourished. One is pregnant, about three weeks along. Jack, one of these girls was beaten repeatedly over a period of weeks, if not months."

"Anything that will help us identify them?"

"We ran what prints we could get and got two hits," Valerie said. "Thelma Reeves and Alyssa Bell. One of the others has a distinctive tattoo that will help if you can find a way to track it down."

"What's the tattoo?" Jack asked.

"An eagle," she said.

"That doesn't sound distinctive," he said.

"It covers her entire back," she said. "And the detail is amazing. I wouldn't think a lot of tattoo artists could do this kind of work."

"Send me a picture," Jack said.

"Already have," she said. "It should be in your mailbox."

"Nothing on the other two?"

"One of them has given birth," Valerie said.

"A mother, then," Jack said. "That may help."

"We may have to run DNA if you can get something to match it to," Valerie said.

"Which one was pregnant?" Jack asked.

"Alyssa Bell," she said. "She's young."

"How young?"

"Seventeen."

Jack closed his eyes and calmed himself. "Send me everything you have. We have to catch this guy."

He lowered the receiver to the phone and turned to Maureen.

"One of them was pregnant?" she said.

"A seventeen-year-old girl." Jack started typing her name into the computer. "Alyssa Bell."

He found her quickly. Her prints were on file because she had been picked up for shoplifting when she was fifteen. The girl in the picture was sad and frightened. The case was ultimately dropped because the store owner who caught her did not press charges. There were no other incidents. She had either been scared straight or had gotten better at stealing. She had vanished five months ago. Her parents were concerned about the girl's boyfriend at the time, but there was no evidence he was involved in her disappearance.

Jack wrote down the address and typed in the name Thelma Reeves.

Like Alyssa, Thelma was in the system because of a run-in with the law. She had been arrested for a DUI on two occasions. The second time was nearly three years ago, resulting in property damage when she struck a parked car. She had spent six months in jail and another year on probation. Eight months ago her roommate reported that she had left their apartment at ten o'clock and never returned.

Jack added her address to his notebook. Neither report mentioned dogs, but he knew they weren't the focus. Details left out by loved ones more concerned with the family member or not recorded by the officer, considering them unimportant.

He pulled up his email and lookcd at the image Valerie had sent him. The victim's back was bare and the eagle tattoo was spread across it. The head was at the base of the woman's neck, its wings stretching from shoulder to shoulder, the body and talons taking up most of her upper body. Valerie had been right. The level of detail in the artwork suggested a highly skilled tattoo artist. Jack printed the image.

"I want you to hit some tattoo parlors and see if you can find who did this." Jack handed the printed page to Maureen. "If you get lucky, see if they have her name."

"Whoever did it should know her name." Maureen studied the image. "That size tattoo would take more than one visit."

"While you do that, I'm going to take care of the notifications," Jack said. "And I'll see if I can get more details about their disappearances."

59

The drive back to the neighborhood where Dawn Callahan had vanished was filled with cursing and gesturing at the other drivers on the road. The idea that Jack dismissed him the way he had, touched a nerve with Shaun. The older detective was supposed to be training him, not sending him on the types of errands he had done when he was a uniformed officer. Canvassing the neighborhood to find out who might own a large pickup truck was grunt work, and he had already done his time as a grunt. He needed to complete his training so he could have his own cases assigned to him.

He parked at one end of the block and stepped out onto the street, slamming the car door. He stood next to the vehicle taking in the surroundings. There were ten homes on either side before the next intersection. He had no way of knowing how far Dawn had walked before being abducted or which direction she may have gone once she reached the other end of the street. He walked up the driveway of the nearest house and cut across the walkway to the front door. He knocked loudly and stepped back.

"What?" The man who answered the door was in his early fifties and sported a beer belly that he had been working on for a number of years.

"I'm Detective Travis with . . ."

"I've already talked to the police," the man interrupted.

"I know, sir," Shaun sighed. "I just need to know what vehicles you own."

The man pointed to the driveway where a four-door sedan and an old rundown Mustang were parked. "There you go."

"No trucks?"

"No," the man said. "Just what you see."

"Thank you," Shaun said.

The man shut the door.

Shaun repeated his questioning at the next twelve houses receiving protests that they had already been questioned at nearly every one. He skipped the victim's home and walked up to their neighbor's. He knocked and stepped away. There was barking followed by a female's voice yelling at the offender to be quiet. When the door opened, the girl was struggling to keep the dog calm, pulling back on its collar and giving repeated commands to sit. She looked up at one point, an apology written into her expression. Shaun immediately recognized her.

"Detective Travis." He held up his badge. "Shelly isn't it? From the Stevens' clinic?"

"Yes." She smiled. "I thought I recognized you. What brings you to my home?"

"I'm here to ask you about what happened to your neighbor." Shaun pointed to the Callahan's house.

"My neighbor?" Shelly looked out toward the house he indicated. "What happened?"

"You don't know?"

"I just got home from work," she said.

"Your parents didn't tell you?"

"They're out of town for the week," she said. "You're kind of freaking me out. What happened?"

"Your neighbor, Mrs. Callahan, disappeared last night," Shaun said. "You didn't see anything did you?"

"Oh, my God," Shelly's eyes grew wide. "No. I didn't see anything. But I don't go outside much. Watched TV most of the night."

"You didn't walk the dog?"

"Not last night," Shelly said. "I just let her out back."

"Do you usually walk her?"

"Sometimes," Shelly shrugged like she was admitting to taking the last cookie from the cookie jar. "Maybe a couple of times a week. It's hard when that's what you do literally all day."

"I'm not judging." Shaun smiled, handing her a card. "Thank you for your time. And keep your eyes open. If you think of something, give me a call."

60

Maureen had no idea how many tattoo parlors there were until she was tasked with finding one particular tattoo artist knowing it was possible the victim may have gotten her artwork in another city altogether. The first dozen or so parlors Maureen visited provided her with little information. All of them were impressed with the art in the photo she showed them. Two claimed they could have, but had not, done the work.

She parked in front of yet another parlor, its neon sign announcing what they did inside the brick and glass building. Maureen walked in to see a bald man with almost every inch of exposed skin sporting a tattoo. He was sitting behind a short counter covered with three-ring binders, in front of a wall covered with drawings, all showcasing the work he had, or could, do. He looked up as Maureen entered and smiled as any salesperson is trained to do.

"You in the market for a tat?" The man asked.

"Sorry to disappoint you." Maureen held up her badge. "I'm after information."

"What kind of information?" He sat up a little straighter.

Maureen pulled out the copied paper and dutifully unfolded it. She turned it toward the man. "You know anyone who might have done this tattoo?"

"Paul Spencer." The man said the name without hesitation.

"Paul Spencer?"

"He's the best." The man looked at the image, running his fingers along the design. "I'm good. But Spencer's the best. This is definitely his work."

"How can I know for sure?" Maureen asked.

"I watched him do it," the man said, handing the paper back to her.

"Where can I find this Paul Spencer?"

Maureen was given an address almost ten miles from where she was, with dozens of parlors between them. After a short debate with herself, she decided it was worth a shot. She drove the most direct route and found the parlor sandwiched between a BBQ joint and a laundromat.

Unlike the parlor she had just left, this place had customers waiting and a receptionist answering the phone and making appointments.

"May I help you?" The receptionist barely looked at Maureen. "Do you have an appointment?"

Maureen held up her badge. "Do you have a Paul Spencer working here?"

"He's booked into the middle of next . . ." The woman raised her head and stopped when she saw the badge in her face.

"So, he works here," Maureen said. "I need to see him. Now."

"Just a minute," the woman said. She pushed away from the small desk and stood. Passing through a doorway, she vanished, returning a short time later with a muscular man at her side. She pointed at Maureen and took up her previous position.

"Paul Spencer?"

"Yes," Paul said. "What's this about?"

Maureen held up the image of the eagle tattoo. "Ever see this before?"

"That's my work," Paul Spencer said, looking at the image. "If I recall, that one took five visits. She was determined. Why do you want to know? Looking for yourself?"

"No thank you," Maureen said. "We're looking for the name of the girl with the tattoo."

"Her name?" Paul said, his eyes moving rapidly. "I'm not going to get her in trouble am I?"

"No, sir," Maureen said. "She's not in trouble."

"You have a picture of her back," Paul thought aloud. "But you don't know her name. She's dead isn't she?"

Several eyes shifted to Paul. Maureen did not respond.

"She is," Paul closed his eyes. "I wondered what happened to her."

"You knew her?"

"I dated her a couple of times," he said. "Even thought things were going pretty well, then suddenly she wouldn't answer her phone. I thought she was ghosting me."

"When did you date her?" Maureen asked.

"Oh," Paul said. "When did she die? She may have ghosted me after all."

"Answer my question," Maureen said. "When did you date her?"

"Seven or eight months ago," he said. "Right after I finished that tattoo. She said she wanted a couple more. When did she die?"

"We haven't determined that yet," she said. "We found her yesterday. But she's been dead a while. What is her name?"

"Oh, yeah," Paul said. "Juanita Alvarado."

"Do you know her family?" Maureen said. "Where she lived?"

"No," Paul said. "We hadn't gotten that far. She would just meet me here when I closed. Never took her home."

"Do you know anything about her?" Maureen asked. "Besides her name?"

"She liked to drink," Paul said. "And she was allergic to peanuts or something."

"Not too helpful," Maureen said. "But thanks for the name."

"Don't mention it," Paul said. "Should I, you know, stay in town or something?"

"You going somewhere?" Maureen asked.

"No."

"Did you kill her?"

"No."

"We'll be in touch if we need you." Maureen handed him a card. "In case you think of something else."

61

Jack parked at the apartment complex listed as Thelma Reeves' address. Her roommate, Katie Ingram, had reported her missing eight months ago. There was a chance the woman didn't even live there anymore. Jack approached the apartment and knocked.

The door opened and a woman in her mid to late twenties stood there staring at him with a scrunched brow and pursed lips.

"Katie Ingram?" Jack said.

"Kat!" The woman yelled over her shoulder and let the door close. Jack shifted his foot forward to prevent it from latching. "There's a guy here to see you!"

A moment later another woman pulled the door open. She was dressed in sweatpants and a t-shirt. Her eyes were almost closed as if drunk or half asleep.

"Katie Ingram?" Jack repeated.

"Yeah," she said. "I'm Katie. Who are you?"

Jack held up his badge. "Detective Malory."

"Did I do something?" Her eyes widened. "I mean, I don't remember doing anything wrong."

"No," Jack reassured. "I just need to talk to you about your roommate."

"Tracie?" Katie looked back into the apartment at the other woman. "What'd she do? I mean, she's right here, you know?"

"I heard that," Tracie said from within the apartment.

"Not that roommate," Jack said. "I want to talk to you about Thelma Reeves."

"Thelma?" she said. "I mean, she left me with a lot of unpaid bills. I almost lost the apartment. Is she in trouble or something?"

"No," Jack said. "She's dead."

"Dead?" Katie said. "My God. How?"

"I was hoping you might answer some questions," Jack said. "May I come in?"

"I mean, sure." Katie stepped to the side to allow the detective to enter. "But I don't know how much help I can be. I mean, I haven't seen her in months."

"Eight months," Jack said. "That's when you filed a missing persons report."

"That sounds right," she nodded.

The two of them sat in the living room. Katie on a sagging sofa next to Tracie who was reading a textbook. Jack opted for a threadbare armchair that in no way matched the sofa. He shifted his weight a couple of times but could still feel the springs in the cushion.

"And she never contacted you after that?" Jack asked.

"No," Katie said. "The detective I spoke to said he thought she had run away to avoid paying her rent."

"Is that what you thought?" Jack said.

"It didn't seem right," Katie said. "I mean, she seemed fine."

"Did she take her belongings with her?"

"No," Katie said. "I mean, that's why I didn't think the detective cared much. She didn't take anything. I mean, even her purse was here. But he was convinced and I didn't know what else to do."

"She left her purse?" Jack said. "Was her ID in it?"

"Everything was in it," Katie said. "Driver's license. Credit cards. Cash. I mean, the only things she took were the clothes she was wearing and the dog."

"Dog?" Jack's eyebrow rose. "She had a dog?"

"Technically, it was our dog," Katie said. "I mean, we picked it out together. Each paid half. I mean, sure, she walked it more. But it was ours. And she just took it."

"Are you saying she was walking the dog when she disappeared?" Jack asked.

"I mean, yeah," Katie said. "She was walking him."

"What kind of dog was it?" Jack asked.

"A Springer Spaniel," Katie said. "Why?"

"I can tell you that Thelma did not run away," Jack said. "She was taken the night she disappeared. The man who took her takes the dogs as well."

"She's been dead all this time?" Katie's eyes welled up. "I mean, I feel so guilty for being mad at her."

"Don't," Jack said. "You didn't know. You did the right thing. You reported it. The detective should have done a better job."

"And I got rid of her stuff," Katie said. "I mean, most of it anyway."

"I was hoping you might be able to help me reach her family," Jack said. "Do you have an address or a phone number?"

"Thelma grew up in an orphanage," Katie said. "Never adopted. I mean, it was really sad. She didn't have any family that she knew of. I mean, I thought maybe she had found a relative and that's why she left. I guess not."

"Here's my card." Jack held it out for her. She took it and studied it's front. "Call me if you remember anything."

Katie nodded, never taking her eyes off the card. Jack let himself out.

62

The Bell's home was a split-level, sitting on a corner lot. Craig and Laura Bell were in their early forties and had five children ages nineteen to ten. Alyssa was their second, the oldest of the two girls. Mrs. Bell answered the door when Jack knocked, showed him to the kitchen where she seated him at the table, and served him iced tea.

"Craig will be home soon," Laura repeated for the third time since Jack had identified himself. Jack wasn't sure if she didn't want to have to repeat everything to her spouse or if she was afraid of what Jack might have to tell them, but she would not allow him to begin until her husband arrived.

"You have a lovely home." Jack looked around the kitchen, his gaze settling on the refrigerator which was covered with school photos of their kids held on with magnets. Each face stared back at him with a toothy smile that suggested happiness. Jack found himself focussing on one photo in particular, that of a teenage girl with curly hair and bright blue eyes. Her smile seemed to be the broadest of them all, the most genuine. Jack knew without asking that it was a picture of Alyssa.

"Thank you," Laura said. She busied herself wiping off already clean counters. When she reached the end, she reversed course and wiped them again. Jack worried she might take off the finish.

The front door opened and a stampede of footsteps reverberated through the house, some going up and others going down the stairs. The kids were home. One set of steps entered the kitchen and Jack turned to see their oldest son standing next to the island. He stared at

Jack for a long moment before opening the refrigerator, taking a soda, and vanishing the way he had come. His steps told Jack he had gone down to the lower level.

"Craig Junior," Laura said. "He's been a tremendous help since . . ." She stopped her thought and started rinsing her rag in the sink. "He prefers Theo. Doesn't want to be confused with his father. Theodore is his middle name."

"Mrs. Bell?"

"Please, call me Laura," she said. "Everyone does."

"Laura," Jack said. "Would you like me to wait outside until your husband arrives? I seem to be making you nervous."

"No." She smiled weakly. It somehow made her look more sad. "Not at all. He'll be home soon."

"Okay," Jack said. He turned back to the glass of iced tea. He sipped from it and held it in his hands to give them something to do.

The whining motor of the garage door opener penetrated the walls to the kitchen. Laura straightened and started for a door on the far side of the kitchen. "That's him."

Jack stood next to the table where he had been sitting and waited as she stepped out into the garage, presumably to warn her husband of his presence. He could hear their voices, Craig asking questions, Laura having no answers. A moment later, the couple entered the kitchen. Craig placed a small case on the counter and leaned in, kissing his wife on the cheek.

"Laura tells me you're a detective," Craig said. He crossed the room to him. "I'm Craig Bell."

"Detective Jack Mallory," Jack confirmed what his wife had told him.

"You're here about Alyssa, aren't you?" Craig gestured for Jack to sit as he pulled out another chair and did the same. Laura reluctantly took the seat next to him.

"I am," Jack said.

"Is she okay?" Craig asked. "Will she be coming home soon?"

Jack looked at the couple. Their cautious optimism was betrayed by the fear in their eyes. The detective took a deep breath. "I'm sorry to inform you . . ." The mother wailed. ". . . that we found your daughter's body yesterday evening."

"No!" Laura cried out. "No. No. No. Not my Alyssa. It can't be."

Craig put his arm around his wife's shoulders and pulled her close to him. He was trying to remain strong, but his hands shook and there was a spasm in the skin below his right eye. His lips quivered as he spoke. "How?"

"I can't discuss the details," Jack said. "But she was murdered."

"No." Laura cried into her husband's chest.

"She was found in a shallow grave near some other victims," Jack said.

"How long ago was she killed?" Craig asked.

"We don't know yet," Jack said. "I can let you know later today."

"Why?"

Their eyes were drawn to the doorway between the kitchen and the rest of the house. Theo stood there, his hands balled into fists.

"What does it matter?" He said. "If she was killed yesterday or five months ago? What does it matter? She's dead. I told you she hadn't run away. I told you she needed us. And now she's dead. Are you happy?"

The boy turned and ran out of the house, slamming the front door. They could hear a car start and tires squeal as he drove away.

"He's angry," Jack said. "It's not unusual in these situations."

"He's right," Craig's chest fell. His voice broke. "We assumed she had run away. That she would come to her senses and come home. We reported her missing, but we didn't make fliers or get on the news. We just waited for her to come back."

Jack looked into the man's eyes. He seemed to age years in a matter of minutes. "I hate to do this, but I need to ask you some questions. About the day of her disappearance."

"I understand," Craig said.

"First," Jack said. "Can you think of anyone who might have had a problem with your daughter?"

"No," Craig said. "Everyone loved Alyssa. She was so popular."

"What about the unpopular kids?" Jack said. "Maybe one of them was jealous of her popularity? Or was upset because she rejected them?"

"I don't think so," Craig said.

"Did she have a boyfriend?" Jack said. "Maybe he wanted more from the relationship?"

"No," Craig said. "She wasn't allowed to date until she was seventeen."

"And she was sixteen when she disappeared?" Jack said.

"Yes."

"No," Laura said.

"What?" Craig said.

"That's not right," she said.

"What are you talking about, Laura?" Craig said. "What's not right?"

"Mrs. Bell," Jack said. "Is something in your husband's statement not right?"

"She had a boyfriend," Laura said.

"What?" Craig said. "What do you mean she had a boyfriend? We told her no. Not until she was seventeen."

"That was so unrealistic," Laura said. "All of her friends were dating when they were fourteen or fifteen. Alyssa wanted to date. A boy asked her out. She was upset at the thought of saying no. She liked him. So, I told her she could date him."

"You what?" Craig said. "Laura, you helped her disobey me?"

"We started dating when we were sixteen, Craig," Laura said. "Why would you deny her that?"

"To keep her safe," Craig said. "So she could be here with us right now instead of dead in a ditch."

"Don't make this my fault," Laura said. "Don't you dare make this my fault."

"I'm sorry," Jack said. "But I have more questions. And I will need the boyfriend's name."

"Mitch Dodson," Laura said.

"Mitch Dodson?" Craig said. "Are you serious?"

"You can discuss that later," Jack said. "This is going to sound like an unusual question, but did you have a dog? One that vanished when she did?"

"We did," Craig looked at him, confusion in his eyes. "How did you know?"

"Was she walking the dog that night?"

"Yes," Laura said. "She walked him most nights. What does that have to do with her being killed?"

"It appears she was killed by someone who targets women while they are walking their dogs."

"But they're supposed to keep them safe," Laura said. "We always felt better when she took King with her."

"What type of dog was King?"

"A Mastiff," Craig said. "Alyssa loved that dog. It was one of the reasons I thought she was safe. I didn't think anyone would go near her with King around."

"I have to ask one more question," Jack said. He turned to look Laura in the eyes. "Did you know Alyssa was pregnant?"

63

Long shadows stretched across the lawn in front of the duplex that was listed as Juanita Alvarado's home address. Maureen parked and walked up to the door that stood open. She could hear several voices through the screen, speaking rapid-fire Spanish over one another. When she knocked on the wood frame, everything went silent.

A Hispanic girl, eleven or twelve years old, appeared at the far end of the room beyond the entrance. She said something over her shoulder then walked the rest of the way to the door.

"What do you want?" The girl stood with her hands on her hips and spoke through the screen.

"Are there any adults home?" Maureen asked.

"That depends." The girl tilted her head to one side and studied the detective's face.

"On what?" Maureen asked.

"On what you want," she said.

Maureen chuckled. "I'm looking for the parents of Juanita Alvarado."

"Juanita isn't here," she said.

"I know," Maureen said. "I'm not looking for her. Just her parents."

"Wait here," the girl ordered. She left the room and Maureen could hear voices again, though not as loud as before.

A few minutes later a man appeared and walked to the door, the girl at his side.

"This is our father," the girl said. "Juanita is my sister."

"Your sister?" Maureen remembered Juanita as being in her late twenties when she found her DMV record.

"Half-sister," the girl clarified. "After Juanita's mother died, our father married my mother."

"And what's your name?"

"Carmela."

"Nice to meet you, Carmela."

The man looked at the girl with concern. She said something to him in Spanish, and he nodded his understanding, followed by a long string of Spanish. The girl nodded repeatedly as he spoke. When he finished, they both turned to the detective.

"He wants to know if you know where Juanita is," the girl said.

"What's his name?"

"Roberto."

"Seems like he had a lot more to say than that," Maureen said.

"He did," the girl said. "But that was the most important."

"Because that's the one you want answered?"

The girl shrugged.

"We found her," Maureen said.

The girl told her father. Roberto said something in return.

"Where is she?" the girl said.

Maureen looked at the young girl, then the father. She did not want to make a notification to a child but did not know another way. She took a deep breath and said, "I regret to inform you she's dead."

The girl's eyes teared up. She turned to her father and whispered the news. There was no doubt as to what she told him. His face seemed to break as agony wrenched what hope he had left for his daughter from him. He spoke quickly between fits of crying. The girl, barely holding on herself, put an arm on his shoulder and tried to comfort him.

"He wants to know what happened," Carmela forced out between sniffles. "And where is she?"

"She was murdered," Maureen said. "We're looking for her killer. As for where she is, she's at the city morgue. I know this is a lot to ask, but I need you to answer some questions."

"What?"

"When did you last see your sister?"

"Four months ago."

"Did she have any enemies?"

"No."

"Are you sure?" Maureen asked. "Maybe you should ask your father."

"She didn't have enemies," Carmela said. "Anything else?"

"Did she have a dog?"

"A dog?" Carmela looked at Maureen like she was crazy. "Yes, she had a dog."

"What kind was it?" Maureen asked.

"A bulldog," the girl said.

"Was she walking the dog when she disappeared?" Maureen asked.

Carmela spoke to her father and he responded. "We don't know."

"But the dog is gone?"

"Yes."

Maureen handed Carmela her card and asked her to call if she thought of anything. She walked out to her car, sat behind the wheel, and held her head in her hands.

64

Maureen pulled into the parking garage underneath the department and parked in her usual spot. A few stalls away she saw Shaun standing outside his car. She gathered her things and walked over to him.

"Not going in?"

"I was just waiting until you got here," Shaun said.

"Waiting for me?" Maureen said. "Why?"

"He kind of pissed me off," Shaun said. "Thought it would be better not to be alone with him. Less likely to say something stupid if there's a witness."

"Okay, then," Maureen smiled. "You ready?"

When they entered the war room, Jack was at the whiteboard writing in the details for Thelma Reeves and Alyssa Bell. He did not stop when the others walked in. He did not acknowledge them at all. They settled in at the table and waited.

"Alright." Jack finished and put the marker down. "Maureen, were you able to find out who did the tattoo on our victim?"

"I did," she said. "And he knew her name. Dated her a couple of times before she disappeared. Thought she ghosted him when she stopped coming by."

"Any chance he's our guy?" Jack asked. "More than one of the victims had tattoos."

"I thought of that," Maureen said. "But he could have admitted doing the tattoo without ever mentioning they dated. If he knew she was dead, he would know that would make him look suspicious. So I concluded he didn't know. I'll check his alibi, but I'm sure he didn't kill her."

"Anything else?"

"The victim's name is Juanita Alvarado," Maureen said. "She vanished four months ago. She had a bulldog that went missing with her. She lived with her father and a half-sister. And maybe others, it's hard to say."

Jack took the marker and started writing in the information Maureen gave him. He finished and turned to Shaun.

"Did you find anything?"

"There were only three trucks on the street," Shaun said. "Only one has a cover over the back, but the owner is an eighty-two-year-old army vet who walks with a cane. I asked if he ever loaned the truck out and he made it very clear that no one was ever taking his truck from him."

"So, the vehicle in the doorbell video was not from the neighborhood," Jack said.

"Not that street anyway," Shaun said. "I didn't continue beyond that. There were just too many streets feeding into that one."

"The killer could live in the area," Jack said. "You should have kept searching."

Shaun bit his lower lip to calm himself before continuing. "I did find something of interest."

"What's that?" Jack said.

"The next-door neighbor of the girl who was taken," Shaun said. "She is one of the assistants from Stevens' clinic. Shelly. Shelly Nichols to be exact."

"She lived next door?"

"Yes."

"Maybe Dawn Callahan wasn't who he was after."

65

The phone in the war room screamed and Jack grabbed it.

"Mallory."

"There's a Craig Bell on the line for you," the switchboard operator said.

"Patch it through," Jack said. He waited until the call connected. "Mr. Bell? What can I do for you?"

"My son's been arrested." The man's voice cracked.

"Arrested?" Jack said. "For what?"

Jack remembered hearing the squealing tires as the boy drove away. It was easy to assume he was picked up on reckless driving charges. Or speeding to such an excess that an arrest was warranted.

"Assault," Craig said.

Not what Jack expected at all.

"Assault isn't really my area, Mr. Bell." Jack shrugged to the other detectives. "But tell me what happened."

"Apparently, Theo knew Alyssa had a boyfriend," Craig said. "And when he heard Alyssa was dead, he got it in his head that Mitch Dodson was responsible. He went to the boy's house and attacked him."

"How bad?" Jack asked.

"I don't know," Craig said. "Theo called me from jail. He didn't tell me anything more than I told you."

"Is there a reason he thought Mitch was responsible?" Jack asked.

"I don't know," Craig said. "He's angry. He was close to his sister. Very protective. He needs someone to blame. Otherwise, he'll blame himself."

"Thanks for calling, Mr. Bell," Jack said. "I'll talk to the Dodsons. If Mitch isn't injured too badly, maybe I can get them to drop the charges."

"Thank you, detective," Craig said. "This is too much for our family right now."

Jack hung up and stood, stretching his back and rolling his head around to relieve the tension in his neck. He looked at the others and noted the sagging shoulders and drooping eyelids.

"Go home and get some rest." Jack pulled his jacket from the back of his chair. "In the morning I want the two of you to go to Stevens' clinic and find out where he was last night when Dawn Callahan was taken."

"You think he might be the killer?" Maureen asked.

"If Shelly was the intended target last night." Jack pointed at the whiteboard. "Add his wife, Judith, and that's two connected to him. Plus two of the dogs were microchipped at his clinic. We should get a warrant for his records. See how many of our victims used his clinic."

"I'll work on the warrant," Maureen said. "If we can get it before we go in the morning, we can get it all out of the way in one trip."

"I'm going to go check on this boyfriend of Alyssa Bell's," Jack said. "The brother had an idea he was responsible for his sister's death. I want to see if I can learn why."

Jack headed out the door purposely avoiding the captain's office as he moved toward the exit.

He arrived at the Dodson's home and sat in his car reading the report that had been filed. Theo had sped to the house, parked in the yard, and jumped Mitch who was in the driveway playing basketball with a friend. The friend tried to intervene but was unable to stop him. Theo punched him in the face, possibly breaking the boy's nose. That was when he called 911. But, according to the report, Mitch was much worse off.

Jack walked up the driveway, looking at the tire tracks in the grass. He rang the bell and waited. A woman answered the door.

"Mrs. Dodson?" Jack asked.

"Who are you?" The woman eyed him with suspicion.

"I'm Detective Jack Mallory." He held up his badge. "I'd like to speak to your son."

"He's resting," she said.

"Mom," a voice came from behind the door.

"You should be in bed," the woman said.

"Let him in," Mitch said. "Come in, detective. I'll talk to you."

His mother let Jack in, with a defiant 'mother protecting her young' look.

"Thank you, ma'am," Jack said.

"Don't thank me." She walked to the next room.

"Have a seat, detective." Mitch gestured to a chair across from the sofa he was headed to.

Jack moved to the chair, examining the boy as they walked. He had a black eye, bruises, and cuts on his face, a split lip. He walked with a limp and held his arm close to his body. He had truly taken a beating.

"Thanks for giving me your time." Jack sat in the over-stuffed leather seat.

"No problem." Mitch lowered part way then fell into the sofa. He took a moment to adjust himself for comfort. "But it won't do you any good."

"Excuse me?" Jack studied his face. "What won't do any good?"

"Your questions," Mitch said. "I'll answer them, but I'm not going to press charges. I won't let my mom either."

"May I ask why?"

"Theo learned his sister was dead." Mitch looked down toward his feet. "He needed a punching bag, and I was it. It hurt like hell. But not as much as he hurts. Alyssa meant the world to him."

"That's pretty understanding of you," Jack said.

"Yeah, well he and I have been friends since we were kids," Mitch said. "If he needs a punching bag, better me than some other guy."

"I need to ask you some questions anyway." Jack scooted forward to the edge of the seat. "But not about Theo, or today."

"Alyssa?"

"Yes."

"You want to know if I hurt her?" Mitch said. "If Theo was right to beat the crap out of me?"

"I was going to work my way up to that question," Jack admitted. "But since you brought it up."

"I was crazy about Alyssa," Mitch said. "Theo and I have been friends for years. And a couple of years ago I looked at her and it hit me. She was pretty, smart, and funny. And I couldn't stop looking at her after that. It took me two years to get up the nerve to ask him if I could ask her out."

"And he said yes."

"No," Mitch grinned. "He said, 'Over my dead body.' But I wore him down. He finally gave me his blessing."

"But her parents didn't know."

"Her mother figured it out after a week or so," Mitch said. "But nobody told Mr. B."

"Were you afraid of Mr. Bell?"

"No," Mitch said. "Nothing like that. Just didn't want him to ground her."

"Do you think he could have found out and hurt her by accident?" Jack asked.

"Mr. Bell?" Mitch said. "No way. He wouldn't lay a finger on his kids. He's not that kind of guy."

"What about if he found out Alyssa was pregnant," Jack said.

"What?" Mitch sat forward. "She wasn't pregnant."

"Her autopsy showed she was three weeks pregnant when she died," Jack said. "Maybe she just hadn't told you."

"No way," Mitch said. "Wasn't possible."

"Using protection isn't a hundred percent guarantee," Jack said.

"Doesn't matter," Mitch said. "We didn't need protection. We never slept together."

66

Detective Maureen Weatherby stood on the corner, outside the department when Shaun pulled up to the curb. She held a tray with two coffees in one hand and an envelope in the other. Putting the envelope in her mouth she opened the passenger door and joined him inside. Handing him a cup of coffee she buckled in. Shaun pulled away and steered toward Stevens' clinic.

"Thanks for this." Shaun held the coffee up.

"Thanks for driving." She placed the envelope on her lap.

"It only makes sense," he said. "I've been there before."

"Do you think he could have done this?" she asked.

"Who?"

"The vet," Maureen said. "You've talked to him. Does he seem the type?"

"I don't know," Shaun said. "He drives the right kind of truck. His wife may be one of the victims. He's connected with some of the other victims."

"But what about him?" she said. "Did you have a gut feeling? Did he seem to be hiding something?"

"Maybe," Shaun said. "But I want to look at his alibi and serve the warrant to see if he has a connection with the other victims. Then we can see if the facts support whatever opinion we form."

Arriving at the clinic, Shaun found a parking space that was near the side of the building. He could see Keith Stevens' truck in the same place the veterinarian had parked it before. The two detectives stepped out of the car and started for the entrance.

"Hold on," Maureen said. She altered her course and walked to the doctor's truck. From the passenger's side, she peeked into the cab. Following the body of the vehicle, she stepped up to the back of the truck and, with the light from her phone looked through the rear window of the cover. She turned sharply and returned to where Shaun waited for her. "No sign that he had a girl in there. Though I didn't expect to find anything that easy."

The two of them entered the clinic and asked to speak to Keith. He was with a patient, so they took a position near the hallway that led back to the examination rooms where they could see everything.

The staff went about their business as if there weren't two detectives watching their every move. Nancy sat behind the desk greeting everyone as they entered, checked them in, and asked them to sit. She would call the name of their pets when it was time for them to go back. When they came out, Nancy checked them out, scheduled next appointments, and collected payments.

Other staff members came and went, taking animals and their owners to rooms or bringing them out again. One of the women stopped at the desk to chat with Nancy almost every time she entered the lobby. From the way she spoke to the customers, Shaun deduced that she was one of the veterinarians, which meant she was Samantha Bedford.

The assistant Shaun knew as Tanner walked through the room leading a Bernese Mountain Dog. He missed a step when he saw the detectives. His eyes were locked on Maureen which made Shaun smile.

"I think you have an admirer." Shaun tapped her arm and motioned his head toward the boy.

When Maureen looked over, Tanner averted his eyes and walked more quickly. The detective elbowed Shaun in the side. "Stick to the case. I don't need a matchmaker. Besides, he's probably ten years younger than me."

A side door opened and Shelly walked in towing a stubborn terrier. When the dog saw its owner, it gave up the fight and raced ahead to greet the woman who scooped it up in her arms and hugged and kissed the animal repeatedly. Shelly reached up and patted the dog on the head before walking away. When she spotted the detectives, she stopped dead in her tracks.

"Hello, Detective Travis." She grinned broadly, tilting her head to one side.

"Hello, Shelly," Shaun said.

"Shelly!" Nancy called out. "Take Mrs. Wainscott to room three, please."

"Yes, ma'am." Shelly looked slightly toward the receptionist's desk. Turning back to the detectives, she smiled broadly at Shaun before moving away, calling out "Mrs. Wainscott?"

The woman was already standing, holding a pet carrier in one hand. The cat inside was frightened and paced the small space. Shelly led them away and down the hall.

"Talk about an admirer," Maureen said.

Keith Stevens emerged from the hallway, quickly focusing on the detectives. It had been three-quarters of an hour since they had arrived.

"What do you want now?" he asked. "I have a full day today."

"We'll try to make it quick then," Maureen said.

"And you are?"

"Detective Maureen Weatherby," she said.

"Another detective," Keith rolled his eyes. "Why couldn't there have been this many detectives working my wife's case? Maybe you could have found her."

"We need to know where you were the night before last," Shaun said.

"Where I was?" Keith said. "You think I did something?"

"Where were you?" Shaun asked. "Specifically between nine p.m. and one o'clock in the morning."

"I was at home," Keith said. "Asleep."

"Can anyone vouch for you?" Maureen asked.

"No." Keith shifted his weight. "Because you never found my wife, I was alone. Have been for almost a year. Now if you'll excuse me, I have patients to see."

"One more thing," Maureen said.

"What?" The veterinarian snapped.

Maureen held up the envelope she had been carrying and slapped it against the man's chest. "Warrant."

"Warrant?" He took the envelope and pulled the papers from inside. "For what?"

"Patient records," Shaun said.

"My records?" Keith said. "You can't take my records."

"Don't worry," Maureen said. "We want specific records. We'll leave you the rest."

"We aren't asking for your permission, Doctor Stevens," Shaun said. "We have the warrant."

Keith breathed in and out sharply. "Fine."

"Do you want to show us where you keep your records?" Maureen asked.

"Nancy!" Keith called out. "Show these detectives whatever they ask for."

"Doctor?"

"Just do it, Nancy!" Keith stormed off, throwing a clipboard down the hall in front of him. The clipboard slid along the floor and crashed into the wall. All eyes fell on the detectives.

Shaun nodded at them and crossed the room to where Nancy waited.

"What's this about?" Nancy asked.

Shaun pulled out a single sheet of paper, unfolded it, and lay it on the desk facing the receptionist. "We need any files you have for these customers."

"You can't just . . ."

"We have a warrant," Maureen said. "You can get them or we will."

"Fine," Nancy stood. "It'll be just a minute."

"I'll go with you." Maureen circled the desk.

67

Jack sat in the war room looking over the timeline once again. He gave Craig Bell the good news that Mitch Dodson was not going to press charges, then took it upon himself to help get the boy released from lockup and back to his family. Theo assured the detective that there would be no repeat of what transpired.

"Stevens had files for every one of our known victims," Maureen announced as she entered the room. She took a seat and lay the folders on the table. "All within the last year."

"And he doesn't have an alibi for the time Dawn Callahan vanished," Shaun said. "Claims he was home."

"Okay. Good." Jack scanned the folders Maureen had brought in. "Even Callahan. I thought she may have been taken by chance. Didn't expect a file for her."

"I didn't either," Maureen said. "Although her last appointment was a year ago. Another week and it would have been out of the twelve-month parameter."

"I learned that Thelma Reeves had a dog," Jack said. "And Alyssa's boyfriend claims they never had sex."

"But she was pregnant," Shaun said.

"That's right," Jack confirmed.

"So we may have the killer's DNA," Maureen said.

"That's what I'm hoping," Jack said. "Unless she had another boyfriend who she was sleeping with, it seems likely."

"Didn't Valerie say she was about three weeks along?" Maureen asked.

"I think that's what she said," Jack said.

"How long is this guy keeping these girls?"

"It seems to be different lengths of time," Jack said. "It may depend on how easily he can handle the victim."

"So fighters may be killed before those who just accept their situation and do what he says," Shaun said.

"Makes sense," Jack said. "Fighters are more likely to try to escape."

"We need a DNA sample from Keith Stevens to compare to the sample from Alyssa's baby," Shaun said.

"Are you sure it's Stevens?" Jack said. "Give me your argument."

"He has had contact with all of our victims," Shaun said.

"They were customers of his clinic," Jack countered. "There were three other veterinarians that could have seen them. Keith may never have met them. Next argument?"

"His wife," Shaun said. "She was the first to disappear. The first victim is usually personal."

"We don't know that she was the first," Jack said. "There may have been a dozen before her that we just haven't found yet. And although first victims are often personally connected to the killer, sometimes they're just random targets. What else?"

"He drives a truck that matches the description of the one captured on video at two of the scenes," Shaun said.

"As do hundreds of others," Jack said.

"He's good with dogs," Shaun said.

Jack just grinned.

"So you don't think it's him?" Shaun asked.

"Oh, no," Jack said. "I'm convinced it's him. All these things add up to a good case."

"But you argued against each one of them," Shaun said.

"Because that's what the defense will do," Maureen said. "Which is why we need to match his DNA to remove any doubt."

"Agreed," Jack said. "Would you work on the warrant?"

"Of course," Maureen said.

"While you do that," Jack said, "I'm going to the morgue to talk to the medical examiner."

68

Walking into the morgue, Jack saw Valerie at the nearest of the three examination tables leaning over the body of a woman with long black hair. Her two assistants were at the far table studying the skeletal remains of another victim. The medical examiner raised her head as soon as she heard Jack enter.

"These are the last two." She made a gesture that did not seem to complement her words, but the detective knew what she meant.

"Do you have anything new for me?" Jack asked.

"We matched dental records to one of the unknowns," Valerie said. "Susan Fredrickson."

"I met her husband already," Jack said. "Her dog was with the first body we located. How long has she been dead?"

"We're estimating three to four months," Valerie said. "We'll know more when labs come back."

"That leaves us with one unidentified, doesn't it?"

Valerie pointed to the far table. "That's what they're working on. It'll probably come down to DNA. Hopefully, she'll be in the system."

"What about all the other details?" Jack said. "Are they the same?"

"We found the same wood shavings in each gravesite," Valerie said. "And the same residue was found on the hands of the three victims we could test. We're going to test the clothing found in the other two graves. I expect we'll find something."

"And the poison?"

"We'll have to wait for toxicology," she said. "But it seems likely. However, this victim wasn't killed by poison."

"How do you know that?" Jack asked.

"She was beaten," Valerie said. "Multiple blows to her back, shoulders, and back of the head. Then she was stabbed repeatedly. I counted twenty-six penetrations. He really wanted her dead."

"Maybe she just wasn't dying fast enough for him."

"No hamburger in her stomach," Valerie said. "Her last meal consisted of dog food."

"Just dog food?" Jack's eyes locked on hers. "You're sure?"

"Completely," she said.

"Wood shavings like animal bedding," Jack said. "Feeding them dog food. He really is treating these women like pets."

"Seems like it," Valerie said.

"But what did this girl do to piss him off?" Jack looked at her face.

"I may have something to help answer that." Valerie walked to the opposite side of the table. "Her feet had mud caked on them and in between the toes. I think she made a run for it."

"She got away?" Jack said. "That would have set him off."

"There's more," Valerie indicated a small cart with bags and jars of evidence. "I found Oleander in the mud."

"Oleander?"

"The plant," she said. "Not just leaves."

"He has plants where he's keeping them?" Jack said. "I guess that's efficient."

"That would be my guess," Valerie said.

Jack returned to the woman's face. "Is this Alvarado?"

"Yes."

"She must have fought hard," Jack said. "Did you find anything under her nails?"

"Yes, we did." Valerie smiled. "We found skin tissue."

"You didn't lead with that?"

69

Knowing there was a chance that the killer was growing his own Oleander, Jack had to have the search warrant amended to include searches of the properties of both Keith Stevens' home and the clinic, in addition to gathering the veterinarian's DNA. After a speech from the judge about not wasting his time and getting it right the first time, Jack walked out with the signature he needed.

They had lost most of the day and getting search teams together would take time so they decided to execute the warrant in the morning. It was a decision that left Jack and the other two detectives staring at the whiteboard. The timeline was filling to the point that any more victims would likely force them to readjust the scale to get everything to fit.

"What's his motive?" Jack said.

"His motive?" Shaun turned to the detective.

"Yeah, his motive." Jack pointed at the timeline. "He's killed eight women, maybe more. Why is he doing it?"

"Assuming it is Stevens," Maureen said, "and his wife was his first victim, his motive for killing her could be any number of things. She may have been cheating on him. Maybe they were having financial troubles and he decided he needed her life insurance."

"Or he wanted to leave her, or her him," Shaun offered. "Could be he didn't want to give her half the business."

"Okay." Jack turned to them. "But how did he go from that to killing all these other women?"

"He liked it," Shaun said. "He killed his wife and liked the way it made him feel. Powerful, excited. He got a thrill out of killing her and he wanted to have those feelings again."

"Or he hated her and he wanted to experience killing her again and again," Maureen said. "These other women are substitutes for his wife."

"But he's poisoning them," Jack said. "He's not choking the life out of them or stabbing them and watching them bleed out. The poison takes time to work. It gives the poisoned person stomach cramps and other issues. It isn't the kind of thing where you pull up a chair with popcorn and watch them die. It could take hours. Not the kind of kill a murderer could claim to enjoy."

"Unless watching them suffer is part of it," Shaun said.

"Maybe it isn't about the kill." Maureen sat up and picked up a couple of the victims' files. "Maybe it's about the women."

"What do they have in common?" Jack said.

"They're dog lovers," Shaun said. "But why would a vet hate women who love dogs?"

"Not dog lovers," Maureen said. "What if he took offense to the way they treated the dogs?"

"He did it for the dogs?" Jack said. "But he's killing the dogs. And his wife was a vet too. Surely she didn't mistreat her dog."

"Not all doctors love their patients," Maureen said. "Some don't like people at all."

"What if his wife wasn't the first?" Shaun said.

"We haven't found any victims taken before her disappearance," Jack said.

"I'm not talking about now," Shaun said. "What if he killed someone five, ten, maybe even twenty years ago? And he's been wanting to do it again but resisted. Then about a year ago something triggered him. He killed his wife. And now he just can't resist anymore."

"How does he pick out the women?" Jack said. "Are they all random choices? Or is there something about these particular women that interests him? Is there something about them that reminds him of his wife?"

"That's impossible to say with the information we have," Maureen said.

"But we were thinking that the assistant," Jack said. "What was her name?"

"Shelly," Shaun said.

"We were thinking that Shelly may have been his target and grabbed Dawn Callahan instead," Jack said. "If he was after Shelly, will he go after her again?"

"We have a patrol car in front of her house," Maureen said. "And she isn't supposed to walk the dog where the officers can't see her."

"And when he sees that," Jack said, "will he look for someone else? Someone more accessible?"

"We should be watching him," Shaun said.

"My thought exactly," Jack said. "Thanks for volunteering?"

"I . . ." Shaun stammered for a second then said. "Fine."

"Good," Jack said. "If you hurry you can get there before he leaves the clinic. Follow him and see if he leads you somewhere other than his home. With any luck, he'll give us a clue as to where he's holding the women he hasn't killed yet."

"Maureen can take over for you in four or five hours," Jack said.

"I can?"

"And I'll take over from her," Jack said. "I'll follow him into work and meet you there when the search teams are ready."

70

Shaun arrived at the clinic shortly before closing. He picked a space so he could see the side of the building where Keith Stevens had parked his truck earlier in the week. Unfortunately, there were three similar trucks parked in that area and the detective could not remember which one had belonged to the veterinarian. He sat back and waited, keeping his eyes on the back door of the clinic.

As the last customer left, employees started to depart in staggered intervals. When the first of the trucks backed out, Shaun had not seen anyone come from the clinic, suggesting they had come from the barn where the larger animals were kept. Assuming Keith would come from the clinic, Shaun did not follow.

It was nearly twenty minutes after closing that Nancy, the receptionist, walked out of the building and to her car. She stood next to the vehicle for a time searching her purse until she found her keys. Once inside, she wasted no time getting on her way. A couple of minutes later and a few more employees drove away leaving the two trucks on the side of the building. Shaun worried for a minute that Keith had been in the first truck to leave.

But just as he was about to panic, the veterinarian stepped out of the building, turned back to lock the door, and walked to his truck. It took him a few minutes to get settled. Backing out slowly, Keith drove away like he had nowhere to be any time soon, a stark contrast to the time Shaun watched him arrive at the clinic.

Shaun followed at a good distance, matching the man's speed so as not to overtake him. The drive was leisurely and the detective found himself growing impatient. After several turns, Keith pulled into his driveway and up the long drive to his home. Shaun parked on the street and watched.

The Stevens' home was a two-story house on over twenty acres of land. There were several outbuildings, including a barn and horse stable. There were plenty of locations to hide his victims. Everything was well-kept and Shaun wondered where the man found the time.

Shaun's line of sight was obstructed at times by trees and shrubs that lined the street and the driveway. Though it hindered his ability to watch Keith's every move, Shaun hoped it kept Keith from noticing the car parked on the street. The detective caught sight of his subject walking toward the horse stable. The obvious explanation would be the veterinarian was on his way to care for the animals. Shaun couldn't help but wonder if the women they were looking for were in there as well.

It was almost an hour later before Keith returned to the house and disappeared inside. For the next three hours, Shaun stared at the house. The sun settled below the horizon and darkness spread over the property. A light in a single window told the detective where Keith was, or at least where it would seem he was. In the shadow of the night, it would be easy for the man to slip out of the house and make his way to the back acreage unseen. Shaun could only watch the single window and hope he was still inside.

A car came over the hill in front of him and Shaun slid down in his seat to make it less obvious someone was in the car as he had done with each passing vehicle. As this car neared, it turned its lights off and coasted to a stop next to him. It was Maureen's SUV and the detective lowered her window and waited for Shaun to do the same.

"Ready to be relieved?" She smiled at him. "Anything I should know?"

"Unless he slipped out," Shaun said, "he's in the house. Only one light on. He went to the stables when he first arrived, stayed nearly an hour. But there's no sign of the women."

"You didn't think he was going to parade them around did you?" Maureen asked.

"No," Shaun said. "Just hoped for something that would help bring an end to all this."

"Well go home and get some rest," she said. "With any luck, it will all be over tomorrow."

Shaun drove away and Maureen did a three-point turn so she could park where he had been. She looked at the single window spilling light then searched the shadows for movement. Seeing nothing, she leaned back and settled in for a long wait.

71

Maureen sat in her SUV watching the night. Although she was law enforcement, she was still a woman alone parked on the side of the road in the middle of nowhere and if they were correct, the closest person to her was a serial killer. She struggled to keep her eyes open but caught herself dozing off more than once. Each time she jerked awake, she grabbed her weapon and searched the darkness for threats.

At half-past two the house had been dark for more than three hours. She hadn't seen any movement other than wildlife and windblown branches until a car came over the hill behind her. With gun in hand, she watched in the mirror as the vehicle approached. The lights went out and the car slowed and coasted to a stop behind her.

Jack stepped out and approached on the passenger side. She unlocked the door and he slipped in beside her.

"Anything?" Jack glanced at the gun in her hand.

"Not a thing." She holstered the weapon. "But then, I didn't expect to see much."

"You should go home and get a few more hours sleep before morning," Jack said. "I asked Shaun to come here with one of the search teams. You meet me at the clinic with the other."

"I can do that," she said. "Try not to have too much fun sitting out here in the dark."

"I'll try." He stepped out of the vehicle. "See you in a few hours."

"Goodnight," she said just before he shut the door. She started the car and drove away, leaving Jack standing on the side of the road.

He walked the short distance to the end of the Stevens' driveway and allowed his eyes to adjust. The moonlight cast stark shadows across the driveway and the buildings beyond. As Maureen had said, nothing moved. He studied the structures, focusing most of his attention on the house and stables, the two places Shaun had seen the veterinarian go. Jack didn't know what he thought he was going to see in the dark and at a distance. He just felt he had to try.

Giving up, he walked back to his car and settled in. He rolled down the front windows to allow the air to circulate, then settled back to watch. Hours later when the sun started to crest the horizon he was still there, waiting.

At about six, Jack saw the first sign of movement from the house. Keith Stevens stepped out on the porch, standing for a short time before walking to the stables. He was inside the outbuilding for just over an hour before he reappeared, brushing at his pant legs with his hands.

He returned to the house and Jack did not see him again until just before eight. Keith climbed into his truck and started down the driveway. He turned onto the street and coasted to Jack's car, rolling down his window.

"Good morning, detective," he said.

"Morning," Jack nodded.

"Is there something you and your cohorts need?" Venom dripped from every word. "I only ask because you were here all night watching me, rather than looking for my wife."

"We're looking for her," Jack said.

"Well, I have to get to work," Keith said. "Are you following? Or is someone already there waiting?"

"I think I'll follow." Jack started his car.

"See you there." Keith accelerated down the street.

Jack turned around and followed, not trying too hard to catch up. He closed the distance gradually, turning into the clinic's parking lot moments after Keith. The detective chose a parking space and stopped just as Keith waved to him before entering the building.

Jack stepped out and stretched his legs as he had done on two occasions while watching the Stevens' home. He was still walking around the parking lot when Maureen pulled in and parked next to his car. She emerged with two coffee cups in her hands, one of which she held out to Jack.

"Thought you might could use some caffeine," she said.

"Thanks." Jack took the offered cup, removed the lid, and inhaled deeply. "Exactly what I needed."

"Anything new?"

"He knew we were watching him," Jack said. "So he didn't lead us anywhere. When does the team get here?"

"They should be here any minute," she said.

They only had to wait about ten minutes before a line of patrol cars flooded the parking lot. They parked haphazardly throughout the lot, the last vehicles parked to block the entrance. Officers congregated in front of the building and waited for direction.

A forensic technician unloaded her equipment and carried it to where the detectives stood. "Where to?"

"When we serve the warrant," Jack said. "You'll need to obtain a DNA swab from the suspect. After that, Maureen will bring you out to search the back of his truck for signs that he has been transporting his victims or their bodies."

"Sounds easy enough," she said. "When do we start?"

"In just a few minutes."

The highest-ranking officer joined them. "The men are ready."

"Okay," Jack said. "They are going to be searching the entire property for places he may be keeping his victims. In addition, Detective Weatherby has photocopies showing what plant we are looking for."

The officer took the copies from Maureen and returned to his team. They passed them and studied the images before starting to spread out.

Jack, Maureen, and the tech entered the clinic. Keith Stevens was standing in the lobby. "What is going on?"

"We're here to execute a search warrant." Jack held out the papers. Keith took them. "We're going to need your DNA."

"My DNA?" Keith said. "What is the meaning of this? Why haven't you put this effort into finding my wife?"

"I assure you, Mr. Stevens," Jack said. "I assure you we are trying our best to find your wife."

"But you seem to think I had something to do with her disappearance," Keith said. "So you're looking here and probably at my home instead of wherever she is."

"And where is she, Mr. Stevens?"

"I don't know," Keith grumbled. "That's why I need you to find her."

"Open your mouth please," the tech said, holding a swab at the ready.

Keith opened his mouth and the tech collected the sample she needed. "All done."

"Are we finished?" Keith demanded.

"Not quite," Jack said. "We're going to need the keys to your truck."

"My truck?" Keith said. "What for?"

"It's in the warrant," Jack said. He held his hand out. "Keys."

Keith dug into his pocket, pulled out the keys, and slapped them into the palm of Jack's outstretched hand. "Are we done? I need to get to work."

Jack handed the keys to the tech. "You go ahead, doc. We'll let you know when we're done."

Keith turned away but stopped. "The men outside. What are they looking for?"

"Victims," Jack said. "Their bodies. Oleander."

"Oleander?"

"That's right," Jack said.

"I don't keep that stuff around," Keith said. "It's too toxic for the animals."

72

The property searches turned up nothing helpful. There were no signs of the missing women or that they had been anywhere at either location other than as customers to the clinic. Jack knew that did not clear Keith Stevens. He could have another property they were not aware of. He could be holding the women somewhere that was abandoned and has no connection to him.

The tech did find signs of blood and tissue in the back of the truck. The samples she took, along with the DNA swab from the veterinarian, were in the lab being processed. They impounded the truck to preserve the evidence and also to retrieve the data from the GPS so they could learn where he had a habit of going, in hopes that they might find the missing women.

"Detective Travis," the chief called out. "My office. Jack, you come too."

Jack looked from the war room to where she stood outside her office door. She did not look happy. "What did you do?"

"Me?" Shaun stood. "What makes you think it was me?"

"She called your name first." Jack pointed out.

The two of them joined Chief Hutchins in her office, each taking a seat when she suggested they do so. Jack sat back to wait, noticing that Shaun seemed nervous. He wanted to ask him again what he had done.

"Gentlemen," she said. "I'll keep this brief."

"Always appreciated," Jack said.

The chief gave him a sharp look that shut him up.

"Detective Travis brought to my attention a case of a man arrested by Detective Peterson, and convicted using the evidence he supposedly collected." The chief shuffled some papers on her desk. "We reviewed the arrest based on the information Shaun gave us and discovered some discrepancies. And as you pointed out there were similar crimes for which another man was ultimately arrested and convicted. As it turns out, as part of a reduced sentence plea, the man confessed to all of the crimes he had committed. One of those crimes was the one Mr. Hopkins was convicted of. No one followed up. No one realized that case had been closed."

"What happens now?" Shaun asked.

"Now it will be taken to a judge and have the conviction thrown out," the chief said.

"That's good news," Shaun said.

"It is," she said. "For Hopkins, it is good news."

"But?"

"But it creates a whole lot of problems for the department," Jack said.

"It does," the chief nodded. "We have to review every conviction Bret Peterson had his hand in."

"All of them?" Shaun said.

"There's no way to know which ones he did by the book and which he didn't," she said. "So, yes, all of them."

"I don't like the way you're looking at me, chief," Jack said.

"Someone has to go through the cases," she said.

"Why me?" Jack said. "I'm on a case. A big case. I don't have time to review old cases."

"You don't have to start until this case you're on is resolved," the chief said. "Or it runs its course. After that, you and Detective Travis can work on Peterson's cases together."

"What about Weatherby?" Jack said.

"They need her back in missing persons," the chief said.

"How about you have Travis and Weatherby go through Peterson's cases?" Jack said. "So I can work homicides."

"My decision has been made, Jack." She crossed her arms. "When you're done with this case, you two are reviewing Peterson's cases."

The two detectives left the chief's office together. Jack grumbled all the way back to the war room and Shaun quickly tried to distance himself, sitting on the opposite side of the table. Maureen looked from one to the other.

"What was that all about?" she asked. "You look pissed."

"Not much," Jack said. "Shaun just dumped a load of work in our laps."

"I couldn't just leave him to rot," Shaun said. "He was innocent."

"He who?"

"I know that," Jack said. "You did the right thing. I'm just pissed that I am still cleaning up after Peterson."

"Who's Peterson?"

"You are new, aren't you?" Jack said.

"Detective Bret Peterson was a bad cop," Shaun said. "Turns out he may have been worse than we originally thought."

"We get to put fresh eyes on every arrest he ever made," Jack said.

"Every one?"

"Yep."

"How long did he work here?" Maureen asked.

"Over twenty years," Jack said.

"Did you say twenty?"

"Average one arrest a week and we're talking about over one-thousand cases," Jack said. "Lucky for us, he wasn't very good at his job. There probably won't be more than five or six hundred."

The phone on the table rang and Jack snatched it up to answer. "Mallory."

"Jack," the medical examiner said, "It's Valerie. I've got the lab results from our last six victims."

"What did you find?"

"As expected, we found the same cleaning chemical residue on their clothing and skin," Valerie said. "The same wood shavings. With the exception of Juanita Alvarado, they all died of Oleander poisoning."

"Nothing unexpected," Jack said.

"The DNA results came back from Alyssa Bell's baby and from under Juanita's fingernails." She said.

"And?"

"They don't match," she said.

"They don't?" Jack said. "So Alyssa's baby may not be her killer's."

"Jack," Valerie said. "They don't match. But we got a hit on the blood from Juanita."

"Who is he?"

"Not a he," she said. "A she. It belongs to Crystal Vaughn."

"Crystal Vaughn?" Jack said. "That's the second time her DNA has shown up on another victim. Are we looking at this wrong? Is she our killer?"

"That's your department," Valerie said. "I can tell you that there was blood under Juanita's fingernails but no tissue that you would expect to find if she scratched someone."

"So she may have had contact with Crystal's blood but not Crystal herself," Jack said.

"That's a possibility," Valerie said.

"But we still need to look at the possibility that our killer is a woman," Jack said. "Or is getting help from a woman. Maybe she lures them in, just another woman on the walking path. Less threatening than a man."

"We still have the possibility that Alyssa's baby is the result of her killer assaulting her."

"Keep me updated," Jack said.

He disconnected the call and filled in his partners.

"I don't buy it," Maureen said.

"Women can be killers," Jack said.

"But from everything I've learned about Crystal Vaughn," Maureen said. "Her kids were her life. She wouldn't just walk away from them without any contact."

"She wouldn't be the first woman to be outwardly a devoted mother and turn out not to be," Shaun said.

"I just don't believe it," Maureen said. "But I'll keep an open mind."

"We need to take a closer look at her life," Jack said. "She may have had a new boyfriend her mother didn't know about. And whether he manipulated her or they chose to work together, she may be a suspect rather than a victim."

73

"**D**etective Weatherby." Louise Vaughn opened the door. "Three visits in a week. I'm going to think you care."

"We do care, Mrs. Vaughn," Maureen said, gesturing to Jack who stood next to her. "Mind if we come in?"

"More news?" she asked.

"More questions," Maureen said.

"If it will help." Louise stepped aside and let them in. "Can I get you some tea or water?"

"We're good," Jack said. "Thank you."

"And who would you be?" Louise looked Jack in the eyes.

"Detective Jack Mallory." He held out his hand.

"Well, Detective Jack Mallory." Louise gave his hand a slight squeeze. "What brings you here today?"

"As Weatherby said, we have questions," Jack said.

"It takes two of you to ask questions?"

"Sometimes," Jack said. "Sometimes it takes two to hear the answers."

Louise considered his response for a minute. "What can I help you with?"

"I was looking through my notes," Maureen said. "And I realized I never asked you about Crystal's relationships."

"I went over all that with the first detective," Louise said. "But as I told him, Crystal wasn't in a relationship. Between work and the kids, she didn't have the time."

"Are you sure?" Jack said. "Maybe she started seeing someone she hadn't told you about?"

"Well if she hadn't told me about him," Louise said. "I wouldn't know about him would I?"

"Sometimes a mother suspects things," Jack smiled. "They have a unique radar for such things. Did you notice anything that made you wonder if she might have met someone new?"

"I'm sorry, detective," she said. "She went from work to here to pick up the kids. We would eat dinner together sometimes, then she would take the kids home and put them to bed. If she met someone new, she never mentioned him, and she never had time to see him."

"What about work?" Maureen said. "Had she mentioned anyone who was paying more attention to her than usual?"

"No," Louise said. "Nothing like that."

"Okay," Jack said, starting to rise. "I want to thank you for taking the time to talk to us."

"Wait," Louise said. "She did have that secret admirer."

"Secret admirer?" Jack sat back down. "What admirer?"

"Who are you talking about, Louise?" Maureen said.

"She had a secret admirer," Louise said.

"Why didn't you mention him before?" Maureen said. "I never saw anything in the original notes."

"Honestly, I didn't think of him," she said. "He stopped bothering her a month or more before Crystal disappeared."

"About the time Judith Stevens disappeared," Maureen said to Jack.

"Tell us about the secret admirer," Jack said. "Do you know who it was?"

"No. He never revealed himself," Louise said.

"What did he do?" Jack asked.

"Crystal started finding notes," Louise said. "First she'd find them on her car. Then on her door. Made her nervous. And then there would be gifts."

"What kind of gifts?" Maureen asked.

"Flowers," Louise said. "Chocolates. Just little things. She would find them on the porch or in the mailbox. It really scared her. She was afraid to go out by herself. But then they just stopped."

"About a month before Crystal disappeared?" Jack said.

"Right," she said. "Do you think there's a connection?"

"I don't know," Jack admitted. "But it's something to look into."

74

The three detectives sat in the war room, each reading through reports and missing persons files. They had found three more possible victims and were trying to tie them to the Stevens' clinic. Jack's cell phone rang, and he regarded it as an unwanted intrusion. The number was local, though he did not know who it was.

"Mallory." His tone reflected his frustration.

"Detective Mallory?" The woman on the other end of the call was timid. Whether that was normal for her or if she was simply responding to Jack's voice was unclear.

"This is him." Jack dialed back his gruffness.

"This is Katie Ingram," she said.

"Okay?"

"Thelma Reeves' roommate," she clarified.

"Oh, Katie," Jack said. "Sorry. I speak to a lot of people."

"I'm sure," she said absently. "Anyway, you said to call if I remembered anything."

"You remembered something?"

"Yeah," Katie said. "At least I may have."

"May have?"

"I don't know if it's relevant," she said.

"Why don't you let me decide that?" Jack said. "What did you remember?"

"A couple of times before she disappeared," Katie said, "I noticed her talking to a guy out on the path."

"The walking path?" Jack sat straight and pulled a notepad closer to him.

"Yes, sir."

"Can you describe him?" Jack poised his pen over the pad.

"Not really," she said. "I never saw his face. But he had a dog. A black and white dog. But why I remember is because the dog only had three legs."

"Three legs?"

"Yeah," she said. "Poor thing."

"Do you remember anything else?"

"That's it," she said. "Sorry, it wasn't more useful."

"No," Jack said. "Thank you for calling."

He disconnected the call and grabbed his notes, thumbing through them rapidly until he came to the page he was looking for.

"Judith Stevens had a three-legged Border Collie," he read.

"What?" Shaun looked up.

"Judith Stevens disappeared eleven months ago with a three-legged Border Collie," Jack said. "Eight months ago Thelma Reeves disappeared after being seen talking to a man with a three-legged black and white dog."

"Border Collies are black and white," Maureen said.

"He's using the dogs of the women he's taken to lure his next victims," Jack said. "What dogs aren't accounted for?"

"Lorissa St. Clair's Australian Shepherd," Shaun said. "And Dawn Callahan's Boston Terrier."

"We need to get the word out to look for a man walking one of those breeds," Jack said.

"There could be dozens of those breeds," Maureen said. "We're going to get calls from all over the city."

"And one of them may be Keith Stevens," Jack said. "Get the word out."

Jack's phone rang again. He saw the name and answered, "Valerie. Do you have something for me?"

"Yeah," she said. "But you aren't going to like it."

"What won't I like?"

"We got the lab results back from what was collected from the Stevens warrant," Valerie said.

"The blood and tissue in his truck don't match any of our victims?" Jack asked. It wouldn't be worst-case scenario. They could still find a victim that matched.

"It isn't even human," she said.

That was worst-case. "Is it canine?"

"No," she said. "It belongs to a deer."

"That doesn't help," Jack said.

"It gets worse," Valerie said.

"What?"

"Keith Stevens is not the father of Alyssa Bell's baby," she said. "And according to the GPS, his truck was nowhere near any of the crime scenes when the women disappeared. And was never at the park."

"So he's a dead end," Jack thought aloud.

"Unless he has another truck," she said. "He wasn't there."

"Okay thanks." Jack dropped his phone to the table.

"What's up?" Shaun asked.

"It looks like Stevens isn't our man," Jack said. "I was just so sure of it. He was the connection between all the victims. But his truck wasn't at the crime scenes. And he isn't the one who got Alyssa pregnant."

"So we drop him as a suspect?" Maureen said.

"Unless we can tie him to another truck," Jack said.

"Another truck?" Shaun said. "When he left the clinic the other day, there was still a truck there. Maybe he has a second one."

75

Jack asked Shaun to drive Keith Stevens' truck so they could return the vehicle to the veterinarian. When they arrived at the clinic, Shaun parked the truck on the side of the building and joined Jack at the entrance with the keys.

"It's not here," Shaun said.

"What isn't?" Jack asked.

"The other truck isn't here," Shaun said. "We may have missed him."

"Maybe he took a late lunch or something," Jack suggested. "Let's see when he'll be back."

They entered the lobby and were greeted with a firm frown on Nancy's face. Jack walked up to the desk while Shaun stayed near the door watching for the truck to enter the parking lot.

"Where is Stevens?" Jack said. "When will he return?"

"Return?" Nancy said. "He's not gone. He's with a patient."

"Are you sure about that?" Jack said. "His truck's not here."

"Are you joking?" Nancy asked. "You took his truck. He drove his wife's SUV today."

"He doesn't have a second truck?" Jack asked. "Maybe one owned by the business?"

"No," she said. "Why don't you leave the poor man alone?"

Down the hall, one of the doors opened and a middle-aged woman walked out practically dragging a large dog on a leash. Keith followed her until he saw Jack waiting for him. He slowed but continued.

"Detective," Keith said. "How do you plan to screw with my life today?"

"We've come to return your truck." Jack held out the keys.

Keith hesitated before taking them. "Am I supposed to thank you?"

"Not at all," Jack said. "But I am curious. What happened to the other one?"

"Other one?" the veterinarian said. "I don't follow."

"My partner said when he was following you the other day," Jack said. "You were the last one to leave, but there was still a truck here. Where is the other truck?"

"Now I see why I shouldn't thank you," Keith said. "You still think I did this."

"Where is the truck?"

"First of all," Keith said. "I only own one truck, unless you want to call my wife's SUV a truck."

"My partner saw it," Jack said. "Where is it?"

"Second," Keith continued. "I am seldom the last one to leave. Usually one of the hands is finishing up in the barn after I leave. The truck your partner saw probably belonged to one of them."

"Which one closed up that night?" Jack asked.

Keith stared at him a moment as if deciding whether to help him. "Nancy. Who closed the barn three nights ago?"

The receptionist typed into the computer amidst an awkward silence. "That would have been Tanner Foley."

"The kid?"

"That kid is twenty-four years old," Keith said.

"We need to speak to him," Jack said.

Keith turned to Nancy.

"He didn't show today." She shrugged.

"Again?" Keith sighed. "Looks like my wife is finally going to get her wish."

"What does that mean?" Jack said.

"She wanted me to fire him," Keith said.

"Fire him?" Jack said. "Why?"

"Said he was paying too much attention to one of the customers," Keith said. "But when Judith vanished, I forgot all about it."

"Which customer?"

"I don't know," Keith said. "Nancy, do you know?"

"It was . . . what was her name?" Nancy thought for a minute. "Oh wait. I know. It was Crystal Vaughn with the Cocker Spaniel."

"And your wife told you to fire him?"

"Yes."

"Did she ever tell Tanner to leave Ms. Vaughn alone?" Jack asked.

"I'm sure she did," Keith said. "She wasn't shy."

"I need his address," Jack demanded. "Now."

76

Detective Weatherby arrived at Tanner Foley's address just ahead of her two partners. The three of them approached the house together, Shaun covering the back as the others climbed the stairs and pounded on the front door.

No one answered. There was no truck in sight.

The property was on the outskirts of town and sat on a twenty-acre plot. It was a lot of property for a twenty-four-year-old working as a general laborer for a veterinarian. Maureen made some calls and learned Tanner had inherited the place from his parents after they were killed in a crash when he was nineteen years old.

The house was in a state of disrepair. The paint was peeling, several shingles were missing from the roof. Some of the windows were broken and boarded from the inside. The land surrounding the building was overgrown with weeds and unkempt shrubs. There were two outbuildings that were in even worse shape than the living quarters. The closest was a long structure, close to the ground, with three doors.

They took the doors one at a time, breaching and searching for the women. Each section was filled with tools, assorted parts, and old equipment.

The second building was a barn. Inside was poorly lit with the failing rays of daylight spilling through cracks in the walls. Shaun found a light switch and flipped it. To one side was a moldy pile of hay. To the other were livestock stalls, a good place to keep prisoners. They opened each to find the decaying remains of horses and cattle. Jack guessed Tanner did not feed the animals after his parents were killed. Again there was no sign of the women or the property owner.

"So, where is he?" Shaun asked. "Looking for another victim?"

"Could be," Jack said. "Get an APB out on him and his truck. Maureen, check with the neighbors. Find out if they know whether he's been here today and when he might have left. I'm going to go to his coworker's house. Shelly, wasn't it?"

"Yes, sir," Shaun said.

"He might be going after her again," Jack said.

"What do you want me to do after the bulletin?" Shaun asked.

"Stay here in case he comes back," Jack said.

77

When Nancy gave Jack the address, she included Tanner's phone number as well. He held the steering wheel in one hand and dialed the number with the other. It rang a half dozen times before going to voicemail. He hung up and called the department asking for a warrant to get the location of the phone. They promised to do the best they could and get back to him.

He raced through town toward the only place they knew he might go. It was a good twenty-minute drive and Jack was doing his best to make it fifteen. Horns blared and tires screeched in near collisions as he maneuvered his way through traffic. When he reached the neighborhood, he reduced his speed and steered toward Shelly's house, sliding to a stop in her driveway.

He ran to the door and knocked frantically. When no one came to the door, he knocked again. His phone rang and he answered before the next ring.

"Mallory," he said between breaths.

"Jack," the officer on the other end of the call said. "We got the warrant."

The door to Shelly's house opened and the young woman stood there with a confused look on her face.

"According to the phone company," the officer continued. "The phone is within five hundred yards of the owner's home address."

78

Shaun watched the others drive away, then called in the all-points bulletin for Tanner Foley and his truck. He put his phone away and stood awkwardly in the middle of the driveway. Not wanting to scare him off if Tanner was to return home, Shaun moved out of sight and started exploring.

He started with the house, walking around the structure and looking into the windows. There was no sign of Tanner inside the house. In fact, there was no sign that anyone had lived there for some time. A thick layer of dust covered every surface that Shaun could see through the dirty windows. Between that and the condition of the barn, it seemed the property had been abandoned since Tanner's parents had died.

Shaun continued to explore the property, finding a storm cellar about fifty yards from the house. With gun in hand, he threw open the door of the concrete structure and walked down the steps into the subterranean shelter. It was empty. He climbed back out and shut the door.

Daylight was waning and Shaun was wondering why he was even there. It was obvious to him that no one lived in the house. It was unlikely Tanner would be returning to a place where he did not live. The detective wanted Jack or Maureen to return so he could go. He had driven Keith Stevens' truck back to the clinic and had ridden to Tanner's supposed address with Jack.

Having nothing better to do he walked farther from the house toward the trees. The shadows cast by the lowering sun seemed darker in one area of the treeline. The detective, having nothing better to do, started walking in that direction. As he neared, he saw that it was a dirt road through the trees, and tire marks suggested someone had been there in recent days. He pulled out his phone to call Maureen but had no signal.

With his gun in one hand and flashlight in the other, he followed the road.

79

Maureen parked in the circular drive of Tanner Foley's nearest neighbor. The man who answered the door was well into his eighties and greeted her with a huge smile. He insisted on inviting her in and pouring a tall glass of iced tea.

"I need to ask you about your neighbor," Maureen said, a little louder than she probably needed to.

"Terrible shame about them," the man said. "They were good people. It's just awful what happened to them."

"You're talking about Mr. and Mrs. Foley?" she asked.

"Yeah." The man waved a finger toward her. "That was their name. Good people, the Foleys."

"What about their son?" Maureen asked. "What do you know of him?"

"That boy?" the man sneered. "Lazy as they come. Doesn't maintain anything at that house. Not since his parents died. Terrible thing what happened to them."

"Have you seen the son lately?" Maureen asked. "Maybe today? Did you see him leave?"

"Did I tell you, Tom Foley's daddy and I were friends?" the man said.

"No," Maureen smiled. "You didn't."

"We served together in Korea," he said. "Lost a lot of friends there."

"I'm sorry," she said.

"But Walter and I made it," he said. "Came back to build our lives. We both married our high school sweethearts and raised families. Bought all this land together. Worked it together. Up til Walter passed. Then it all got divided. His to his family. Mine to my family."

"That's fascinating," Maureen said. "But have you seen Walter's grandson today?"

"I don't think I've seen him more than a few times since his parents were killed." The man said. "Terrible thing . . ."

". . . that happened, I know," Maureen nodded. "But did you see his truck come or go today?"

"It's hard to believe that boy was related to Walter and Tom," the man drifted. "You know, I always suspected that Penny cheated on poor Tom. It's the only explanation for him being so different from his father."

"Did you see his truck today?" Maureen asked.

"Tom would work the land," the man said. Maureen closed her eyes to keep from screaming. The man continued, "all by himself. And that boy would be off doing whatever it is he did."

"Listen." Maureen stood to leave. "Thanks for the tea and the help. But I'm going to have to go."

"Spent most of his time up at that cabin," the man said.

"What did you say?" Maureen turned back. "What cabin?"

"Up in the woods behind Tom's house." The man pointed in the general direction of the hills behind their properties. "There's a cabin. Before we built the houses, we used to stay up there."

"Where is this cabin?"

"Just follow the old road through the trees," the man said. "Can't miss it."

80

Jack scrolled through his contact list and called Shaun. He listened to it ring until it went to voicemail before disconnecting the call. He quickly found Maureen's name and repeated the process, again going to voicemail. He left a message for her to call, explaining that it was possible Tanner was in the area.

He cursed himself for leaving them, for not being there. If they were in danger, it was because he left them in harm's way. Traffic was heavier on the drive back and he struggled to not force others off the road so he could pass.

Reaching the edge of town, traffic thinned and Jack accelerated, leaving the other cars small dots in his rearview mirror. His phone rang and he put it to his ear.

"What?"

"Jack?" Maureen said. "Is that you?"

"You got my message?" he said.

"No," she said. "I called you to see where you were."

"On my way back," Jack said. "Listen. Get back over there. Tanner's phone is pinging from that area. I'd feel better if Shaun wasn't alone over there."

"Well, that's why I called you," Maureen said. "I just got back over here. Shaun isn't here."

81

Large trees forced multiple turns as the road made its way through the wooded land. Shaun walked cautiously, noting the grade of the land was leading him ever upward. Fifteen or twenty minutes in, he wondered if the road led anywhere. He considered going back to wait for the others, but the tire tracks would not allow him to turn back. He had to know what was at the other end.

He came to a wooden fence, the kind used to keep cattle in, but little else. There was a gate that stood open and Shaun continued forward wondering if he was entering or exiting the fenced area. There had been livestock in the barn, so this could be the end of their property line. One thing that stood out was the Oleander that grew along the fence.

A few minutes later he saw faint lights through the lower foliage. He shut off his flashlight so he wouldn't announce himself and left the road to walk a more direct route to the lights.

The sun had not set completely, just enough illumination remained that Shaun could make out shapes. He could see a wooden structure that looked like a hunter's cabin, complete with a porch. Another structure stood just past it, smaller, darker. And in the foreground was the distinct shape of a pickup truck.

Shaun circled away from the cabin and around the vehicle. Staying low in the trees, he made his way to the smaller building. He walked slow, avoiding telltale snaps of twigs and rustling leaves. He took every care to not alert anyone he was there.

At the edge of the small building, he thought he heard movement, and he froze. After a long moment, he stepped up to and around the corner for a look. He saw chain-link, just before a large dog threw itself at the barrier and started barking, causing Shaun to stumble back. Several other dogs chimed in and the silence of the night was lost.

Shaun started to rise when he saw movement in the back of the nearest dog-run. A woman was making herself as small as possible in the far corner. He stepped forward just as a shot rang out. He felt a sting and realized he had been shot. Turning with his gun held up, he heard another shot. This time he didn't feel a thing.

82

"No. No. No. No. No." Tanner Foley paced in front of the dog runs as the animals within barked excitedly. He stopped and looked down at the man he had shot. He poked the man's ribs with the barrel of his rifle. It wasn't the first time he had shot a man who had wandered onto his land. There had been a hunter just last year. And another two years before that.

But this was no hunter. Shaun recognized him as one of the detectives that had come to the clinic. It would not be as easy as dumping the body on the other side of the county as he had done with the others. If this detective was here it was likely the other was nearby, or at least knew where he was. It was a threat that could ruin everything.

Tanner began pacing again. He had to decide what to do, and he had to decide quickly. He could not allow this to destroy everything. He had to protect himself and his property. He came to an abrupt stop.

He had to get rid of the detective. Tucking the rifle under one arm, he dug in his pocket and retrieved his keys. Thumbing through he found the key he wanted and slid it into the padlock on one of the dog-runs. The dog inside jumped against the gate and Tanner snapped his finger and ordered the animal to sit, which it did. He repositioned the rifle then pulled the gate open, holding his hand, palm out, in front of the dog.

"This way," he said, but not to the dog.

In the back of the run, a woman stepped forward slowly. She was frail and dirty, as one might expect a homeless person to be. There was fear in her eyes, a feeling that had become an everyday experience for her.

As she stepped out, Tanner used the rifle to direct her to the side so he could close the gate. He handed her the keys and pointed to another run. She stepped up to the gate and selected a key. The dog inside jumped at her, barking aggressively. She stumbled back a couple of steps. Tanner stepped forward and snapped.

"Sit!" He ordered. The dog slowly sat. To the woman, he said, "Hurry."

She grabbed the lock and tried a key. It did not work. She frantically tried the next key with the same result. She continued through the keys. After each try, she glanced over her shoulder at her captor. She had come to recognize the signs when he was reaching the level of frustration that caused him to lash out. Grinding his teeth, bobbing his head, sharply inhaling; all being exhibited at that moment. She knew what was coming and was bracing for it when the lock clicked and opened. She closed her eyes and sighed.

"Open it," he ordered. He looked at the young woman inside. "Out."

The woman trembled and started to cry.

"Out!" he repeated.

"It's okay," the first woman said to the other. Holding a hand out she said, "Come to me."

Sobbing, the woman moved toward the other and took her hand. The first woman pulled the younger woman to her and away from the gate. Tanner closed the dog run and held his hand out.

"Keys."

The woman handed them to him.

He pocketed them and pointed the rifle at the women. "Drag him to the truck."

The first woman guided the younger toward the detective. Her sobbing became more pronounced, and she physically tried to pull away.

"Do what he says," the first woman advised.

But the woman pulled against the other's hold and set her feet to resist. Tanner stepped forward and struck her in the side with the rifle. She cried out in pain, fell to the ground, and wailed. Tanner stepped forward again with the rifle raised. The first woman threw herself on top of the crying woman.

"Please," the woman said to him. "She'll do it."

"Get it done," he demanded.

"You have to do this," the woman said softly to the other. "He'll hurt you if you don't. Now, get up."

The woman stood and helped the other to her feet. Still crying, she let herself be led to where the detective lay. They approached him tentatively, each taking an arm and pulling. He slid a short distance before the younger woman lost her grip and fell backward. Tanner stepped forward.

"No!" The first woman shouted. "She's okay. We'll do it."

Tanner stepped back again, but she could see him grinding his teeth.

Together, the women struggled to move the man to the back of Tanner's truck. When they reached their destination, they collapsed next to him.

"Open the back," Tanner ordered.

The first woman rose to her feet again and opened the tailgate. She leaned against the vehicle breathing heavily, looking down at the man they had moved, concentrating on the badge on his belt. It made her want to cry along with the younger woman lying on the ground.

"Get him in," Tanner said.

The woman squatted down and made eye contact with her counterpart, "Come on. You can do this."

The young woman shook her head.

"Yes." The first woman pulled on the other's hand. "Get up or he'll hit you again."

"You should listen to her. This has already taken too long." His tone took a sharper tone, "Now, move!"

83

Jack slowed only slightly as he turned into the drive that led to the Foley home. His car slid on the dirt road, and he quickly corrected to keep from ending up in the field. A cloud of dust followed his advance as he sped toward the buildings. He braked hard when he saw Detective Weatherby waiting by her car, weapon at the ready.

He skidded to a stop next to her, and she jumped into the passenger seat. She hadn't even gotten the door closed when he accelerated again. The inertia slammed it shut as he steered toward the trees.

"There's a road up ahead," Maureen pointed. "I assume he went there. The neighbor said there's a hunter's cabin up there where Tanner stays sometimes."

Jack nodded and followed the path into the shadows. Between the canopy of leaves above them and the setting sun, he was forced to use his headlights as a guide, risking alerting anyone ahead of their approach.

Even more disappointing was the way the road zigzagged through the trees, causing Jack to slow to an almost crawl. The idea that it would be faster on foot crossed the detective's mind. As they drove, Jack watched the road. Maureen watched the trees and anything illuminated by the beams of light in front of them. She searched for Shaun and threats, finding neither.

They crested a small hill and saw lights through the trees. Jack attempted to shut off the headlights but missed the switch. A few seconds later a bullet pierced the center of the windshield. He stomped on the brake and threw the gearshift into park. Both detectives opened their doors and rolled into the cover of the night as two more rounds struck the glass.

84

The two women struggled to lift the man into the truck. It was no easy task as he weighed nearly two hundred pounds, not much less than their weights combined. But the first woman Tanner had released to help had done so before. The others had been women. Smaller, but she had not been allowed help then. She had developed a method and although it would not work with the man if she were alone, with help she hoped that it would.

Giving the younger woman direction, they managed to raise the man to a sitting position. She then wrapped her arms around his chest and encouraged her new partner to help her stand. It took tremendous effort, falling twice and starting over before they were successful. Together they turned him to face the truck, then pushed his upper body onto the tailgate. They had to work together to keep him from falling back to the ground.

While the women debated whether they should both try to push him up or if one of them should get into the truck bed and pull, Tanner grew impatient with the delay and raised the rifle to strike.

It was at that moment that a flash of light struck them. Tanner dropped to one knee and pulled his weapon to his shoulder. Headlights. They had taken too long. He fired at the lights stopping their progression. Satisfied, he fired two more shots. He turned back to the women, angry they had failed him.

They were gone. The detective lay on the ground, but the women were nowhere to be seen. He searched the increasing darkness for them. Seeing movement he fired in that direction. There was no scream, no whimper. He had missed.

Hearing movement behind him he dropped and spun. He couldn't see anything in the darkness. Frustrated, he circled the truck and climbed into the cab.

85

Jack ran crouched low to the ground. A fourth shot rang out, and he wondered if Maureen had been the target, or maybe Shaun. Was his young partner somewhere near the building Jack thought he had caught a glimpse of?

He only ran a short distance farther before deciding no one was trying to shoot at him and turned toward the building in question. His eyes had adjusted to the dark, and he could make out shapes. The buildings. The truck. Trying to stay in the shadows he advanced on the small compound. He was nearly there when the truck started. Their target was getting away.

He wanted to fire into the truck, but his instincts kicked in and he worried the man may not be alone inside. Instead, he broke into a run. As he ran, he saw what looked like Shaun laying on the ground. He saw movement to his side but determined whatever it was, it was not coming at him and was not a threat. He saw Maureen illuminated briefly by the truck's lights as she ran forward. The truck moved into the trees and freedom only to come to a skidding halt. Their car was on the narrow road and there was no way through the trees.

Jack closed the distance from behind. Maureen closed in from the driver's side. The truck's door opened and Maureen slowed, shouting for him to throw out his weapon and surrender. A shot struck her and threw her to the ground. Jack did not slow. He was rounding the back of the truck when Tanner slid out and to the ground. The young man spun when he saw the detective closing on him, but he was not fast enough. Jack slammed his body into the man and crushed him against the inside of the truck's door. Wrenching the rifle from his hands, Jack slung the man to the ground and pounced.

86

Jack walked away from the truck with a handcuffed Tanner in tow.

Maureen was sitting up when he reached her. He had shot her in the vest near the left shoulder. It had stopped the bullet, but she was not able to move her arm. Jack helped her to her feet, and they continued back to the compound where Jack had seen Shaun.

A woman kneeled over him, her hands on his chest. She saw the detectives and screamed, "Help me! He's still alive!"

"I've got him." Maureen yanked on the cuffs with her good hand to show she had a firm grip.

Jack nodded and ran ahead to Shaun's side. He fell to his knees and patted Shaun down. The first shot had hit him square in his vest. The second had slipped in under his arm. He had lost a lot of blood and was still bleeding. Jack tore his sleeve and shoved the material into the wound to stop the flow.

"What's your name?" He asked the woman when he was done.

"Crystal," she said. "Crystal Vaughn."

"We've been looking for you," Jack said. "Is there anyone else?"

"A girl named Dawn Callahan is hiding in the trees over there." Crystal pointed. "Dawn. It's okay. They're the good guys."

The young woman slowly showed herself before coming fully into the opening.

"And," Crystal gestured to the row of dog runs. Three women were at their perspective gates, two standing, one sitting. Tears came to Crystal's eyes. "They're hurt."

87

One of the women in the dog runs was Meghan Quinn, the only woman taken without a dog. However, she had met Tanner on the walking trail while walking her friend's dog, who she had been dog sitting for. She had been surprised to see Tanner again. He appeared near her home a week later seemingly as shocked as she. That was why Meghan let her guard down and almost that fast he had tranquilized her.

The woman who could not stand was Angela Case. Jack had spoken to her parents while trying to identify Lorissa St. Clair. He had not gone back to ask the right questions to add her to the list of potential victims. She had seen Tanner several times over the course of nearly a month before he took her. She tried to get away, and he had broken her leg in two places.

The last woman was not known to them before. She had been held for five months and had all but given up on getting out alive. She had been there the longest aside from Crystal.

Crystal held a special place for Tanner. He had tried to court her, to no avail. When Crystal rejected him, he became obsessed. When Judith Stevens found out that he was harassing their customer, she tried to get him fired. Tanner became enraged kidnapping Judith for revenge. She had been there when he brought Crystal. Shortly after that, the veterinarian was dragged away. Crystal never knew what had become of her.

After he began taking women, he could no longer control himself. He liked the power he felt. Also, he felt he was paying them back for the way they treated him. Only Meghan and Dawn did not meet that criterion. Meghan had been walking Karyn Hayes dog. It was Karyn who he planned to take. But after he built the trust with Meghan he had to go through with it. And Dawn was a mistake as the detectives had thought. He was going to take his coworker, Shelly, but in his haste, did not realize he had gotten the address wrong.

Crystal had seen the others die. She realized quickly that Tanner was poisoning the food when he was done with the women. And because of his feelings for her, Crystal was the one he chose to help him when he needed to dispose of the victims, not because he wasn't capable of doing it himself. In his mind, having her help him made them closer. He still had the delusion that she would someday love him.

DNA tests showed that Tanner had fathered Alyssa Bell's child. And when detectives asked Crystal about her, she cried for the young victim.

88

"I would say you're looking good," Jack said, "but I don't want it to go to your head."

Shaun smiled at his partner. "Thank you."

"You have some visitors if you're up to it," Jack said.

"I don't know," Shaun gestured around the hospital room. "My schedule is kind of full."

Jack opened the door. A man and woman entered. Shaun had seen the man before but did not know where. Not until he saw the woman. She was Patricia Hopkins which made the man Jeremiah Hopkins.

"They tell me you're the reason I got out," Jeremiah said. "I wanted to thank you."

"Wasn't me," Shaun said. "Your wife did it. All I did was look after she convinced me to."

"Thank you," Patricia said.

They spoke briefly before leaving. After they were gone, Maureen entered, her arm in a sling. The impact of the bullet had broken her collarbone. "You better get out of here soon. Jack is piling all his files on your desk."

"Those are his files," Jack said. "He's the one who started this mess with Bret Peterson's old cases. I'm saving them for him."

"Oh, good," Shaun said. "Something to look forward to."

Thank you for reading!

Dear Reader,

I hope you enjoyed reading **Dog Walkers** as much as I enjoyed writing it. At this time, I would like to request, if you're so inclined, please consider leaving a review of **Dog Walkers**. I would love to hear your feedback.

Amazon: https://www.amazon.com/dp/B08SGCSZR6

Goodreads:
https://www.goodreads.com/author/show/18986676.William_Coleman

Website: https://www.williamcoleman.net

Facebook: https://www.facebook.com/williamcolemanauthor/

Many Thanks,

William Coleman

Other novels by William Coleman:

THE WIDOW'S HUSBAND

PAYBACK

NICK OF TIME

MURDER REVISITED

THE CONTRACT

Printed in Great Britain
by Amazon

10516852R00171